FIRST CONTACT

ALSO BY EVAN MANDERY

FICTION

Dreaming of Gwen Stefani

NONFICTION

The Campaign

Capital Punishment

PLAYS

Pastrami on Rye and Other Aspects of the Afterlife

FIRST CONTACT

Or, It's Later Than You Think

Parrot Sketch Excluded

EVAN MANDERY

HARPER

NEW YORK • LONDON • TORONTO • SYDNEY

For my best and favorite teachers: James Connolly, Ralph Henderson, and the incomparable Roslyn Goldstein.

And, as always, for the greatest teachers of all: Mathew and Sherry Mandery, my parents.

HARPER

HarperCollins books may be purchased for educational, business, or sales promotional use. For information please write: Special Markets Department, HarperCollins Publishers, 10 East 53rd Street, New York, NY 10022.

FIRST EDITION

Designed by Aline C. Pace

Library of Congress Cataloging-in-Publication Data is available upon request.

ISBN 978-0-06-174977-3

10 11 12 13 14 OV/RRD 10 9 8 7 6 5 4 3 2 1

1

HE WEARS SHORT SHORTS

WHEN RALPH BAILEY, ATTACHÉ to the President, entered the family chambers at 5:26 A.M. with the news that aliens had contacted the American government, the President was on the treadmill.

"Good morning, Mr. President," he said.

"Good morning, Ralph," said the President. "You're up early today."

"Yes, sir. I have important news."

"I have some big news too."

"This is very important, sir."

"Well, so is this. Yours can wait a minute, can't it?"

Ralph wondered about this. It seemed a rather important item, the fact that aliens had reached Earth. The Secretary of State had told him to tell the President straightaway, to get him out of bed if he had to, but setting the agenda for conversations was an executive prerogative of which this president took full advantage.

"I suppose it can, sir," Ralph said.

"Good." The President stopped the treadmill, stepped off, and removed his sweaty shirt. The President liked being bare-chested.

"I ran my five miles in under thirty-five minutes this morning. That's less than seven minutes per mile."

"Yes, sir."

"I haven't done that since I took office."

"It is very impressive, sir. It is a very impressive time."

"Seriously, Ralph, how many men my age do you think could run five miles in under thirty-five minutes?"

"Not many, sir."

"I bet I'm the fastest president in history."

"You might very well be, sir."

WHAT RALPH KNEW AND the President did not was that the treadmill in the family quarters was calibrated in kilometers, not miles. He had thus run five kilometers in thirty-five minutes, which comes out to a little more than ten minutes per mile. This explained the President's absolute preference for the treadmill to running out-side. When the President ran outside, his times were, of course, in the range of ten minutes per mile. The President attributed his diminished fleetness outdoors to allergies and car exhaust and hence preferred to exercise in the controlled, allergen-free, positive-ion-charged environment of the White House, where his improved performances were, he felt, more reflective of his natural abilities. Ralph, who had overseen the installation of the exercise equipment, knew better. He had thought of explaining the error to the President but, wisely, rejected the idea. A longtime jogger, the President was quite invested in his physical fitness and the impor-tance of physical fitness generally. He took enormous pride in the fact that since entering office, he had knocked three minutes per mile off his running times.

THE PRESIDENT POPPED INTO the shower. He emerged glistening, took a towel from the rack, and began the process of drying himself, beginning, ceremoniously, with his hair and underarms.

Ralph felt an increasing sense of urgency to get the news out. He imagined the Secretary would be quite upset with the delay. The Secretary knew how the President could be when he got his mind on something, particularly in the morning when he brimmed with energy, but this was big.

"Tell me, Ralph," the President said as he wiped his chest. "Suppose we were to stage a race among all the presidents of the United States. Ten-k, flat course. Who would you pick to run against me?"

"Just the living presidents in their current physical condition, sir?"

"Ha!" roared the President. "You're obviously not much of a sports fan, are you, Ralph?"

"No, sir."

"It would be meaningless to make a comparison on the basis of two athletes' current physical state. Suppose someone asks you who is better, Kobe Bryant or Oscar Robertson? You're obviously going to pick Kobe. He is thirty-one. Oscar Robertson is seventy-one. So you have to go with Bryant. But in his prime, son, Bryant couldn't have carried the Big O's towel. That's the interesting question, Ralph: Who was better in his prime?"

The President moved the drying process down to his feet. He paid careful attention to a bunion.

"Living presidents would be no competition for me. Who did you have in mind? Carter? Clinton? One of the Bushes? I don't think any of them could run a twenty-minute mile. They couldn't beat me even if you let them run as a relay team." The President laughed. "No, Ralph," he said, "the question is me as I am today against any president at the peak of his physical fitness. If you want to pick FDR, you can have him with his good legs. Now, who's it going to be?"

"I'm not sure, sir. I've never really thought about this before."

This was, of course, true. Ralph had never thought of the question before.

"Well, think about it now," the President said.

As Ralph thought, he understood the question was not really who could offer the President the best race, but whom Ralph could choose without insulting his boss. It would be bad to pick someone who the President perceived as unworthy, not so much because it would make for a bad hypothetical competition, but because the President would be hurt or even outraged that Ralph would think so little of the President as to select for his adversary someone whom the President held in such low regard. It would be particularly bad if Ralph inadvertently chose a former president who was effete, or more relevantly whom the current president believed to be effete. It would be particularly bad to pick a liberal.

Teddy Roosevelt seemed like a safe choice.

"I think I would go with Teddy Roosevelt, sir."

"TR!" the President bellowed. "You have to be kidding me! TR couldn't hold my jock. Everyone thinks TR is such an athlete because he bagged a few moose and took a hill in battle. Let me tell you a little secret: the Spanish had already abandoned the hill. And, besides, TR went up on a horse. He was a fat turd. Have you even seen Mount Rushmore? They only did the faces because they would have needed another whole mountain for TR's ass. I don't think he could even walk six miles. I'd kick TR's butt."

The President snapped Ralph with his towel. It was soapy and wet.

THE PRESIDENT IS NOT without basis in diminishing Teddy Roosevelt's efforts in Cuba. The Spanish had not abandoned Kettle Hill, as the President claimed, but Roosevelt's deeds were widely inflated in the press. He was the only one of the Rough Riders to remain mounted during the charge, primarily because he did not think he could keep up on foot in the tropical heat. Furthermore, the Spanish incomprehensibly kept thousands of soldiers in reserve at the nearby city of Santiago de Cuba, even though the Americans outnumbered them on the battlefield by more than ten to one. Roosevelt was posthumously awarded the Medal of Honor for his actions, but the victory could be attributed as much to Spanish incompetence as to American valor.

While Roosevelt may not have been as much of a hero at San Juan Heights as is popularly thought, he would have been in every other respect a worthy opponent for the President. A sickly, asthmatic child, TR embraced vigorous exercise and literally willed himself to robust health. In pictures of him as an undergraduate, he appears stout and barrel-chested. He wrestled and rowed crew while at Harvard, climbed the Matterhorn at the age of twenty-two despite a bad heart, and boxed well into his forties. At the age of fifty-five, Roosevelt led an expedition to chart the Amazon River, then known as the River of Doubt. This was toward the end of a life during which TR served as police commissioner in New York City, a colonel in the navy, governor of the state of New York, and president of the United States. Roosevelt managed in these various capacities to, among other substantial accomplishments, establish the National Park Service, mastermind the construction of the Panama Canal, and negotiate the treaty ending the Russo-Japanese War.

TR understood in a very fundamental way the importance of living life to the fullest. As Roosevelt liked to say, he sucked the juice out of life.

BY COINCIDENCE I AM eating an orange right now, which I am doing by sucking out the juice but discarding the remains. This is how I like to eat oranges, though it seems like a waste and gives me some pause about the whole live-life-to-the-fullest thing. Any physician worth his salt will tell you the pulp is where the fiber is.

THE SNAPPING OF THE presidential towel suggested to Ralph his choice had been a success, which indeed it was. The President may have dismissed Roosevelt, but he was not insulted. He regarded Roosevelt as an opponent of worthy character, if not adequate swiftness, and he accepted the choice with good humor.

"Who would you pick, sir?" Ralph asked. It was obvious he was expected to ask this.

"That's a thoughtful question," the President said. He began a vigorous two-handed attack on the lower half of his torso as he pondered. "I'd pick Nixon," he said finally.

"Was Nixon particularly fit, sir?"

"No. He was a good bowler. Good poker player, too. Not particularly fast, though. I just think he'd find a way to get the job done."

"But you would beat him, sir."

"I like to think so."

The President lost himself in thought for a moment.

"Imagine if we could have a footrace among all the world leaders throughout history," he said. "That would be a truly fascinating competition. I bet Napoleon could run like the wind. And Gandhi too. He looks swift."

"Sir, I have this news I mentioned."

"In a minute, Ralph. I have one more thing for you."

"Yes, sir." Ralph thought again about the Secretary of State, an impatient man to begin with, sitting in the Map Room waiting for

Ralph to return with instructions from the President, who was at that moment standing stark naked, having dropped his towel to the floor to facilitate his rummaging through the presidential wardrobe. He removed from the drawer a pair of underwear, which had been folded and sealed in the manner a dry cleaner would return a boxed shirt, though this pair of shorts had the presidential seal across it and not the "We ♥ Our Customers" labeling that the local dry cleaner emblazoned across Ralph's dress shirts.

THIS CAREFUL, ALMOST OBSESSIVE attention to laundry seemed, to Ralph, to be an overindulgence, albeit one of many in the White House. The kitchen maintained a reserve of 475 gallons of ice cream in the freezer and had a chef on duty at all times. The former executive chef of a Michelin three-star restaurant in New York manned the graveyard shift in case the President ever wanted an omelet or a cup of gazpacho in the middle of the night. Not only had the President, who prided himself on being an early-to-bed, early-to-rise type, never taken advantage of the overnight *cuisinier*, he ate the same thing for breakfast every morning—Rice Krispies and coffee; ate the same thing for lunch every day—a ham and Swiss cheese from Blimpway; and for dinner had either spaghetti and meatballs or macaroni and cheese. If he had to attend a state dinner, where pasta could not very well be served, at least not in a form he would tolerate, the President would have a bite of the capon or fish that was on the menu, then steal off afterward for a plate of noodles, which he would eat while watching sports.

Knowing of the President's fondness for mac and cheese, the head chef of the White House, himself the former culinary director at a four-star restaurant in Los Angeles, experimented during the first several months of the President's term with various recipes for the dish, arriving ultimately upon a mélange of thin gemelli with diced bits of pancetta, caramelized onion, and roasted asparagus in a creamy Asiago-Parmesan sauce that several White House staffers who acted as taste testers described as the most exquisite thing they had ever eaten, bordering on orgasmic, and which the President rejected in favor of the Kraft product that came in 99-cent boxes. Still, they kept vats of caviar, foie gras, and truffles in the kitchen, in the event the President awoke one evening with a case of the munchies and an epiphany of palate sophistication.

* * *

NOW HE WAS STANDING in front of Ralph, nude but for his underwear. Ralph had witnessed this scene more times than he cared to remember.

"It's bunching."

"Where, sir?"

"Here." The President pulled at the material between his buttocks and turned around so Ralph could have a clearer view.

"Here," he said. "Can't you see?"

"I'm sorry, sir, I can't."

"It's grabbing at me, son. Everywhere I go, it's grabbing and bunching."

"Yes, sir."

"You know the president of the United States can't just fix himself like everyone else. I mean, I sit in meetings six hours a day, and half the time it's up there in my butt-crack. I'm aware of it. You shouldn't be aware of underwear. But I can't just go up there after it. I can't say, 'Excuse me, Mr. Premier of Kazakhstan, my wears are riding up today and I'm going to go and have me a tug.' I can't very well do that, now, can I, Ralph?"

"No, I don't suppose so, sir."

"Well, what are we going to do then?"

"I don't know, Mr. President. I think we may have tried everything."

INDEED THEY HAD TRIED seemingly everything. In the beginning, Ralph tried the offerings of the various popular commercial brands— the Gap and J. Crew, Brooks Brothers and Banana Republic. When it became clear none of these were satisfactory, Ralph did what any good government official would do: he threw money at the problem, thereupon entering a world he had never imagined existed. He bought the President Armani underwear at $89 a pair, Dolce & Gabbana for $109, and Versace at $129 a pop. None worked. The material of the Armani abraded the President's testicles, the Dolce Gabbana rubbed on his thighs, and the Versace bunched just as much as the Fruit of the Loom.

Thereafter, Ralph retained, at considerable expense to Mr. and Mrs. John Q. Taxpayer, Mr. Hirohito Sun of Hong Kong, tailor to the Sultan of Brunei and the Prince of Monaco, the world's most exclusive clothier, who handcrafted suits of the finest gabardine wool for $25,000 apiece, and who, on the rarest of occasions, and for the most exclusive of clients, dealt in the crafting of bloomers. For the President of the United States, Mr. Sun flew to America, conducted a fitting, and created, after four months of research and development, a sui generis composite of silk and cotton—a magnificent, almost historic, undergarment, which the President dismissed after a twenty-second trial as too "nubbly," a word Ralph had neither heard before nor could find in any dictionary.

Ralph sometimes wondered whether this might be an elaborate test of his loyalty, some kind of bizarre hazing ritual, because nobody who had a history with the President, including several people who went back years with him, all the way to his days as commissioner of sanitation, recalled him taking any interest in his underwear. And still, despite the extraordinary efforts undertaken on his behalf, the President insisted he was not difficult to accommodate.

"You know, Ralph, I bet I could walk into the Wal-Mart and get this thing taken care of in two seconds."

"Yes, sir," Ralph said, even though it was most emphatically not true because the President had tried on every kind of underwear Wal-Mart sold by the first April of his presidency. The President failed to recall this because he had since tried some 250 other varieties of underwear, none of which, of course, had been to his satisfaction.

"Wouldn't that be something if I just walked into the Arlington Wal-Mart? That would cause quite a stir. Get those liberals all up in arms."

"Yes, sir."

"Get them talking about raising the minimum wage and the plight of workers in America and all that crap."

"Yes, sir."

"You know, back when I was an alderman, I used to hit the Wal-Mart all the time. I'd always go in there around Christmas and do my shopping. Always made for a good picture in the town paper. Don't suppose I could do that anymore."

"No, sir."

The President changed clothes, first removing the problematic underwear in favor of his familiar boxers, several pairs of which had been with him since his early days in state government and which had become, through repeated wearing and washing over the years, tattered and threadbare.

* * *

AT THE SAME TIME the President complained to Ralph about the bunching in his underwear or, more accurately, at the same time I wrote that the President complained of the bunching in his underwear, I began to notice bunching in my own underwear. This could be an example of the peculiar manner in which life imitates art. The same could also be said of my experience with the orange, although I ate oranges in this manner long before I began writing this book. On the other hand, I have never had a significant problem with bunching other than during a, pardon the pun, brief experiment with boxer shorts in college.

UPON DONNING HIS UNDERWEAR and the remainder of the standard uniform of the American politician—a starched white shirt, blue suit, and red necktie, knotted in the President's preferred half-Windsor—the conversation finally turned to the matter that Ralph had come to discuss.

"So what was it you wanted to tell me, Ralph?"

"Sir, the Secretary of State has asked me to inform you that aliens have contacted the American government."

The President fixed his knot in the mirror. He had high knotting standards.

"Well, tell him to handle it. I'm sure he'll know what to do."

"Sir, the Secretary believes this matter requires your urgent attention."

The President flashed a look at Ralph off the mirror. His ire was up. "Does the Secretary really expect me to drop everything every time some Mexicans try to get across the border?"

"These aren't Mexicans, sir."

"Who are they then? Cubans? I'll be pissed if it's the Cubans again. What did they do this time? Try to make it to Miami in a shoe box? Those damned Cubans can't even build themselves a proper boat."

"Sir, it's not illegal aliens. It's real aliens, from outer space."

The President turned away from the mirror to face Ralph directly. "You mean Martians?"

"I don't think they are actually Martians, sir. NASA has found no evidence of life on Mars. These people appear to have come from several hundred light-years away."

"I'll be damned," the President said. "Martians in my White House." He shook his head and said to himself, "The Lord works in mysterious ways."

Then he asked, "What was the message, Ralph? What did they say?"

Ralph replied without editorializing. "It said, 'Mr. President, would you like to have brunch?'"

2

EVERY LITTLE THING
SHE DOES IS MAGIC

THAT SAME DAY, AT precisely 11:30 A.M., Lois Dundersinger, secretary to the President, entered Ralph's cubicle. Mrs. Dundersinger had worked for the President for thirty-seven years, since his earliest days in politics, and fifteen years longer than there had been a Mr. Dundersinger. Ralph thought she bore a striking resemblance to Andy Rooney.

"The President has asked for his lunch," she said.

"I wondered whether today might be different," Ralph said.

"Mr. Bailey, why should this day be different from all other days?" Mrs. Dundersinger asked this rhetorically, with no evidence of irony.

"Well—" Ralph said, starting to explain the obvious reason, but Dundersinger cut him off with a wave.

"The President has asked for his lunch," she said.

Mrs. Dundersinger was a traditionalist. She wore dresses that extended to her knees, sensible shoes, and addressed every member of the White House staff by their surname, except of course the President, whom she referred to as "Mr. President." Mrs. Dundersinger's conservatism could be endearing and presented no problem for Ralph, except for her insistence on making the President's calls from a rotary phone. Mrs. Dundersinger liked to count the clicks in order to make sure she did not dial a wrong number on the President's behalf.

Supervising the installation of a rotary phone became Ralph's second major project after the President took office, only succeeding in time consumed and importance the vexing underwear initiative. Though the White House had a highly competent technical staff, the rotary phone was simply incompatible with the modern wiring in the West Wing. Ralph attempted one day to explain to Dundersinger the difficulty of employing 1970s technology in the twenty-first century. He analogized it to the difficulty of causing the dimmer switch in the Oval Office to regulate a candle as opposed to an electric light. Mrs. Dundersinger either did not understand or did not care to understand the problem, and nonverbally insisted that it was imperative that she place the President's calls on a rotary phone. She did this by making the most disturbing acerbic face, a puss so sour it could have wrinkled the skin of an olive or a baby or something else uncommonly smooth.

The problem was whereupon resolved by the White House employing—at a salary of $57,000 a year—a full-time employee, one Edna Peachpit of Wichita, Kansas, with the sole responsibility of translating Mrs. Dundersinger's rotary calls into touch-tone data. Mrs. Dundersinger's phone was not connected to a phone line. It was connected to a small machine in Ms. Peachpit's office, which displayed the number to be dialed. Ms. Peachpit then placed the call in the normal, modern fashion.

Mrs. Dundersinger was not informed of the arrangement.

"THE USUAL?" RALPH ASKED.

"Yes," said Mrs. Dundersinger. "The usual sandwich."

The usual, as mentioned, was a ham and Swiss sandwich from Blimpway. It was necessary to procure the sandwich at Blimpway because the White House chef had been unable to produce an effort that met with the President's approval. One early effort—a sumptuous *croque monsieur*—had nearly led to the head chef's dismissal. The President did not like the French. Other subsequent efforts fared no better.

With a sense of resignation, Ralph put on his blazer, passed security, and walked to the Blimpway on L and Fourteenth. There was a Subbie three blocks closer to the White House, but the President did not like their mayonnaise. Sometimes Ralph resented the inconvenience, but that day he did not mind the walk. He played Green Day's "Wake Me Up When September Ends" on his iPod. The song seemed to have special meaning now. Ralph watched with interest and wonder as the people of Washington went about their business: a woman contentedly walked down the sidewalk brandishing an overstuffed Lord & Taylor shopping bag, a man in a suit sprinted down the street perhaps late for a meeting, another man cleaned up after his beagle. Each was oblivious to the change in their reality. Ralph wondered whether the tardy man would still be running if he were aware aliens had contacted Earth.

When Ralph arrived at the sandwich shop, it was already crowded. The lunch rush, which Ralph knew all too well, starts early at Blimpway. But things were moving even more slowly than usual. At the head of the line, a gentleman was exercising the strictest of scrutiny over the production of his sandwich, with the apparent agenda of getting a little bit more of everything.

"A few more," the customer said, his nose pressed to the sneeze guard as the sandwich artist applied the tomatoes.

"A few more," he said, as the onions were dispensed.

"A little more," he said, with respect to the hot peppers and olives.

The counter boy obliged, until they got to the meat. At the request to add another slice of ham, he balked.

"I'm only allowed to put on four slices," he said.

"Just one more slice," the customer implored.

"Those are the rules."

"You have nerve. The sandwich is so thin."

Presently, the manager was summoned. He explained that four slices of meat per sandwich was store policy. If the gentleman wanted more meat he could pay for an extra-thick sandwich. The customer repeated his charge that the owner had gall serving such a meager sandwich—"flimsy" was his word—and said he could easily take his business elsewhere. The customer became further enraged, the manager more indignant, and for a moment, just a moment, that ham sandwich became the most important thing in the universe.

The two men argued the question whether the sandwich was too thin or just right with passion and aplomb. But since it was not a question to which any objective answer existed, neither side could get the better of it, and soon, inevitably in some ways, the matter deteriorated into name-calling. The customer said something about the manager's Muslim heritage—he was, in fact, Muslim—the manager replied that he did not need the patronage of the homeless— the customer was, in fact, homeless—and soon the customer threw a napkin dispenser at the beverage refrigerator and stormed out of the store.

The napkin dispenser made a sickening thud against the cooler but, since the door was constructed of plastic, did not break anything. So the lasting damage of this dramatic conflict was only a displaced napkin dispenser and the unpaid-for and unclaimed one-slice-too-thin sandwich, which sat upon the counter looking rather pathetic.

The manager stared at it, apparently unsure of how to dispose of it.

"I THINK HE'S THINKING of selling the sandwich."

The comment came from a woman standing behind Ralph on line. Absorbed in the drama at the counter, Ralph had not noticed her before. She was pretty.

"He must know he can't get away with selling it," she continued, "but I think he's wondering whether he can put back the meat. After all, it hasn't been eaten."

Ralph smiled. He stepped forward and placed his order for the President's sandwich and his own. He received each without event or controversy. He decided to sit down and eat his own tuna sandwich before returning to the White House. Moments later, the woman appeared at his table.

"Mind if I join you?" she asked.

Ralph saw now that "pretty" did not do her justice. Her beauty was radiant.

"Please," he said, and removed his earphones as she sat down and unwrapped her veggie sub.

"You must be really hungry," she said.

"Why do you say that?"

"You bought two sandwiches."

"One is for my boss," Ralph said.

"That's nice of you to pick up lunch for your boss."

"It's kind of part of my job."

"Your boss makes you buy him his lunch?"

"Sort of. His secretary usually asks."

"How often?"

"Every day."

She seemed quite bothered by this. She pursed her lips and scrunched her eyebrows. Somehow, impossibly, this made her even more attractive.

"Does he at least pay for your lunch? Since he makes you go out for him every day, the least he could do is spring for your sandwich."

"No, he doesn't do that."

She scrunched again.

"Actually, he doesn't even pay for his own lunch," Ralph said.

She said, "I don't think I would like your boss very much."

Ralph thought of protesting, but took a bite of his sandwich instead. "What do you do?" he asked, after he finished chewing.

"I'm a law student at Georgetown."

"What type of lawyer do you want to be?"

"I want to help the poor," she said. "I mean, I guess I'll have to work in a firm for a few years, but afterward I'd like to go to Legal Aid or some other kind of legal services agency. I really just want to help people somehow."

Ralph shook his head. "No," he said, "you definitely wouldn't like my boss."

The woman smiled and extended her hand.

"I'm Jessica," she said.

He said, "Ralph," and took her hand. She had soft skin and long, elegant fingers. They sent a charge of electricity through Ralph's body.

"What were you listening to?" Jessica asked.

"Green Day."

"Let me see your iPod," she said. "I like to imagine the iPod as the soundtrack to people's lives. It makes ordinary life a bit more like the movies. You can tell a lot about someone from the songs she or he chooses."

Ralph nodded and handed over the iPod. She inserted the earphones and began nodding to the music.

"Green Day is cool," she said. "I didn't know they covered 'Cracklin' Rosie.'"

Ralph reached to take back the device.

"I must have had it on shuffle. That's embarrassing."

She held on to the iPod.

"It's okay. Green Day and Neil Diamond. I like that."

She scrolled through his playlist, reading as she went along.

"The Beatles, solo Lennon, Dire Straits, Crosby, Stills & Nash, Rush. You have eclectic taste in music." Then she stopped and looked up.

"The Police," she said. "I believe the Police may be the greatest rock band of all time."

"I agree."

"Are you really a fan?"

"I am," Ralph said.

"Then let me ask you this: What principle did they use to order the Synchronicity songs? Why was *Synchronicity I* number one and *Synchronicity II* number two?"

"Because one came first," Ralph guessed, playing along. He found the banter engaging.

"You mean it was written first?"

"I don't know."

"Do you remember which one is which?"

"I think the one about lemmings and the Loch Ness monster is number two."

"Do you remember what the other one is about?"

"No."

"Is it even about synchronicity?"

"I don't know," Ralph said. "Right now, I am feeling uncertain about everything I have ever known."

"And thus," Jessica said, with a wave of her elegant hand, "right now, somewhere else in the universe, someone is experiencing the exact same feeling."

THE ACCURACY OF THIS claim depends on what is meant by "exact." It is certainly not the case that somewhere else in the universe a man named Ralph Bailey and a woman named Jessica Love were falling for each other over subs and Dr Pepper. If one demands this level of precision in the quest to find meaning, disappointment is inevitable. At a slightly greater level of abstraction, however, seemingly meaningful coincidences abound. There were, for example, many people in the universe falling in love at that very moment. On the planet Tukaloose, a young male and female *crigler*, a species that looks more or less like giant squid, made snappy repartee about popular music while enjoying sandwiches of *politzcar*, which tastes more or less like tuna, in a restaurant called Grestline, which is the Tukaloose word for a dirigible. Dirigibles are an important and popular mode of transportation on Tukaloose. Grestline operates in direct competition with Matzater, a similar chain of restaurants that offers virtually the same menu and the same quality food. *Matzater* is the Tukaloose term for an underground rail system. These sadly, fell into disfavor following the advent of the zeppelin but continue to evoke a romantic nostalgia and a hearty appetite.

I DON'T EAT MUCH meat or fish, but I think the tuna at Subbie is better than at Blimpway. I could be wrong. My best friend, Ard, swears by the tuna at Subbie and thinks Blimpway is crap.

FULL DISCLOSURE: I HAVE changed the names of Subbie and Blimpway. To be safe, I also changed the names of Grestline and Matzater from their Tukaloose analogs. Tastes can be subjective, especially when it comes to tuna salad, and I am accordingly reticent to disparage the good names of the sandwich shops here at issue. To be safe, I have also changed the name of my aforementioned best friend. His real name is Ira J. Kaufman.

Ard and I have been friends for twenty-five years. The plurality of that time has been spent debating the moistness of various snack products. We also like to play instant lottery scratch games, drink cream soda, and say funny names like "Bunny Glamazon." Ard is very good at rationing beverages. He always has some soda left at the end of a meal. If you ever want to see him in action, try the MacKing on 71st and Broadway. On Sundays he likes to go there for coffee and a bacon, egg, and cheese biscuit.

THE NAME MACKING HAS been changed.

* * *

BACK AT THE BLIMPWAY on L and Fourteenth, Jessica discoursed further on synchronicity.

"It's such an awesome idea," she said. "We all think whatever we're doing is so crucial that our problems are the most important in the world. But no matter what we are doing, somewhere else someone is doing the exact same thing at the exact same time. If you think about that, all of a sudden a sandwich doesn't seem as if it could ever be significant to anyone."

Her speech hung in the air for a few seconds as they both paused to consider the enormity of the thought. When the moment passed, Ralph understood it was his obligation to say something next. He said the first thing that came into his mind.

"Do you think the Police are popular on other planets?" he asked.

"I don't know," Jessica said. "Perhaps we'll find out soon."

Ralph regretted his question. The aliens were a matter of national security. She would have interpreted it as a joke, but it was the kind of joke that got White House staffers in trouble. He wondered also what she meant by her reply, but Jessica quickly changed the subject.

"Let me ask you something else," she said. "This is truly the most important question in the history of the universe. Forget cold fusion and general relativity, this is the question someone should get the Nobel Prize for answering."

"Go ahead."

"Would Sting have been Sting if he hadn't changed his name?"

Ralph smiled. "You mean if he had remained Gordon Sumner?"

"Right," she said. "And I ask this question with the greatest of respect for Sting. I have all of his solo albums. I love *Dream of the Blue Turtles*, *Ten Summoner's Tales*, and *Brand New Day*. I gotta be honest, I didn't love . . . *Nothing Like the Sun*. I didn't get "Englishman in New York." But I didn't hate it either, and that says a lot. The man has been making music for thirty years and I've hated none of it and loved almost all of it. I am a huge fan. But the plain truth is there aren't a lot of famous Gordons. I defy you to come up with two famous Gordons."

"There's Gordon Jump from *WKRP in Cincinnati*."

"OK. That's one, I suppose."

"Lord Byron's middle name was Gordon."

"That's a middle name. I bet he had a normal first name."

"George."

"You're still at one."

"There's Gordon Moore."

"I don't know who that is."

"He invented Moore's law—you know, computers double in speed every two years."

Jessica rolled her eyes. "I said famous."

Ralph racked his brain.

"Got it," he said. "Gordon Lightfoot."

"Gordon Lightfoot is famous?"

"I think you're selling him short," Ralph said. "He had something like eight gold records."

"Why do you know that?"

"I love 'The Wreck of the Edmund Fitzgerald'?"

"What are you, sixty-eight years old?"

"I'm twenty-four."

"Well, you have an old soul." Jessica smiled ever so.

Ralph nodded thoughtfully. Then he said, "Lightfoot was a big talent. But I take your point. There are not a lot of famous Gordons."

"Thank you," Jessica said, touching her heart. "That's very big of you."

"My pleasure."

"The power of a name is awesome," Jessica said, resuming her train of thought. "Do you think Stewart Copeland ever sits in bed at night and wonders if things might have been different if he had come up with the name Sting first? It's not like anyone had dibs on it. Einstein could have called himself Sting."

"It's not as if Stewart Copeland had a bad life. Dad in the CIA, private schools in the Middle East, toured the world in an all-time great band."

"Of course not. He's had a great life. But he's not Sting. He doesn't sell out Madison Square Garden. No one goes around humming 'Miss Gradenko'."

"Maybe it's not a good song."

"Or maybe it's a great song but we've just been trained to think 'Every Breath You Take' is great."

"Because the record companies didn't think they could sell a guy named Stewart?"

Jessica flared her eyeballs. "Can you think of any famous Stewarts?"

"Stuart Little?"

"I suppose that makes my point," Jessica said.

"I suppose," Ralph said, and hummed the chorus to "Miss Gradenko." "It's a pretty catchy tune," he said. "If only he had named himself Flea or Slash or some other one-word name."

Jessica smiled. "It'll be interesting to see what sort of music the aliens admire," she said. "And what else they value too."

HERE'S THE CHORUS TO "Miss Gradenko":

> Is anybody alive in here?
> Is anybody alive in here?
> Is anybody at all in here?
> Nobody but us in here . . . Nobody but us in here.

I have no idea what the song is about.

"WHAT'S THAT?" HE ASKED. Ralph absorbed Jessica's words. He was sure he had heard wrong or misunderstood.

"I said it'll be interesting to see what art and music the aliens value," Jessica said. "We've had thousands of years to develop our conception of beauty. Now these people will come and give us an entirely fresh assessment. It doesn't mean theirs is right and ours is wrong. It'll just be interesting to see what they think."

Ralph stammered. "You know about the aliens?"

"Oh my goodness," Jessica exclaimed. She reached out and touched Ralph on the arm. "That was so insensitive of me. Did you not know?"

"No, I knew. I just didn't realize it was public knowledge."

"It's been on the Internet all morning. They sent an e-mail last night with a video attachment to this high school kid in Chicago. He sent it to everyone he knew. Pretty much the whole world knows now."

"An e-mail? A video? How do you know it's authentic?"

"I don't know," she said. "It just seems sincere. I never had any doubt. I hope you don't think I'm a wacko, but I always knew this day would come. The universe is such a big place. It was just a matter of time. They sent this sweet, peaceful message. It is the way I always imagined it."

For a moment, Ralph lost himself in her eyes. Impossibly, this beautiful woman had a searching, joyful soul. Everything about her seemed magical. He wanted to lean across the table and kiss her right then and there, but duty called him back.

"I need to go," he said. "I have to get back to work."

"Don't forget your iPod," she said, as she handed it to him. "And your boss's sandwich."

He took the iPod and the sandwich and turned for the door.

"Wait," he said. "How will I find you?"

"You'll figure it out," she said.

He wondered, but she seemed confident. "Tell me one other thing," he said. "You said there was a video. What do they look like? What did the alien look like?"

"Dark hair, braided, thick facial hair," she said. "A bit like a rabbi."

Ralph nodded, exited Blimpway, and walked briskly down Avenue L toward the White House, thinking as he traveled that the world was changing faster than he had ever imagined possible. How many of these people knew? Did the woman with the Lord & Taylor bag know? Did the man cleaning up after his beagle know too? Did they just go on with their lives as if nothing had happened? He had presumed the dozens of people who passed him on the street were all operating in blissful oblivion, shopping and walking their dogs, but maybe they each knew all along and still chose to go about their business. Who knew what to believe?

Ralph walked faster. As he crossed Sixteenth Street, he glanced down at his cargo and noticed that Jessica had written her phone number across the wrapper of the President's sandwich, and the pace of change seemed to accelerate further still.

3

I THOUGHT I'D RAISE MY SPIRITS WITH A LITTLE CHAMPAGNE BRUNCH

When Ralph returned to the West Wing, the White House senior staff had already assembled in the Roosevelt Room. They were waiting to begin a meeting with the President, who had been behind schedule all morning because at the start of his day he lingered for fifteen minutes too long with a group of Eagle Scouts. The President, himself a former Eagle Scout, had special fondness for all Boy Scouts. This was touching, but as a result of his dallying with the scouts, the President was late for a meet-and-greet with the national spelling bee champion, in turn late for a photo opportunity with the Stanley Cup champions of the National Hockey League, in turn late for a meeting with the prime minister of Luxembourg, then late for a meeting with a high-profile lobbying group of rock stars and actors who wanted the United States to buy the Amazon rain forest, late to meet the First Lady and a renowned upholsterer about changing the couches in their weekend home on the Chesapeake to which they were scheduled to leave later that afternoon, late for a reception with the ambassador of Tahiti, late to talk to a midwestern congressional delegation about relaxing the standards required to call a farm product "organic," late for a haircut, late to have tea with the chairman of the Federal Reserve, late to call and wish the First Mother a happy birthday, and finally, now, late for a session with the senior staff about how to respond to the whole alien situation.

Ralph was out of breath when he entered the Roosevelt Room. "They know," he panted. "Everybody knows. The aliens sent some kid a video. It's all over the Internet."

The press secretary, Martha Jones, gestured for Ralph to sit down. "We know," she said. "We're not sure everyone buys it, though. The person who forwarded it to me thought it was a hoax."

The chief of staff, Joe Quimble, said, "Apparently not everybody thought it was a hoax. In one morning, it's already the most downloaded video in the history of the Internet."

"Well, it's real," said David Prince. "People have a way of sniffing out the truth in these things. Call it a collective intuition." David was the deputy chief of staff, and the closest thing Ralph had to a friend in the West Wing.

"What's in the video?" Ralph asked.

"It isn't much," Joe Quimble said. "It's less than a minute long. Basically they say hello and that they come in peace."

"The production quality isn't very good," added Martha Jones. "It's just a crappy straight-to-camera shot. We should put them in touch with our media people."

"Does the President know?"

"Yes," Martha said. "He asked the Secretary of State and Secretary of Defense to join us for this meeting. They're waiting next door. He wants to coordinate a tactical and political response—just as soon as he gets off the phone with his mother."

Softly, Martha added, "Len Carlson is coming too."

Joe Quimble said, "I hate that guy."

LEN CARLSON WAS THE President's political consultant, and the mastermind behind his election. At the start of the campaign, the President—then a little-known senator—was polling last in a crowded field of Republicans. Carlson adroitly positioned the President as a moderate in the conservative-heavy Republican field, largely by emphasizing his openness to abortion for victims of rape and incest. This attracted attention and set him apart from the other candidates. Then, after the President shockingly won the primary, Carlson had him tack back to the right for the general election. This maneuver consisted almost entirely in emphasizing his blanket opposition to abortion, including for victims of rape and incest. The press did not explore the arguable tension between these positions. The strategy worked, which was all that mattered.

Carlson would have been heralded by the press as a genius, if it knew that he existed, which it did not. Carlson was obsessively reclusive. This allowed him to take on clients of differing persuasions without his engagement creating difficulties for the candidates. Included among these were the President's immediate predecessor, a lifelong Republican who at Carlson's urging won nomination through the Democratic primaries, and the President's predecessor's predecessor, a liberal Democrat who ran on a bring-back-prayer-in-school platform.

The joke among the dozen or so people inside the Beltway who knew of Len Carlson's existence was that with $100 million for television advertising, Carlson could get Nixon reelected president, despite the impeachment and being dead.

With $200 million, the joke went, he could get him elected as a Democrat.

THE SPECTER OF CARLSON'S presence cast a pall over the political team as it waited for the President to get off the phone with his mother, who was giving her son substantial grief about her birthday gift, a magnificent Jean-Paul Gaultier evening gown, unfortunately purchased in a size eight instead of a size ten, the size the First Mother had worn for her entire adult life. The First Mother tearfully concluded the President was sending her a message about her weight. In truth, an assistant had reminded the President of his mother's birthday, searched for the gift, and arranged for its delivery. His participation consisted entirely of saying okay to these arrangements. Of course, the President could say none of this to his mother. He spent several minutes trying to calm her.

In the Roosevelt Room they did not know the details of what detained the President. They just waited.

"I wonder why they came to Earth now," David Prince said softly, thinking aloud. "What's significant about this particular moment in our history?" This was a natural question for Prince, who had been a college history professor, with a tenure track job, when he decided to volunteer some time for the President's first senate campaign. His interest in the campaign was academic; he wanted to see how politics worked. Before David knew it, he was in charge of research on the campaign, then the legislative director in the Senate, and soon after that a key member of the White House staff. Ralph wasn't entirely sure David shared the President's politics.

"Maybe they were just in the neighborhood," Martha Jones said with a smile.

"In *Star Trek*," David said, "the Federation makes first contact when a planet develops faster-than-light-speed travel."

"That's quite a bit beyond us technologically," Martha said. Neither Martha nor Joe Quimble seemed very interested in exploring this issue, but Ralph found David's question intriguing.

"In the movie *Contact*," Ralph said to David, "it was the transmission of television programming that triggered the alien response."

"They're a bit slow on the draw if that's the case," said David.

"They were in *Contact* too. In fact, part of the message they sent back was footage of Hitler opening the 1936 Olympic Games in Berlin. That was the first image ever transmitted by television. It took the *Contact* aliens more than fifty years to get a message back to Earth."

"Remember in *Galaxy Quest*," said David, "how the aliens had seen all the episodes of a *Star Trek*–like show but thought it was real, and decided Tim Allen, who played a character like Captain Kirk, should lead them through a crisis?"

"*Galaxy Quest* wasn't bad," Ralph said.

"Well," Joe Quimble said, "I hope they didn't see a bunch of *Sanford and Son* reruns. They might think Earth is a giant junkyard."

"Seriously, though," David said. "Why would they come now? We've been transmitting messages into space for almost a hundred years and listening for responses all the while. What has happened recently that's special?"

"Nuclear weapons?" Ralph suggested.

"The first atomic weapon was detonated more than sixty years ago," David said.

"Space travel?"

"The Russians launched a human into space in nineteen sixty-one."

"So what then?"

"It's just as likely something sociological as technological," David said. "It's exciting to be alive for this, and more exciting still to have a front-row seat."

Ralph said, "I hope it's not like that *Twilight Zone* episode where the Kanamits come to Earth because they want to harvest humans. That story always creeped me out."

"'To Serve Man,'" David said. "I loved that episode."

Martha Jones cut them off. "I hate to interrupt your little sci-fi convention, but the President is coming."

THE PRESIDENT ENTERED, FOLLOWED by the Secretary of State, the Secretary of Defense, the National Security Advisor, and finally Len Carlson. Everyone stood.

"Please sit down," the President said. They sat and awaited his guidance.

"Ralph," the President said, "do you have my lunch?"

Ralph took the ham and Swiss sub to the President. The President opened the wrapper and stared disapprovingly at the sandwich.

"There's hardly any meat on this," he said. "Did you bother to check this?"

"I did, sir. The sandwich seemed fine to me, Mr. President."

"How can it be fine? There's barely any meat." The President removed the top slice of bread and thumbed through the sandwich.

"There are only four slices of meat here."

"Sir, I believe there have always been exactly four slices of meat. That is the company policy."

"I could have sworn there used to be more."

"I don't believe so, sir."

"Well, is there any way to get more meat?"

"Yes, sir. You can pay two dollars and fifty cents more for an extra-thick sandwich."

"Then let's do that in the future. Can you take care of that, Ralph?"

"Yes, Mr. President."

Ralph ran a quick calculation in his head. The President's directive would cost him approximately seven hundred dollars over the next year, and something on the order of three thousand more if the President won reelection.

"All right, folks," the President said between bites, "what are we going to do about this alien nonsense?" He had a dab of mayonnaise on his chin. No one pointed it out.

The Secretary of Defense spoke first.

"Sir, our satellites have not detected any sign of weapons. Nevertheless, I have placed the military on alert. I recommend you issue a directive bringing us to our highest state of readiness."

"So ordered."

Joe Quimble raised his hand. "Mr. President, with all respect, that may not be necessary. The aliens have done nothing to suggest any hostile intention. Our actions may send the wrong signal. Mobilizing the military could be misinterpreted."

"Point noted," said the President. "But there's no reason to take any chances. You know what Jack Frost said, 'Good Fences Make Good Neighbors.'"

Here followed the most awkward of silences, which only Martha Jones had the nerve to break. "Sir," she said, "you have a spot of mayonnaise on your chin."

The President wiped it off. "Mr. Secretary of State, what say you?"

The Secretary of State went way back with the President, even further than Lois Dundersinger did, all the way back to the President's days as sanitation commissioner, when he, the Secretary, was starting what would later become the largest chicken-feed company in the United States.

"Sir," the Secretary said, "our allies are looking to us for guidance. The nations of the world are waiting to see what we will do before they choose their course of action."

The President nodded. He turned to his trusted political advisor. "What do you think, Len?"

Len Carlson had been munching, some might say irreverently, on a cruller coated in powdered sugar, the substantial remainder of which he now devoured in a single bite and washed down with a swill of coffee. He stood up from his chair and made a halfhearted effort to clean his lapel. This effort consisted of a single outward brushing motion with his left hand, which did not disturb the detritus on his lapel but created on his right shoulder a curious blend of confectionary sugar and dandruff. As he paced the room, speckles of this mélange floated to the ground like a soft winter flurry.

"Sir," Carlson said, "this is the defining moment of your presidency."

Few could disagree with this. Ralph saw several members of the staff nod their heads approvingly. This was not always the case when Len Carlson spoke.

"This is a critical opportunity to shore up our support among Jewish voters and reestablish the credibility of our commitment to Israel."

Heads stopped nodding. David Prince silently mouthed the word "Israel" several times.

"Go on, Len," said the President.

"Mr. President, your numbers have been dropping since the terrorist attack on Jerusalem last year. People feel our reaction was too slow and not sufficiently forceful. This is your opportunity to prove to America and the world that we stand by our allies."

"So what do we do?"

"Lots of media, a flashy state dinner, big emphasis on the Jewish thing—dreidels, beanies, the works."

The President said, "I like it."

THE DISCUSSION SENT THE cabinet into a trance, which Joe Quimble snapped out of first.

"If I may, Mr. President," he said. "It seems to me we may be missing the real import of this event. This is a unique moment in human history. We have confirmation for the first time that we are not alone in the universe—"

Len Carlson interrupted. "That doesn't mean there isn't a political opportunity here."

"We should be thinking about the message we want humanity to send these visitors," said Quimble.

"We should be thinking about the political message we want to send the American people," Len Carlson replied.

"We should be thinking about history," said Quimble.

"We should be thinking about your legacy," said Carlson.

"We should think about the future."

"We should think about now."

"Mr. President, this is much bigger than you."

"Mr. President, nothing is bigger than you."

"This is crazy! We don't even know if they're Jewish!"

Heads had been darting back and forth in tennis-match fashion between Carlson and Quimble. Thus no one realized at first it was the normally unassuming David Prince who had shouted these last words. For a moment even Len Carlson was stunned.

"Excuse me, Mr. President," David continued, calmer now, "but we have no reason to believe the aliens are Jewish. So the man in the video has black hair and a ponytail. That doesn't mean he's Jewish. It wouldn't make any sense. Judaism is six thousand years old. These people are coming from thousands of light-years away. They probably left before Abraham was born."

"You mean Moses," said the President.

Ralph felt David deflate.

"Yes, sir," he said.

"Whether they are Jewish or not is beside the point," Len Carlson said. "People will believe these people are Jewish. Thus how you treat them will determine whether or not you are reelected."

The President considered the matter. He sat silently in his chair, tapping his finger on his upper lip, absorbing everything he had heard. The staff waited anxiously, knowing the President's next words would inalterably shape the future of human history.

Finally, he spoke.

"They did say they wanted to have brunch."

"Sir?" asked Quimble.

"I've never heard of anyone having brunch who wasn't Jewish."

"Mr. President," David said quietly, "lots of people have brunch who aren't Jewish."

"Well, I don't know any. Where does the word come from anyway?"

"It means breakfast and lunch."

"Well, I never heard that word when I was a kid. We had breakfast and then we had lunch, like the Good Lord intended. First I heard of brunch was when I got into national politics. I'll say the same thing today I have always said: Don't understand it, ain't gonna eat it."

"But, sir, whether or not you like brunch isn't really the point."

The President rose and put his fist to the table.

"It's decided," he said. "We're going to proceed on the assumption our new friends are Jewish until proven otherwise."

"A judicious decision, Mr. President," Len Carlson said, reaching for a jelly-filled cruller.

"We still need to send a reply to the aliens," Joe Quimble said.

The President looked to Len Carlson. He was chewing his donut.

"Say 'shalom,'" Carlson said.

The President nodded approvingly. "Make sure that gets out to the media," he said.

THE ASSOCIATION OF BRUNCH with the Jews is yet another counter-historical, anti-Semitic defamation, like Jews' responsibility for the death of Jesus, with the notable difference that pretty much everyone likes brunch, so no one gets too agitated about the error. The word is, in fact, British, a term of student slang, which originated in the mid 1890s. It is a portmanteau, of course, of "breakfast" and "lunch."

I would like to invent my own portmanteau and have advocated strongly with friends who live in Seattle that the Space Needle be renamed the Sneedle. I worry, though, I may be forgotten by history, as was the Oxford student who, in a flash of brilliance, came up with "brunch," which is really snappy, and the best sounding of the several meals one can eat between breakfast and lunch. These include second breakfast, elevenses, and the Indian meal tiffin. If you go to Seattle and hear somebody saying they're taking the monorail to the Sneedle, please know that's my doing.

As the professional bowler Jacques explained to an ignorant Marge Simpson, "It's not quite breakfast, it's not quite lunch, but it comes with a slice of cantaloupe at the end. You don't get completely what you get at breakfast, but you get a good meal." It is most decidedly, most emphatically, not a Jewish thing. Dim sum brunch is an enormously popular meal at Chinese restaurants worldwide. They serve stuffed buns and dumplings from passing carts and, almost inevitably, a slice of cantaloupe at the end.

DAVID PRINCE AND RALPH lingered in the Roosevelt Room.

"Can you believe this?" David asked.

Ralph smiled and shook his head.

"I can only imagine what the history books will say," David said.

Ralph nodded and smiled again.

"You're glowing," David said.

"What do you mean?"

"You met a girl."

"What makes you say that?"

"It's all over you. I can see it in your eyes and in your face. Don't try to deny it."

"It's true," Ralph said, with a silly grin. "I met this great girl at the sandwich shop today."

"Does she like you?"

"I think so. She gave me her number on the President's sandwich wrapper."

"Are you going to ask her out?"

"I don't know," Ralph said.

"Are you kidding me?" David asked. "You're not seriously saying you're not going to ask her out, are you?"

"I don't know," Ralph said. "With everything going on it just seems like such a—frivolous thing to be thinking about. And, besides, the President depends on me . . ."

"To get him his lunch."

"All the same, he depends on me, and I feel a sense of duty."

"Well," David said, somewhat mischievously, "the President is going out of town this weekend, so it would be the perfect time."

"I don't know," said Ralph.

"Let me tell you something, Ralph. When I was a history professor, I was always struck by one thing. Historical moments are over in a flash. Caesar ruled an empire—then, snap your fingers, and he's a Shakespeare play. Genghis Khan ruled half the world and, snap, hardly anyone remembers who he is. We're about to live through history and it's incredibly exciting. But don't make the mistake of thinking life stops because of any of this. It doesn't. It just keeps coming at you, faster than you could ever imagine."

"Okay," he said, pensively. "I'll give her a call."

Ralph wondered about what David said. His thoughts returned to the men and women he had seen earlier that afternoon walking the streets of Washington. Ralph's instincts were always to do what was expected of him, to fulfill his responsibility. But perhaps if those people's lives could go on as normal, even in the face of the most dramatic shift in their reality, so too could his own. Perhaps David was right.

"Okay," Ralph said pensively. "I'll give her a call."

David smiled a wide grin, which infected Ralph, and soon he could barely contain his excitement at the prospect of seeing Jessica again.

4

HERE IN MY CAR, I
FEEL SAFEST OF ALL

IN THE RIGHT-HAND LANE of the Trans-Galactic freeway, puttering along at 40,000 miles per second, less than one quarter the speed of light and just above the highway minimum, Maude Anat-Denarian was having a bad day.

It started when she decided to drive all the way to the Trader Planet in Orion to shop for groceries. Maude had a love-hate relationship with Trader Planet. The idea of being able to buy everything in the universe in one place was grand in theory, but odd in practice. It seemed unnatural, at least in Maude's view, to go to a single place to fill a shopping list that read:

- ☑ Seltzer
- ☑ Succotash
- ☑ Trans-Warp Coil

- ☑ Frozen Fish Fillets
- ☑ Epsom Salts
- ☑ Pencil Sharpener
- ☑ Portable Cold-Fusion Generator Filter
- ☑ Baby Formula
- ☑ Cremation Urn

But you could get it all at Trader Planet. You would even find the urn and the formula in the same aisle, #684, arranged and titled by a store manager with a macabre sense of humor: "Birth/ Death."

Maude Anat-Denarian did not care for irony.

MAUDE FINISHED HER SHOPPING in a reasonable amount of time. She found the right filter for the fusion generator and fought through the beverage section, securing the seltzer without incident. She found the formula and the urn for her friend Edith, who had had a baby and lost her great aunt in the same week. They even had the brand of succotash she liked.

The trouble began at the checkout. The man ahead of her on line got into an argument with the cashier over the price of a one-pound can of dangonsheel, a meat substitute that tastes like ham. They had to call over the manager and get a price check. Since Trader Planet is almost five miles long, it took nearly twenty minutes for the manager to travel from one end of the store to the other. The customers in line behind the man did passive-aggressive things like exhaling and muttering under their breath.

THIS WAS ALL HAPPENING at precisely the same time the homeless man was fighting the powers that be at Blimpway about the quantity of meat in his sandwich. This is not as much of a coincidence as it might first appear. Lots of people in the universe like ham and ham substitutes, which can be expensive. There are often disputes over price.

AT TRADER PLANET, UNLIKE Blimpway, the customer is always right. When the manager arrived, he happily resolved the price dispute in favor of the customer. The customer thus saved approximately a half dollar on the can of dangonsheel. The manager even threw in a free gallon jug of a new concentrated prune juice, which hadn't been selling well.

This was all fine for the customer, but of no help to Maude. During the nearly twenty minutes it took for the manager to arrive, most of the customers lost patience and went to other cashiers. Maude stayed. Immediately next in line, Maude felt trapped. She figured if she abandoned her position the manager would arrive the very next moment. So she stayed in line, and thus ended up waiting out the full twenty minutes.

For some reason, the cashier could not ring up another customer while they waited. This required a sophisticated technological advance beyond the store computer's capabilities.

IT SHOULD BE NOTED that in point of fact, Trader Planet did not sell items in either one-pound cans or gallon jugs. The people of that region of the universe used the Natriccian system, which, by coincidence, is identical to the Metric system. For convenience, I have converted all mass and volume to the English system of weights and measures.

THINGS GOT WORSE STILL in the parking lot. They have every modern convenience at Trader Planet, including shopping hoverwagons equipped with antigravity lifts that can be used to hoist the heavier items. These are free of charge, save a modest deposit of a ditron, a coin equivalent to the quarter, which is inserted into a female lock attached to the handle of each hovercart. The coin is retrieved by inserting a male key, one of which is attached to the rear of each wagon. The idea is that when the shopper brings back her hovercart, she pushes her cart into line, using the key from her cart to release a coin from the next cart in the queue.

This kept the carts stacked neatly and saved the Trader Planet the expense of hiring cart boys. In the past, this function had been performed by the Zosmodians, a reptilian species from a six-dimensional universe with photosynthetic skin, a talent for spackling, and the ability to travel across time and space. The Zosmodians worked cheap, and generally off the books because few of them had visas, but they were nevertheless regarded as undesirable laborers. This was because, though they possessed the ability to travel through time, they always showed up five minutes late. This defect in their chrono-ambulatory capacity was why they had never parlayed their natural abilities into fortune. When they showed up, for example, to bet on the Andromeda Derby, with knowledge of which space eel won, they arrived tardy as usual, and after the close of pari-mutuel wagering.

For their part, the Zosmodians had a good attitude about the whole thing. They figured it was part of God's master plan, and spent lots of time in the distant past, when people appreciated quality spackling and weren't in so much of a hurry.

FOR THE LIFE OF her, Maude couldn't get the coin back. She tried everything—jammed the hovercart closer, jiggled it up and down, even applied some of her lip balm to the key as a lubricant. Nothing worked. After five minutes of grappling, she considered giving up, but if her mother taught her one thing it was that a ditron is a ditron. So she went back inside the store, waited fifteen minutes to get someone's attention, asked for help, waited fifteen minutes more for someone to actually help her, walked back into the parking lot, then watched in disbelief as a bespectacled, pimply teenage boy released the ditron in less than a second.

"You were putting the key in upside down," he said, handing Maude the coin.

BY THE TIME MAUDE finally headed home, fish fillets and Epsom salts safely in tow, she was a full two hours behind schedule and more than a little upset. Truth was she was upset even before the whole Trader Planet price-check and parking lot fiasco began. That morning, she had received a call from her son's physics teacher who said Todd, her son, was failing the course. Though she did not say so to the boy who helped her, Maude believed her distress over this telephone call was what had impaired her ability to retrieve her ditron from the shopping wagon.

The teacher said Todd paid little attention in class and would often draw sketches in his notebook during lectures. He had failed each of the first three tests and, without a remarkable turnaround, would have little chance of passing. Furthermore, the teacher said he had spoken with Todd about his situation after class and the boy had shown almost no concern. The teacher thus felt he had no choice but to contact the parents.

This news upset Maude greatly, of course, and her first reaction was to call her husband. She resisted, though, because Ned was away on business in another galaxy and the phone charges would have been substantial. Now she was supremely upset. She had to speak with Ned, roaming charges be damned.

MAUDE DIALED. NED ANSWERED after the second ring. His voice sounded concerned. "What is it, Maude?" he asked. "Is everything okay?"

"How did you know it was me?"

"Caller ID, Maude. We've been through this before."

"It's just so spooky to have someone answer the phone with your name. It was never like that growing up. You always said, 'Hello,' and then the person would identify himself or herself or you would ask, 'Who is this?' and then they would tell you. There's no mystery anymore. You can't surprise anyone."

"Honey, can you get to the point? You know I'm on a mission."

She wanted to tell him about how long it took to finish the shopping and about her trouble with the ditron. Ned could be comforting about things like that. But she could tell from his voice she needed to cut to the chase.

"It's Todd. His teacher called and said he is failing physics. I called the school and it turns out he's failing three of his courses. They say he's daydreaming in class and is unconcerned with his performance."

"Have you spoken with him about it?"

"No, I just found out this morning. In any case, I wanted to speak with you first."

"Well, I'm glad you called."

"I really think we should talk to Todd together, face-to-face."

"That's going to be difficult. I'm not going to be home for almost a month."

"Can't you come home just for a day or two? You work so hard all the time. I don't see why they can't give you a few days off."

"We're in the middle of a crisis right now, honey. We just made first contact with a species and the dominant power sent back a very confusing message. It is just one word and it isn't in their native language. We're trying to discern their intended meaning."

"And this is more important than your son?"

There was a long silence and, given the rates, an expensive silence at that.

"I'm sorry," Maude said. "That wasn't fair of me."

"It's okay. I know my being away is hard on you and Todd. It's just that they really need me here right now."

"What does the Ambassador say about the message?"

"You know how he is. Everything is fun. Nothing to worry about. He finds the matter amusing."

"If he's not worried then you shouldn't be worried either."

"I wish I could help myself. I'm just not built that way."

"Well, I love you just as you are."

"I love you too, Maude. Listen, how about I give Todd a call later on? It's not as good as being there in person, but I can set aside an hour and have a good, long chat with him. I'll try to figure out what's going on."

"That sounds fine."

"And I'll be home in a few weeks."

"I know."

This soothed Maude. Even so, her husband knew it was best to end these conversations with small talk.

"What did you do today?" he asked.

"I did some shopping. I'm on my way home right now."

"Did you remember to get seltzer?"

"I did."

"Well, I love you. Drive carefully."

SAYING THIS WAS SUPERFLUOUS, almost ridiculously so, given Maude Anat-Denarian was perhaps the most careful driver in the universe. She stopped fully at every stop sign, always signaled before turning, and believed speed limits were to be approached only in the event of emergency. As a policy, she drove at least 10,000 feet per second below all posted maximums.

She had developed an impenetrably thick hide to the people who flashed her with their bright lights and cursed as they passed her car. She distracted herself by listening to Intergalactic Public Radio. She particularly enjoyed the afternoon program on good gardening practices. That day's show was devoted to cultivating broccoli. An avid gardener and fan of broccoli, Maude settled in for a good listen.

Unfortunately for Maude, Nelson Munt-Zoldarian was not so cautious a driver. In fact he was intentionally reckless. Munt-Zoldarian liked to get people, particularly women, to rear-end him. What he would do, and what he did on this occasion, was to drive along a highway in hyperwarp and then brake quite suddenly, leaving the driver behind him very little time to avoid an accident.

This was dangerous behavior to say the least, but Munt-Zoldarian had learned to exploit a loophole in intergalactic traffic law. By any honest assessment, when Maude Anat-Denarian slammed into the back of Nelson Munt-Zoldarian's car at a speed of approximately 8,000 feet per second, causing all twenty-eight airbags to inflate, it was one hundred percent Nelson's fault. This was true of each of the thirty-seven prior accidents in which Munt-Zoldarian had been involved. Despite this, Munt-Zoldarian had never been found at fault and would not be found so on this occasion. This was because the law said that when a driver strikes another driver in the rear of the car, the striking driver is adjudged to be at fault.

No one, not even Lionel Hut-Zanderian, the greatest legal mind in the Orion galaxy, could explain how this rule had come to be adopted. It was one of many, many things in the universe that could be observed, but not explained.

It could also be observed, but not explained, that Nelson Munt-Zoldarian had parlayed his "career" as an accident victim into a fortune amounting to the equivalent of approximately fifty million dollars. This was particularly difficult to accept given the fact that many decent, hardworking people in the universe lived in poverty or near poverty without the benefit of modern amenities such as painless dentistry, no-run panty hose, and levitating luggage. Nevertheless, Munt-Zoldarian had his money. This was why at the time of the accident he was driving a Mercedes Ben-Zantarian, one of the nicest cars in the universe.

Driving an especially nice car helped Munt-Zoldarian in his work because when the police would arrive at the scene to take a report, the officer would never suspect someone driving a Ben-Zantarian of purposely damaging a car costing the equivalent of approximately a hundred thousand dollars. It also helped Munt-Zoldarian to target women because the police had a preconception that women were inferior drivers. Munt-Zoldarian would speak politely to the police in the presence of the women victims, but would privately roll his eyes to the officers, who always understood. They would draft a report, which would invariably favor Munt-Zoldarian.

In the matter regarding Maude Anat-Denarian, the report simply said this:

Party of the Second Part (Maude Anat-Denarian) struck Party of the First Part (Nelson Munt-Zoldarian) in rear of vehicle. Party of the Second Part is unharmed. Party of the First Part complains of neck pain.

This one-sided account of the accident would effectively ensure that Nelson Munt-Zoldarian would receive a settlement of somewhere between $1 million and $5 million, depending on the Party of the Second Part's resolve and, more relevantly, the coverage limits of the Party of the Second Part's insurance policy.

It was yet another outrage the police accident report was dispositive of the conflict. Police officers were not experts in accident reconstruction. More often than not, these cases boiled down to one person's word against another's, and the police were no better than anyone else at assessing credibility. Lionel Hut-Zanderian called the use of police reports in courtrooms "scandalous," but by and large the practice went unchallenged.

GENERALLY SPEAKING, MUNT-ZOLDARIAN'S VICTIMS did not help their own causes. This was particularly true in Maude Anat-Denarian's case. Maude might have chosen to focus on her well-established, almost comical, caution as a driver to develop the operative hypothesis that she had not been the cause of the accident. This might have led her to realize the Ben-Zantarian in front of her, which appeared to be stopped in the road, was in fact stopped in the road and not just traveling slowly, as its driver contended. It might have emboldened her to challenge the conclusory and one-sided report prepared by the investigating police office. It could also have led her to investigate, or at least have prompted her attorney and insurance carrier to investigate, the rather suspicious intergalactic driving record of Nelson Munt-Zoldarian.

Instead, Maude developed the operative hypothesis that the accident had indeed been her own fault. Honest woman that she was, Maude recognized she had been rather upset over the news regarding her son, her husband's absence, and the ordeal at the Trader Planet. All of this had led her to focus too intently on the gardening program on the radio and to fantasize about the possibility of good results in her garden. Rather than defend herself, Maude concluded she had caused the accident, in whole or in part, by daydreaming about broccoli.

5

I THINK WE'RE
ALONE NOW

THE EVENING FOLLOWING THE day aliens made first contact with humans, Ralph Bailey stood outside the White House anxiously waiting to begin his first date with Jessica Love. It was crowded on the street, but once Ralph spotted Jessica, he could not take his eyes off of her. Pennsylvania Avenue became, in essence, a long runway, which Jessica traversed in a brimmed red beret and overcoat, which she wore to combat the chill of the autumn air. Several men checked out Jessica as she walked, but she did not notice. She had only Ralph on her mind. When she spotted him, she accelerated her pace. He beamed as she drew near.

"Hi," she said.

"Hi."

"This was a good place to meet."

"I'm glad it suits you."

"So where are we going?" she asked playfully.

"I thought we would just stay here."

"You mean outside the White House?"

"No," he said, gesturing toward the presidential home. "I mean inside the White House."

Jessica's face lit up. "This is so cool," she said. "You arranged an after-hours tour?"

"A personal one," Ralph said. He felt mischievous.

RALPH LED JESSICA TO the West Gate security checkpoint. As they approached, a Secret Service agent said, "Good evening, Mr. Bailey."

"They know you?" Jessica asked.

"They do."

"Do I need to show identification?"

"Just a photograph," Ralph said. "The rest has been taken care of."

The agent asked, "Are you Jessica Love of Harrisburg, Pennsylvania?"

"I am."

"May I see a picture identification?" Jessica produced her driver's license, which the agent ran through a scanner. He watched the results on a computer.

"You're clear to proceed." The agent passed Jessica's bag through a metal detector and handed her a visitor badge. She thanked him.

"A pleasure, ma'am. Have a great evening."

"Thanks, Tom," Ralph said.

"You're welcome, sir."

"I'm flabbergasted," Jessica said as they walked across the front lawn. "We just walked in the main gate of the White House. He knew I was from Harrisburg before I even showed him my driver's license." Jessica pulled his arm. "Tell me," she said, "what do you do?"

Ralph stopped and faced Jessica. "Look," he said, "I expect you don't like the President very much. The truth is I go back and forth myself. Is it okay, just for tonight, if I am a twenty-four-year-old kid who has access to a really cool place to take a girl he really likes?"

Jessica nodded. "That's totally fine."

Ralph said, "Thank you," and they started walking.

"I bet you don't like him because he makes you pay for his sandwiches."

Ralph gently shoved Jessica and they both started to laugh. When they began walking again, Jessica's arm somehow became entwined with his.

"Now," Ralph thought, "everything is right in the universe."

WHETHER THIS IS TRUE is a matter of perspective. On the planet Bildungsruinia they have a saying: "Everything is exactly as it should be." The Bildungsruinians are polyamorous, live for thousands of years, and have conspicuously fertile soil that supports crops of candy corn and jelly beans. The Bildungsruinians have another saying, which was coined after Gilbert Arnot-Friedinian struck his shin against a step stool, which one of his wives left out in the middle of the kitchen. What he said was: "Life stinks."

This suggests the perspective that the rightness of the universe is really just a question of one's own lot in life, but even this rule has its exceptions. Case in point: Gottfried Leibniz, the seventeenth-century German mathematician and philosopher. Leibniz profoundly said, "This is the best of all possible worlds." Yet he was a short, bandy-legged man with a stoop, best-known for his ability to sit for days in the same chair. Of Leibniz, the duchess of Orleans graciously said, "It is rare to find learned men who are clean, do not stink, and have a sense of humor."

AT THE MASSIVE FRONT doors, Ralph bowed and said, "After you, my lady."

Jessica smiled. "Thank you, kind sir," she said.

Inside the Entrance Hall, the light of the twin eighteenth-century chandeliers made Jessica's cheeks glow. She stood facing the Grand Staircase and gaped. "It's magnificent."

"Best of all, everything you see is made of chocolate," Ralph said. "It's all eatable. I mean it's edible. I mean you can eat everything you see."

"Seriously?" she asked, playing along.

"Of course. In 1801, the Oompa Loompas, who were terrific at building chocolate structures but quite small in stature, were in great danger from predators. So President Adams said to them, 'Come and live with me in peace, away from the Whangdoodles and Hornswogglers and Vermicious Knids.' And they came and constructed the White House out of creamy milk chocolate. Unfortunately Chester Arthur ate most of the East Wing, so they had to rebuild. To make the structure sturdier, they mixed in pralines."

Jessica punched him in the arm. "The Secret Service is going to think you're crazy."

"Don't worry," Ralph said. "They can't see us. The pralines block video reception." He whispered in her ear, "Don't tell anyone, though. It would be bad for national security if that got out."

"You mean someone might come and steal the national chocolate."

Ralph nodded. "Exactly."

RALPH FIRST TOOK JESSICA downstairs to the creepy corridors of the White House basement and the Mary Todd Lincoln Bedroom.

"The room was furnished in the style of the high-Miltown period," Ralph explained. "Most of the pieces are attributed to Hoffmann-La Roche."

"Do you have any idea what the high-Miltown period is?"

"None whatsoever."

"So why do you know this?"

"You know the saying, 'Those who don't know history are doomed to repeat it.'"

Jessica nodded as she examined the room. "Why are the walls padded?" she asked.

"For the same reason the bedroom is in the basement."

"Why is the bedroom in the basement?"

"This is where they used to send First Ladies who could not control their behavior."

"A mini-sanitarium for the wives of presidents. That's charming."

"I didn't make the history," Ralph said. "I just repeat it."

At this moment, a raccoon darted out from one of the heat vents and scampered from one end of the bedroom to the other. The creature startled Jessica and she jumped into Ralph's arms, where she lingered for a moment too long after the danger had passed.

WHEN I WAS SIX years old, I took a tour of the White House with my parents and when we were in the Mary Todd Lincoln Bedroom, a raccoon made a similar impromptu appearance. It is the kind of event that makes an indelible impression on a six-year-old and I remember every detail vividly. I remember people were quite startled and my mother nearly jumped out of her skin. I remember people decompressed in a peculiar way by reminiscing about an event that had occurred only moments before. And I remember several jokes being made about Richard Nixon, which I did not get, but laughed at anyway in the spirit of the moment and because I recognized the name of someone my parents disliked.

The repeat appearance of a raccoon so many years later is not as coincidental as it might appear at first blush. Calvin Coolidge's wife had a pet raccoon named Rebecca who started a family, which for the next century chewed through the wiring in the walls, pilfered unguarded cheese, and generally gave the White House maintenance crew fits.

It does make me question, though, the old saw Ralph repeated about people who don't know history. The implication is that people who *do* know history will *not* end up repeating it either by not doing the thing of historic moment or doing it better so the consequences are different. But I'm not so sure.

People who say, "Those who don't know history are doomed to repeat it" are actually saying, "Don't fight a two-front war in Europe." It's really a veiled shot at Hitler for trying the same thing Napoleon had unsuccessfully tried a century before. But what was Hitler supposed to do? He didn't choose to be born in Germany with its tenuous strategic position. Once he made the highly questionable decision to conquer the world, he had no choice but to fight in Europe. That's where he lived.

The principle attributes too little weight to the twists of fate that truly drive the force of history. It wasn't Hitler's ignorance that sealed his fate, it was his bad luck (good luck from a more global perspective) of being born on the same plains land as Napoleon, which anyone who has ever played Risk knows is nearly impossible to defend. The thought that knowledge is sufficient to alter the course of destiny is laughable when one thinks about the infinite, arbitrary, and powerful forces at work.

I mean, suppose someone could have gotten to Grace Coolidge and explained to her the problems with keeping raccoons in the White House—both the problems raccoons had caused in important government buildings throughout history and the problems her own beloved Rebecca would cause in the future. What difference would it have made? Another raccoon still very well might have gotten into the White House ventilation system and made a family, and anyone who owns a home knows once raccoons get in there's not much that can be done. They are persistent and resilient creatures. My neighbor once had one in his attic. He trapped the critter, released him in a forest thirty miles away, and, believe it or not, the little guy was back in the attic three days later.

RALPH TOOK JESSICA UPSTAIRS, to the more upbeat parts of the house. He showed her the Library, the Vermeil Room with its collection of Hummel figurines, and then the famous Blue Room.

"This has always been used as a reception room, except during the Truman Administration when J. Edgar Hoover used to keep his corsets here," Ralph explained. "Interestingly, the blue fabric used on the furniture is EZ Wipe, just like in nursery schools."

"Cute," said Jessica.

They walked to the Map Room. "FDR used to use this as a situation room, but now it's a room where the President and First Lady entertain guests," Ralph explained. "It is decorated in the Chippendale style, which flourished in the late eighteenth century."

"Do you have any idea what the Chippendale style is?"

"None at all," said Ralph.

Finally, he escorted her to the West Wing. The executive offices mesmerized her.

"Now this impresses me," she said. "This is where it really happens."

It was quiet in the West Wing, and Jessica quickly noticed.

"Where is everybody?"

"The President is at his place on the Chesapeake for the evening," Ralph explained. "When he leaves the White House, some of the staff go with him."

"What about you?"

"I didn't go this time. The others can take care of him okay."

"How often do you get time off?"

"This is the first time since the President took office."

"You mean in three years this is your first night off."

"Sounds like a great job, doesn't it?"

"How's the pay?"

"Not too good."

"Where do I sign up?" Jessica asked.

"I bet we could use another lawyer."

"I bet you could too. Show me around."

RALPH SHOWED JESSICA THE press briefing room, and the chief of staff's office, and the little kitchen area where staff members microwaved their soup and snack-sized Beefaroni. He showed her the Roosevelt Room and explained how it used to be called the Fish Room because that was where FDR used to mount his fish, and how Nixon named the room in FDR's honor, but got rid of his fish, and that the biggest of the formerly mounted fish, a mackerel, was in storage in the basement. Then he revealed the pièce de résistance.

"Oh my god," she said. "This is the Oval Office." Tentatively, she asked, "Can we go in?"

"Of course."

Jessica walked to the center of the room on the rug with the presidential seal, and took a full, Marlo Thomas turnaround.

"It's magnificent," she said.

"In the morning, when the sunlight streams in from the east, it's almost mystical."

"I can imagine," she said.

Jessica pointed toward a cubby. "Is that where Clinton and Lewinsky did it?"

"Yes," Ralph said, leading her over.

"Who cares where the executive orders are signed," Jessica said. "I want to see where Clinton took his dates."

"It isn't so exciting anymore," Ralph said. "The President doesn't even allow real sugar in the West Wing." He rifled through the coffee station. "Sometimes the President's secretary smuggles home packets of Equal by stuffing them into her brassiere. Would you like some?"

"That's okay," Jessica said.

Together, they walked to the President's desk. Jessica caressed the top. "This is from the HMS *Resolute*," she said. "The *Resolute* was an abandoned British ship the Americans discovered and returned to England as a gesture of goodwill. Queen Victoria commissioned the desk and gave it to Rutherford Hayes."

"I'm impressed," Ralph said, smiling.

"When I was a kid I wanted to be president," she said.

"Me too," Ralph said. He pointed to the desk. "Why don't you try it out?"

"Really?"

"Sure."

Solemnly, Jessica sat down. She wiped her palms across the top of the desk and arched her back against the chair to feel the full power of the furniture. Ralph sat down on one of the sofas and watched.

"How do you like it?" he asked.

"It suits me just fine," she said.

"And you suit it," he said. "I don't think that desk has ever looked better."

Jessica blushed. When the color faded from her cheeks, she turned more serious. "What would you do if you were president?" she asked.

"I would get a beautiful woman to sit behind the desk and I would sit on this sofa and look at her all day." Ralph pointed at her. "You would do quite nicely."

"No, seriously, what would you do?"

"I am trying very hard not to be so serious."

"Just for a moment."

Ralph took a breath and exhaled. "If I were president of the United States," he said, "I would place a tax on people who have too much."

"Too much money?"

"No, just too much in general. You know, people like Tiger Woods. Here's this guy who is good-looking, plays golf better than anyone else, and has a billion dollars. On top of all that, he marries this unbelievably beautiful Swedish woman. That's too much."

"So you'd tax him?"

"Yeah. I'd take away the girl and give her to a homely guy who couldn't get a date. Tiger would still have plenty. It's only fair."

"And you think you could sell this to the public."

"Absolutely. It would be much more popular than a monetary tax. Take Warren Buffet, for example. No one begrudges him what he has. Sure he's worth fifty billion dollars, but he looks like Warren Buffet. So no one minds that he has so much money. It's people like Tiger and Brad Pitt and George Clooney who the IRS should be hitting. If Jennifer Aniston arrived at your house instead of a rebate check, people would really start to buy into the tax code."

"I like it, but I'm not sure the American people will buy it."

"Do you have a better idea?"

"Yes," she said matter-of-factly.

"And what is that?"

"What I would do," Jessica said, "is give every American a stuffed animal."

"You mean like a teddy bear?"

"It doesn't have to be a bear. It could be a lamb or a dog—just so long as it's stuffed."

"Why?" Ralph asked without any hint of skepticism. He expected her answer would warm his heart, which it did.

"People who grow up with stuffed animals are more gentle and caring," Jessica explained. "They're completely dependent on you, even more so than a real pet. A cat could do pretty well on its own, a dog can go feral and survive, but a stuffed pet has no life without its owner. Having responsibility for something powerless teaches you empathy."

"What type of stuffed animal did you grow up with?" Ralph asked.

"I had a soft little porcupine."

Ralph grinned, but Jessica cut him off. "Don't you dare laugh! I would have died for Booda. I used to worry there would be a fire in my house. Booda would have been the first and only thing I took on my way out. If need be, I would have risked my life to save him. The thought of him burning was unbearable to me. The world would be a better place if everyone thought of other people's suffering in the same way."

"I wasn't about to laugh," Ralph said. "I think what you said is nice." So nice he wanted to go over to the Resolute and kiss her.

"I bet the President didn't have a stuffed animal growing up."

"I wouldn't know. He has certainly never mentioned it to me."

Jessica softened. "I bet you did, though. I bet you had a stuffed bunny rabbit."

This woman was incredible. "You're right, though I don't know how you knew that," Ralph said. "His name is Bun-Bun. He's still with me."

"Well, perhaps Bun-Bun can meet Booda someday."

"I'm sure he would like that."

THE BRITISH CLAIM THE Teddy Bear took its name from King Edward VII, who went by Teddy, but every patriotic American knows the real story is that Theodore Roosevelt, while bear hunting in Mississippi in 1902, spared the life of a cub whose mother had been killed during the hunt. The episode was depicted in a popular cartoon, which in turn inspired a store owner named Rose Michtrom to create a toy bear. She wrote the White House requesting permission to name the bear "Teddy," permission President Roosevelt freely granted.

This was another of the many ways in which TR really got it, although it is impossible to imagine Roosevelt foresaw the massive proliferation of stuffed animals that would ensue over the following century, including bears, cats, dogs, snakes, alligators, rabbits, zebras, monkeys, birds, horses, several extinct species including dinosaurs of every kind, several species that never existed such as the unicorn, and, of course, not to be forgotten, the occasional, improbable porcupine.

"So WHAT ARE WE going to do now?" Jessica asked.

"Are you getting antsy?"

"Well, a private tour of the White House and sitting behind the president's desk is fine, but a girl likes to be impressed."

Ralph had prepared for the moment. He pulled a large wicker basket from the closet. He spread a picnic blanket across the carpet and laid out china plates and two thin candles, which he lit with a lighter from his pocket.

"How does a Chinese food picnic in the Oval Office sound?"

"It sounds just wonderful," Jessica said. She got up from the desk, walked over to the blanket, and sat down cross-legged. "What are we having?"

"General Tso's Chicken."

Jessica started to speak, but Ralph cut her off. "It's vegetarian," he said.

"How did you know?"

"I just guessed. I know how you tree-huggers are."

He dished the food onto a plate. "Here," he said. "Have some General Tso's Lite."

She took the plate. "Let me ask you a question," she said. "If it's made with tofu, is it still General Tso's Chicken?"

"You mean is chicken an integral part of the dish?"

"Right. If it's made with tofu, can it be General Tso's Tofu or tofu prepared in the style of General Tso or did General Tso only like chicken?"

"I don't know. How do you get a food named after you anyway?"

"That's a good question. How many people can you think of who do have foods named after them?"

"Napoleon has a pastry," Ralph said.

"Julius Caesar has the Caesar salad."

"I always thought that was Sid Caesar."

"No, it was definitely Julius."

IN FACT IT WAS the Italian-American restaurateur Caesar Cardini (1896–1956) who created the salad—sans anchovies—at his Tijuana restaurant in 1924. Cardini lived in San Diego, but ran the restaurant in Mexico to avoid Prohibition. As with every great invention, disputes have arisen over where the credit truly belongs. Among others, Cardini's business partner, Cardini's brother, and the mother of one of Cardini's sous-chefs claim credit for the recipe, but the weight of historical evidence is with Cardini himself. Julius Caesar is almost certainly not involved, except as the inspiration for Mr. Cardini's first name. Looking back, it is almost impossible to imagine Mr. Cardini could have foreseen the massive proliferation of Caesar salads, including salads topped with chicken, salmon, and fresh grilled tuna, and the explosion of salads generally, including the Waldorf salad, the Cobb salad, and the unfortunately named Watergate salad, a fruity mélange of pineapple, nuts, marshmallow, and whipped topping, which fell out of favor in the late seventies, but has enjoyed something of a renaissance of late, coinciding with the decision to turn the old hotel into condominiums.

"MAYBE YOU HAVE TO be a brutal tyrant to get a food named after you," Jessica said.

"There is the Shirley Temple."

"But that's clearly the exception."

"Or the exception proving the rule."

"Just think of all the great people who never had a food named for them."

"In that way," Ralph said, "Sting may have hurt himself. It's easy to imagine someone named Gordon getting a food named after him—Chicken Gordon Bleu, for example. But it's hard to imagine a food with Sting in the name—Shrimp Sting—it just doesn't sound very elegant."

"You know, there's a *Simpsons* episode on this. Mr. Burns has takeout Chinese and he says something like, 'General Tso, you may have been a ruthless tyrant, but you make a delicious bird.'"

Ralph's heart skipped a beat. "You like *The Simpsons?*"

"I do," she said with mock indignation. "I hope that isn't a problem for you. I can deal with this whole working-for-a-Republican-president thing, but not liking *The Simpsons* would be a deal breaker." She stood up theatrically.

"Oh no," Ralph said, looking up. "I love *The Simpsons*. I was hoping you did too."

Jessica sat back down. "Well," she said, playful again. "If you like *The Simpsons* so much, then enough with this derivative banter."

"The part about Sting was original."

"Inadequate. The central thrust was the General Tso thing. That was derivative."

"*The Simpsons* have covered just about every funny thing there is in the universe."

"There's a *South Park* episode to that effect. That's a funny idea—that there's nothing original to laugh about."

JESSICA AND RALPH DID not and could not know about the Spinocoli, one of the most ancient species in the universe, a race of monkey-like creatures who, aside from occasional lemonade breaks, spend their waking hours typing compulsively and randomly. Over the eons, they have written everything imaginable, including *Hamlet*—twice—the *Koran*, and a comedy routine, beloved on the planet Rigel-Rigel, about a man who shot a moose.

"I THINK EVERYTHING HAS happened before," Ralph said. "I think everything we experience has been experienced by someone else somewhere in the universe—every grief has been endured, every idea has been explored, every joke has been told."

Ralph took a bite of food, chewed thoughtfully, and continued. "But that doesn't make the experience any less meaningful to us. It doesn't make the joke any less funny—just told, not unfunny. That people have experienced the same things before doesn't diminish the quality of our experience or our ability to enjoy life. The mistake is to pretend these things haven't happened before, that we are somehow unique. That's too arrogant. Really, it's just a matter of perspective."

Someone else might have found this speech a bit melodramatic or juvenile, but Jessica had fallen in love with Ralph, as he had fallen in love with her, and she hung on his every word.

"One thing I take from that is we should enjoy every moment to the maximum."

"I agree with that in the abstract," Ralph said, "but I haven't practiced that principle. I worked too hard when I was in school, and I work too hard now. When you work at the White House, it becomes your entire universe, and everything in it seems profoundly important. Every day is like life and death. I never used to think of myself as being so serious, but working here I have a powerful sense of duty."

"To get the President his lunch," she said with a smirk.

"Exactly."

"Well, how about just for tonight we act as if the world is going to end tomorrow?"

"It could happen," Ralph said. "The aliens are lurking in orbit as we speak."

"Don't worry," Jessica said. "They have good intentions."

"How can you be sure?"

"I don't know," she said. "I just am."

"Are you one of these people who thinks things always work out for the best?"

"Not always," Jessica said, "but mostly."

"I don't understand that," Ralph said.

"What's not to understand?"

"Well, what evidence is there to suggest things always work out for the best?"

Jessica shrugged. "What evidence is there things work out for the worst?"

"I'm not sure that's the only alternative," Ralph said.

"Isn't it?" asked Jessica.

Jessica reached across the blanket and touched him on the lips with her index finger. "How would the Secret Service feel about us making out on the President's carpet?" she whispered.

Ralph gently kissed her lips. "I told you," he whispered. "The pralines block video transmission."

She started to sing softly. "*I think we're alone now. There doesn't seem to be anyone around.*"

"Tiffany?" he asked.

"Tommy James & the Shondells," she said, and as night fell on the White House, Ralph and Jessica shared their first kiss.

6

WORKING IN THE LAB
LATE ONE NIGHT

PROFESSOR JOHN FENDLE-FRINKLE'S EVENING of research in theoretical physics began like most; by removing wet laundry from his desk. This had been a "socks and underwear" day in the Fendle-Frinkle household. The Professor moved aside six sets of undershorts and three pairs of soggy socks, including a particularly wet pair of hosiery Mrs. Fendle-Frinkle had placed directly on the yellow legal pad containing the Professor's current calculations.

The Professor set the socks and underwear down on a small foldable tray table. This table had been designed and marketed as a place for people to rest their microwavable dinners while they watched television. In the Fendle-Frinkle household it was used exclusively as a place for the Professor to temporarily rest laundry while he contemplated the nature of the universe. Mrs. Fendle-Frinkle could have used the tray table in the same manner—thus sparing the Professor's papers some unnecessary smudging—but she chose to use the desk instead, leaving it to her husband to clear his work space. Earlier in the marriage, the Professor protested this practice, but he had long ago capitulated on such matters. In fact, when the Professor finished his work for the evening, he would return the socks and underwear to their original places on the desk.

Professor Fendle-Frinkle noticed some of his underwear contained holes, several of which were rather large. Professor Fendle-Frinkle noticed this because Mrs. Fendle-Frinkle had drawn rings around the holes with a pen. The Professor paid the ink circles little attention. Professor Fendle-Frinkle did not care much about socks, underwear, or any of the other quotidian details of life.

When he finished dealing with the laundry, the Professor sat down, at long last, at his desk. A black leotard hanging from the overhead clothesline dripped water onto his head, so he moved his chair to the right. In this position a second leotard—this one aquamarine—dripped water onto his head, so he moved the chair slightly to the left. Finally, he managed to find a narrow dry space between the soggy nylon bodysuits.

The Professor's desk was situated between the Fendle-Frinkles' washer and the Fendle-Frinkles' dryer. There was no choice but to place the desk along the same wall as the washer and dryer; the basement was quite small to begin with and one wall was occupied by the boiler, another by a slop basin, and a third by a set of plastic bins containing Mrs. Fendle-Frinkle's old shoes. It would have been possible, though, to put the desk to the left of the washer or to the right of the dryer. But the Professor's wife insisted on keeping the desk between the two appliances. She found the space useful for transferring clothing.

Because the dryer vibrated when it ran and because the washing machine produced a high-pitch squeal during its spin cycle, the positioning of the desk led to further disruptions of the Professor's work whenever his wife ran the washer or the dryer or, as was the case that evening, both.

When clearing clothing from his desk, the Professor sometimes wondered why his wife didn't put the underwear in the dryer together with the other clothing. He had asked his wife about this once. She had offered an explanation, something about elastics, which he did not understand at the time and had long since forgotten. The Professor also wondered, from time to time, why his wife did not run the wash during the day, since she did not work and spent most of the day watching soap operas. He had asked her about this once too. For this his wife offered no explanation. The Professor suspected, correctly, it was a passive-aggressive way for his wife to express disapproval of his work and, perhaps more relevantly, him.

On top of everything else, the vibration of the dryer caused the lightbulb above the Professor's head to flicker on and off. This single bulb, fastened to a socket hanging tenuously from the ceiling by a slender wire, was the sole source of light in the basement. Mrs. Fendle-Frinkle had steadfastly opposed the placement of a lamp in the cellar, saying it would disturb the aesthetic milieu. It would have been of no use anyway since there was but a single socket in the basement and it was fully engaged that evening by the washer and the voluble, vibrating dryer. So the Professor sat in intermittent periods of darkness, which sometimes lasted for no longer than an eye blink, but sometimes lasted for twenty or thirty seconds.

MY OWN WORK SPACE is far more pleasant than the Professor's. I have a quiet room at the top of my house with a big wooden table I use as a desk, a new computer with a flat-screen monitor, and two windows that offer excellent cross-ventilation. And I always have plenty of light. This is in part because of a special lamp I purchased to combat depression.

I am mostly a happy person, but I get down from time to time about politics and the environment and the general direction of things. I worry whether any of the enterprises to which I devote my time—like writing and teaching and bowling on Thursday nights— really make any difference. I think this metaphysical angst is quite typical of our times. It is arguably the defining characteristic of this generation. Just this morning I received an e-mail from one of my students, a very nice young man, asking me the meaning of life. I get these e-mails a lot.

For whatever my two cents is worth, I think the problem is affluence generally and, more specifically, having the time and money to watch television and movies. I mean, if you lived in ancient Sumer or during the Depression there just wouldn't have been time to think about the meaning of life. You'd worry about how you were going to eat and provide for your family. I could be wrong, but I don't think farmers experience much metaphysical angst. I think at the end of the day they collapse into bed, too physically tired to think. But if you live in modern America—and are not a farmer— there is ample time for dangerous, destructive questions like "What does it all mean?"

Movies and television only make matters worse. They create the impression everyone is attractive and perky, everything happens for a reason, and, most insidiously, the expectation that every moment will be interesting and entertaining. In the movies things are constantly happening, conversation is snappy, and music is always playing in the background.

That's not real life. Real life is eating a bowl of cereal by yourself before you go to bed or sitting in traffic on the way to your grandmother's for Thanksgiving or waiting in line at the Department of Motor Vehicles. There's nothing intrinsically wrong with any of these pursuits—they are certainly no worse than tilling the soil for twelve hours a day—but judged against the expectation of constant gratification and the illusion of grand purpose, they can seem quite unsatisfying. They certainly do to me.

One day a few years ago, in the back of an issue of *The New Yorker*, I saw advertised a special lamp designed to combat depression. I had heard of such lamps and the company (Swedish) seemed reputable enough since it advertised in *The New Yorker*, so I plunked down $225 plus shipping and handling for a Realite Full-Spectrum Lamp. It arrived three days later and looked nice enough, but more or less like a fluorescent lamp. I called the company and asked whether there had been some mistake. They said there was no mistake, research shows lamps of this sort are effective at combating depression, and I should give it a try. I did and still use it. It works pretty well, but I did get depressed for a few days over spending $225 on a fluorescent lamp.

NEEDLESS TO SAY, THE basement was not the ideal working environment for a theoretical physicist, and in fact there was other space available in the house. The Fendle-Frinkles had a small three-bedroom home. The husband and wife slept in the largest of these bedrooms, except on evenings when the Professor was required to sleep elsewhere because of his snoring, her insomnia, or her general dissatisfaction with him. The second bedroom was employed, somewhat reasonably, as a guest bedroom. The use seemed a bit less reasonable when one considered the Fendle-Frinkles had not had a guest in eleven years, but the Professor was glad for the extra bed on the nights when his wife evicted him from the master bedroom.

The third bedroom was another matter entirely. The Fendle-Frinkles had no children so the room could easily have been used as an office. It was a converted attic, a minuscule room with a short ceiling on the top floor of the house. But though it was small, it had a window that looked out over a ledge where birds liked to perch and sun themselves, and a view of the single tree in their tiny backyard. The Professor, who liked birds very much, envisioned hanging a small feeder from the window. On a sunny day it would be a splendid place to have a sit and a look and a think. It would have made a fine office indeed.

In fact it was used as a yoga and oatmeal room. When the Professor had first lobbied to use the room as an office, many years ago, his wife insisted she required the room as a place to practice her yoga. She made a great show of converting the attic into a yoga studio, furnishing it with mats and candles and a proper drapery over the window, but to the Professor's knowledge had never actually performed yoga in the room.

After three years or so of disuse for the Tantric arts, the Professor made the argument, in something of a lawyerly fashion, that the room had been abandoned for its stated purpose and he should be allowed to claim it as an office. His wife protested she had every intention of getting back to yoga and if he performed physics in the room, the feng shui of the space would be permanently spoiled.

The pretense she would return to the practice of yoga became difficult to maintain as several more years passed without exercise or contortion. So Mrs. Fendle-Frinkle thereafter contended she required the room for the proper storage of the whole-grain, macrobiotic oatmeal that had become the staple of her diet. She contended that a constant, particular level of humidity was required in order to maintain what she termed the "integrity" of the oatmeal. The Professor, one of the three or four smartest men in the universe, had never heard the concept of integrity applied to hot cereal. When he inquired as to its meaning, he was told he would not understand. But he capitulated, of course, and his wife went through an elaborate charade of installing a humidifier and a dehumidifier and a sensitive monitor to maintain the proper moisture level at all times. So it was that the space the Professor coveted for his office became occupied by yoga mats, humidifiers, and macrobiotic oatmeal.

By the by, the Professor tried the oatmeal once and thought it tasted like sawdust. One time, in a puny act of revolt, the kind to which impotent husbands are reduced, the Professor secretly stored one of his wife's canisters of oatmeal in their dank basement and later substituted it for the moisture-regulated attic-oatmeal without her knowledge. She ate it and made no mention of tasting any difference. The Professor tried it too and thought it tasted, just as before, like sawdust.

I SHOULD PAUSE FOR a moment to say I have taken the liberty here of translating certain terms for the convenience of the reader since the Fendle-Frinkles do not live on Earth. They live on the planet Rigel-Rigel, the very same planet that has just contacted Earth and is home to Maude and Ned Anat-Denarian. To be more specific, the Fendle-Frinkles live in the town of Chewelery in a small subdivision, which used to be okay until the Rashukabia got in. The Rashukabia are an ethnic subgroup that loosely translates as "Dutch." It should be said the Rashukabia neither look, sound, nor act Dutch. It is simply the best translation available. The planet name Rigel-Rigel has been translated for these pages in a similarly imperfect fashion. The actual name contains six letters and three sounds that are not present in English.

Some of the translations, however, are better. For example, the Rigelian term for what I have referred to here as feng shui is also unpronounceable and unspellable in English, yet it corresponds to the art of arranging furniture to enhance the spiritual energy of a room. Its practice is associated, as on Earth, with the kind of people who worry about the environment and eat things like macrobiotic oatmeal. Through a remarkable coincidence, yoga is called yoga on Rigel-Rigel and its practice is largely similar to that on Earth. One popular position is called *Huinatulana*, which, loosely translated, means "downward facing dromedary."

THE PROFESSOR SAT DOWN for his evening's work between the squealing washer and the vibrating dryer, underneath the flickering lightbulb in, all things considered, a rather good mood. He had long ago released his anger over matters such as the wet laundry on his desk and the oatmeal and yoga mats lying fallow in what should have been his office. He was just happy to have some free time to think about his research, which he loved, and his current project, which he found particularly engaging and which was, by any measure, quite important.

No sooner had he sat down than his wife began to scream from upstairs.

"John!" she screamed. "John!"

The lightbulb flickered off and she screamed his name again.

After years of living in the house, Mrs. Fendle-Frinkle knew screaming from across the house was an inefficient method of communication. Under normal circumstances it was difficult to hear someone two stories away; with the washer and dryer running it was virtually impossible. The Professor had explained this many times, but still his wife insisted on screaming from across the house.

"Hold on," the Professor shouted, and he walked upstairs. His wife was sitting in bed watching television with the volume turned all the way up.

"What is it, Evelyn?"

"There's no toilet paper upstairs," she said without shifting her focus from the television set.

He could take the laundry on the desk and the shaking of the dryer, but the gross inefficiency of this drove the Professor crazy. If his wife needed toilet paper she could have walked down to the basement and gotten it herself. This would have been a total of two trips: one trip down and one trip up. The Professor, who had already walked up once, now had to walk down to get the toilet paper, back up again to put it in the bathroom, and back down to resume his work: a total of four trips. He muttered the whole way and made the mistake of mumbling the word "shrew" within earshot of his wife. Earshot should have been a radius of six inches or so since his wife had the television turned up so high, but Evelyn had extraordinary perception when it came to criticism of her. She turned down the volume of the television set and the Professor understood immediately he had made a mistake.

"What was that, honey?" she asked saccharinely.

"What was what?"

"I thought I heard you say something."

The Professor popped his head back into the bedroom.

"No, love. I didn't say anything. Nothing at all."

He knew she didn't believe him. And he knew he would pay a price for his insubordination.

"Wash done yet?"

"No, still running."

"Make sure you fold the clothes in the dryer."

"I will."

"And transfer the wash after it's done."

"Of course."

"And turn the dryer back on."

"Not a problem."

"And don't forget to turn off the buzzer. I don't want it to go off while I'm sleeping. You always forget to turn it off."

In fact the Professor had forgotten precisely once, seven years earlier.

"I'll be sure to turn it off. Anything else?"

He turned, starting to walk away, thinking he had gotten off rather easily. He should have known better.

"What are you working on down there?"

The Professor turned back. "Oh, this and that," he said. "You know, same old nonsense."

"Still tackling the big problems in theoretical physics?"

"I suppose."

"I worry about you," she said in a tone that sounded concerned, though the Professor knew better.

"Why is that?"

"I worry that no one pays attention to your work. It could get depressing sitting in the basement every night working on these unimportant problems without any recognition. You might think your life has amounted to nothing. That could really get someone down."

The Professor liked to believe every living organism possessed a unique talent. His wife's unique talent was to masquerade in an expression of genuine interest or concern a devastating critique of a person that reduced his life to rubble—a spectacular sort of disingenuousness.

It was as if when John Wilkes Booth assassinated Abraham Lincoln, he said, instead of "*Sic semper tyrannis*" (which is Latin for

"Thus be it ever to tyrants"), *"Hic quidam salve tu vente"* (which is Latin for "Here is something to aid your digestion").

OF COURSE ON RIGEL-RIGEL they had never heard of the highly literate assassin John Wilkes Booth or the great President Abraham Lincoln. There was a man named Abraham Lincon-Lindle who lived on Rigel-Rigel, but he worked in a factory that manufactured paste.

NOW MRS.' FENDLE-FRINKLE, EVELYN, was both right and wrong in what she said. She was right in the sense that the Professor was a failure in his profession, and his failure was in large part attributable to his personal character.

At one time in his life the Professor had been a graduate student of great promise. Later, he secured for himself a teaching position in a well-regarded university. This was how he first came to be referred to as "the Professor," a moniker that stuck with him even after he lost his post.

In the academy on Rigel-Rigel it is what they like to call "publish or perish." It is expected that professors, especially young professors without tenure, will write and publish lots of articles in top journals and hence bring prestige to their university. This was most decidedly not the Professor's style.

The Professor was a simple man. He did not have any aspirations to be rich or famous. He liked jelly beans and strawberry rhubarb pie, which had entirely different names on Rigel-Rigel but tasted basically the same as on Earth. He liked to take walks in drizzling rain. And he liked to think about physics. He didn't care much about the practical consequences of the problems he thought about—he wasn't trying to come up with a more efficient warp engine or a better electric toothbrush, for example—he just liked thinking about an interesting problem, even if it was the kind of problem that might take a long time to solve or might have no solution at all. As it was, he had been thinking about the same problem for thirty-two years.

He was in this sense a bit like a man on Earth named Andrew Wiles who devoted most of his adult life to proving Fermat's Last Theorem, a mathematical conjecture that went unsolved on Earth for four hundred years. This problem was referred to on Rigel-Rigel as Ascribanta Alianta, which roughly translates as "The Elementary

Conjecture in Number Theory." It was one of the first things every Rigelian student learned in second grade.

What Professor Fendle-Frinkle had in common with Wiles was an abundant reservoir of perseverance. Left to his own devices, Professor Fendle-Frinkle could think about a question for days. He didn't require much sleep. When he did sleep he continued to think at a subconscious level. He would awake continuing the same thought as before he went to bed. He thought about the kinds of problems that were so complex it might take a year to resolve a small subproof. The long haul did not deter him, though. Once, he became so excited by the improbable sight of a dollowarrie flying over an upside-down rainbow (right-side up by Earth standards) that he lost a train of thought eighteen months in the making. This did not discourage him either. He simply picked up where he had been a year and a half earlier and started again.

This kind of stick-to-itiveness is remarkable and admirable but not well suited to a successful career in academia. Academics need to publish. Even Professor Wiles, the admirably persistent Fermat guy, put out a paper from time to time. On both Earth and Rigel-Rigel, a few organizations, such as the MacArthur Foundation and the Institute for Intertemporal Studies, provide funding for geniuses to sit and think all day. Unfortunately, the Professor had never lucked into a situation of this kind. He just sat and thought without funding, and without writing.

The Professor's colleagues literally begged him to publish, even a sub-subproof in a second-tier journal would have done, just something to show the tenure committee. But the Professor could not be persuaded. He had no interest in describing his reasoning to others, or educating the public, or dealing with an editor at a journal. All of this seemed to him like a waste of time. He put it this way to his colleague Professor Sibilant-Sislakean of the mathematics department: "Which would you rather do: solve a Sudoku puzzle or write an essay explaining how you solved it?"

THEY ACTUALLY HAVE SUDOKU puzzles on Rigel-Rigel, which by co-incidence are called Sudoku puzzles, though the puzzles that are labeled "easy" in the local papers are a 25-by-25 grid and start with only four numbers as clues.

* * *

NEEDLESS TO SAY, THE Professor did not get tenure. Now, since even theoretical physicists have to eat (and since the Professor had a wife to support), he took a job teaching introductory physics in a private secondary school. This was a bit like Niles Bohr teaching subtraction to six-year-olds.

Professor Fendle-Frinkle didn't mind the job. Since he didn't like teaching, or communicating with other people in general, and since he was smarter than just about everyone in the universe, it made little difference to him whether he was forced to teach fifteen-year-olds or advanced doctoral students in theoretical physics at Chewelery State. To the Professor, all of it was a waste of time. He would just as soon have worked in a mitten factory. In some ways, he would have been happier there. All he wanted was a job that earned him enough money to eat and gave him time to think. In a mitten factory, there is lots of time to think.

Of course, making mittens is not the kind of job one expects for a prodigy in theoretical physics, nor for that matter is teaching in a high school for the children of wealthy government officials. By any objective measure, the Professor's career was a failure. The soubriquet "Professor" was itself subtly derogatory. The students and teachers universally referred to him as "the Professor," because they knew he had once taught at a university and been denied tenure. Not only did they not understand he was one of the smartest people in the universe, they thought he was a bit dim because he could not manage to keep his shoelaces tied. "Professor" was their ironic way of diminishing a man who seemed to have made very little out of his professional life. Long story short, when Evelyn said her husband's professional life was a failure, she was right about that.

But Evelyn was wrong, clearly wrong, in characterizing the Professor's work as unimportant. One could argue, in fact, the Professor was working on (and had been for thirty-two years) the most important problem in the history of the universe.

A PRACTICAL CONSIDERATION PREVENTS discussion of this problem in detail here. This consideration is that only a half dozen people in the universe could understand the Professor's calculations, and certainly no one on Earth, not even Stephen Hawking, who is the Lucasian Professor of Mathematics at Cambridge, Isaac Newton's old job.

Best I can, here's the gist of it: It had long been proved that following a period of expansion the universe would begin contracting. This was a byproduct of the Big Bang. It was as if the universe were a balloon, and the Big Bang was a big fat guy in a circus who blew it up quickly, but got a bit lightheaded and forgot to hold the balloon shut. The air was slowly seeping out of the balloon. Some people speculated the balloon had been filled up several times, in effect creating multiple universes, a new one each time the carnival came to town, every twenty billion years or so. Some scientists on Earth had speculated about this possibility, but others believed, or rather hoped, the universe would instead expand indefinitely.

On Rigel-Rigel, however, it was understood by all that the universe alternately expanded and contracted. It was also known that the rate of expansion and contraction did not change evenly. The universe got bigger quicker and quicker and would also get smaller at an accelerating pace. It was further known the universe would ultimately be reduced in size to a microscopic dot, a so-called Singularity. This made some wealthier folks on Rigel-Rigel quite anxious. They worried it would diminish the property values of their homes. For example, many people in the nicer neighborhoods surrounding Chewelery worried that after the Big Contraction they would be living, literally, right on top of the Rashukabia.

Not everyone found this news discouraging. Several developers saw an opportunity to build very low-cost condominiums. They could put up a hundred thousand units on less than a square micron. By and large, though, the Contraction was regarded as bad news.

But while it was known the universe would inevitably contract, and while it was known the Big Contraction would accelerate once it began, it was generally believed on Rigel-Rigel that the universe had begun contracting but only slowly, and that the end of the Contraction—the return to the great Singularity—was still a long way off in the future. Most Rigelian physicists believed it would take about as long for the universe to contract as it had taken for it to expand, which meant it would be about another 14 billion years before the Rashukabia got in.

The Professor knew better. He had hypothesized thirty-two years earlier the rate of contraction might be faster than people had predicted. He theorized that after the universe shrank below a certain critical mass the Contraction would proceed much,

much faster than people realized. That evening, after getting the toilet paper for Evelyn, the Professor concluded his calculations. The proof consisted of six lines on his yellow pad. It showed the Contraction, instead of taking 14 billion years, would take about eighteen months. Things would seem pretty much normal through the following summer, after which people would begin to notice little things out of the ordinary, like being able to ride a bicycle from one galaxy to another.

Many people would have become agitated by completing a proof of this kind. They might claim credit in the scientific community or clamor for the government to do something. This, most decidedly, was not the Professor's style. For one thing, he knew there was nothing to do about the situation. The proof was irrefutable, the outcome inevitable. And he cared not at all about being credited for his work. In fact, after he completed the proof, which had been the work of his life for three decades, the Professor crumpled up the sheet on which he had written the proof and threw it in the garbage.

Then he began thinking about the next problem on his agenda. They had these trinkets on Rigel-Rigel, tiny glass cylinders with small models of space-faring vessels inside them. The Professor had long wondered how the manufacturers accomplished this, and his attention now turned to this problem. He spent another hour or so sitting at his desk thinking about this. Then he put the underwear back on top of his desk so his wife would not get mad. Then he went upstairs to the kitchen and had a slice of strawberry rhubarb pie.

7

MEETING WITH HIS
SO-CALLED SUPERIOR

LATE SUNDAY MORNING, THE President returned from his short weekend and summoned Ralph to the Oval Office. He was wearing a flannel shirt and dungarees and appeared at first glance to be quite relaxed. The Chesapeake had that effect on the President. Ralph imagined he had spent the previous day fishing from his boat or hitting golf balls into the bay or running along the beach.

The President greeted Ralph warmly.

"Sit down, sit down," he said and gestured for Ralph to sit on one of the sofas, which Ralph did as the President took a seat opposite him. "I've been doing a lot of thinking," the President said. "There's something about the bay that gives me clarity of thought. Camp David is nice enough, but there's no substitute for being near the water." The President went on, but Ralph did not hear the rest of what he said because he noticed then that on the arm of the President's sofa was a pair of Ralph's own underwear.

To make matters worse, the underwear was not even modestly concealed. It was in full view, resting on the arm of the sofa, where it appeared to have been folded and quite neatly placed. Under different circumstances, it might have been possible for Ralph to steal back into the Oval Office during a break in the President's schedule and lift the bloomers from the couch. But if the President had not already noticed the underwear he would soon enough. Discovery was inevitable. So Ralph did not even make a perfunctory effort at a bottom-of-the-ninth, Hail Mary, buzzer-beater-type play. He did not even do what most people do in uncomfortable moments such as this, which is to ignore the situation and hope it will go away. In fact, while the President spoke, Ralph stared directly at his underwear.

AS HE STARED, RALPH wondered how he had made the mistake. Forgetting underwear is not the kind of thing a man often does. When he does he generally notices it quickly and says something to himself like, "I have forgotten to wear underwear."

Ralph went over the events of the night before in his mind. It had all been innocent enough. After dinner, Ralph rustled up some blankets and bedclothes. They changed into their pajamas in separate rooms, made camp on the floor, and stayed up most of the night talking. In the morning, they were greeted by glorious sunshine streaming in from the east. They woke, drank coffee, and talked for a little while more. Then they changed, Ralph in the coffee-cubby, Jessica in the office, and left.

Looking back, Ralph now recognized he forgot to put on the clean pair of underwear he had packed for himself. In fact he put his pants on directly over the pajama bottoms. That Ralph did not notice this, and hence recognize he had left his change of underwear by the Equal, was all the more astonishing given that Ralph had floated back to his apartment and showered before returning to work. Somehow, Ralph failed to have a moment in which he said, "Oh, I am wearing pajama pants under my slacks." He attributed this to the delirium of love. He also recalled what Hans Shruman, parliamentarian of the student government, wrote in his college yearbook:

SEMPER
UBI

SUB
UBI

This is Latin for "always wear underwear."

ALL THE WHILE RALPH reflected, the President continued talking. During this time, Ralph did not pay much attention to the substance of what the President said. He did, however, remain on alert for certain key words and phrases he expected to be uttered, such as "fired," "disgraced," and "federal charges." He heard no such expression. In fact the President seemed to be in the best of spirits. He paid no attention whatsoever to the incriminating underwear. Rather, the President was talking about the situation with the aliens.

"So," the President said. "After a great deal of soul searching I have decided Len Carlson is right about the visitors to our planet. I prayed long and hard on this question, and God assured me they are most definitely men of faith, and almost certainly Jewish."

Ralph didn't know what to say.

He wanted to ask the President whether God had really told him the aliens were Jewish.

What he actually said was: "Yes, Mr. President."

This is pretty much always a safe thing to say when conversing with the president of the United States.

The President had more to say.

"Ralph," he continued, "I've been thinking a great deal about your place in all of this."

"Mine, sir?"

"Yes. You have been a faithful servant to me since I took office. No president could have asked for any more loyal service than that which you have rendered to me. I am very grateful to you."

"Thank you, Mr. President."

There was still no mention of the underwear and the President did not seem upset. In fact, he was smiling. He seemed almost playful.

"Now, Ralph, I know you didn't go to college so you could have a career getting someone's lunch and taking care of their dry cleaning. I mean you could have gone to Harvard for that, right?"

Ralph smiled, but the President laughed heartily. He had a general anti-elitist sentiment, and a specific distaste for Ivy League institutions. The President had graduated from a state agricultural college and believed his public education had fundamentally shaped the man he was. He liked nothing better than to poke fun at people who were, as he called it, "the children of educational privilege" almost as much as he liked to make fun of the French. He found these jokes uproariously funny no matter how often he made them, which was often since more than half of the West Wing staff had attended Princeton, Harvard, or Yale. Brown, however, was conspicuously underrepresented.

THAT WAS A GRATUITOUS shot against Brown and I really don't know why I took it. It seems out of place, so much so that I went back to the section with the aim of deleting it. Instead I ended up leaving the insult and writing this additional section exploring why I wrote the insult in the first place. Even after this further reflection, I have no insight to offer. I think it is an example of one of the many, sometimes hurtful, things we all do in spite of ourselves.

RALPH SAID, "THAT'S A good one, Mr. President."

Still caught up in the bonhomie and humor of the moment, the President said, "I like you, Ralph. I don't trust most of these people around me. I don't trust how they think. I don't even trust how they dress. You're a different story. You remind me of me."

"Sir?"

"You're an honest kid, Ralph, and you're relentless. Once you start on a project, you don't let up until the problem is solved. I like that. I see a lot of myself in you."

"Thank you, sir."

"I have been thinking for some time about elevating your level of responsibility. You can't spend eight years in the White House just looking after me. You have too much potential. I'm going to start having you do some policy work for Quimble. You'll do this in addition to your regular duties through the election. If that goes well, you can work full-time in the chief of staff's office next term."

"Thank you," Ralph said, still with an eye on the underwear.

"Quimble is entirely in favor of this. Your official title will be Assistant Chief of Staff. How does that sound?"

"It sounds fine, Mr. President."

"As your first assignment, I'm appointing you as point person for the logistics of the aliens' arrival. We need a White House staffer to coordinate the response of the various agencies. Secret Service, State, Defense, and CIA are all going to be involved. I want an honest broker in charge, someone I can trust implicitly, and that's you, Ralph." He smiled. "Besides, I don't want the first person our visitors meet to be some wonk from one of those schools in New Haven or Cambridge. They'll fly back home tout de suite. I want a regular honest Joe. Someone just like you and me."

"Yes, sir."

"I have always thought of us as kindred spirits. You know, picking ourselves up by our shoelaces and all."

"Yes, Mr. President. I'll do my best, sir."

The President nodded. "I know you will."

The President had still more to say.

"There's one other thing, Ralph. Now that you're an official member of the executive staff, you'll have a place in the chain of succession."

"Sir, I thought only the cabinet was in the line of succession."

"That's what everyone thinks," the President said. "Everyone knows the vice president succeeds the president and after that the Speaker of the House and so on. The list is actually a lot longer. A few years ago I convened a commission on continuity in government. After they issued their recommendations, Congress secretly revised the Presidential Succession Act to include all of Congress and anyone designated by executive order. You know, nuclear Armageddon and all."

"Sir, aren't I too young? Don't you need to be thirty-five to be president?"

"There's a provision that in the event of a national emergency—defined as the simultaneous death of more than four people in the order of succession—persons are eligible to serve who would otherwise be disqualified because of constitutional infirmities. That's the lawyer word for it—'infirmities.'"

"Is that constitutional?"

"Some of the lawyers in the commission asked that. The way we figured it, if something like this ever happened, people wouldn't be asking a lot of questions."

Ralph couldn't argue with that.

THE PRESIDENT PRESSED THE button on the intercom. "Lois," he said, "can you come in?"

Mrs. Dundersinger walked in carrying an executive order, which the President examined after donning his reading glasses, and then signed.

"Congratulations," he said. "You are now nine hundred forty-ninth in the presidential order of succession."

"Congratulations," said Mrs. Dundersinger, and she walked out of the room. She paid no heed to the underwear.

The President stood up from the couch and offered Ralph his hand.

"Thank you, Mr. President," Ralph said, shaking.

"You're welcome, Ralph."

The President walked back to his desk. Ralph understood this as his cue to leave, but could not resist asking the obvious.

"Sir, may I ask a question?"

"Yes, Ralph," the President said, turning back to face him.

"I'm very grateful for all of this, but why today of all days?"

The President returned to the sofa and lifted the underwear off the couch. "I would be lying," he said, "if I didn't say this had something to do with it."

"Sir?"

"You did it, Ralph. You found the perfect underwear. Someone else might have given up after all this time, but you stuck with it and you succeeded. You demonstrated a tremendous amount of perseverance and great loyalty. These qualities say a lot about a person."

"Thank you, sir."

"I have to say I was particularly impressed you got me a smaller waist size. When I tried them on earlier this morning, I didn't think I'd be able to fit into them. But with all the running I have been doing I was able to get into them just fine. I never would have thought of trying a smaller size, but the snugness was exceedingly comfortable. And it's good incentive to keep up the running. Maybe soon I'll be as thin as you."

"Yes, sir."

"Do you know where you'll be able to get more of these?" the President asked, gesturing to his pants.

"Yes, Mr. President," Ralph said. "I think I know a place."

8

DON'T WANT TO BE AN
AMERICAN IDIOT

So IT WAS, BY virtue of his serendipitous failure to put back on his underwear, Ralph Bailey became the first human to meet an extra-terrestrial being. His charge was to resolve the hundreds of protocol issues that need to be addressed before a state visit. The President of the United States would be the first to officially greet the visitors and would receive all of the attendant glory, but on all such occasions there are myriad details to be sorted out in advance, details that are left to lower-level functionaries quickly forgotten by history.

It may be true, for example, that only Nixon could have gone to China, but before he got there his staff spent weeks debating important matters such as what Nixon and Zhou Enlai would wear when they greeted each other at the airport (they wore suits), what they would have for dinner (they had Chinese), and what theatri-cal performance they would attend in the evening. Nixon strongly advocated for *Carousel*, which was his wife Pat's favorite musical, but in fact they watched a ballet called *Red Detachment of Women*, about the liberation of a peasant girl and her rise in the Communist Party. This was more or less the plot of every play, movie, and dance piece performed in China during the Cultural Revolution. Beijing was not exactly Broadway.

With respect to the visiting aliens, the White House had already decided, unilaterally, what food would be served and what the entertainment would be. But other details remained to be negotiated, such as what the alien ambassador and the President would wear—it was important, for example, that the colors of their ties not clash—and, of course, the numerous, complex issues regarding security.

At the President's direction, Joe Quimble asked Ralph to meet with the alien ambassador's deputy to begin preliminary discussion of these matters. So for the second time in three days Ralph was standing on Pennsylvania Avenue, in front of the West Gate, with a tremendous sense of anticipation. It was a magnificent day in the nation's capital, cool but not too cool, with abundant, glorious sunshine—precisely the right sort of weather for making history.

I SAY PRECISELY THE right sort of weather for making history because history is rarely made on hot or humid days, particularly since the advent of air-conditioning in the late 1920s. It is simply too tempting to sit inside or just hang out by the pool. It was, for example, chilly when the Japanese attacked Pearl Harbor, blustery when the Americans stormed the Normandy coast on D-Day, and downright frigid for the Battle of the Bulge in December 1944. On the other hand, it was a characteristically sticky day in Cuba in the summer of 1898 when Theodore Roosevelt and his men took San Juan Hill. This may explain why the ten thousand soldiers in reserve in Santiago de Cuba never got into action.

WAITING ON THE SIDEWALK, Ralph did not know what to expect. He had a preconception based on the circulated Internet video about what the alien would look like, but no clue how he would arrive. Would a creature simply materialize in front of him, transporting down to the planet as on *Star Trek*? Would he and the alien be able to speak with each other directly or would they have to rely on some sort of sophisticated translation device? He simply had no idea.

So Ralph alternated between looking down the street and up into the heavens. As he did, a young man walking down the street stopped in front of him and asked, "You Ralph Bailey?" The man looked to be in his late thirties. He was dressed casually, in khaki pants, an unbuttoned corduroy overshirt and a Green Day T-shirt. The T-shirt said,

American Idiot
Don't Want to Be One

"How do you know my name?" Ralph asked warily. He presumed it was a lobbyist or one of the countless people who wanted to get something from the President. With one eye, he continued looking down the street and up into the sky for signs of the alien visitors.

The man said, "I'm Ned—from Rigel-Rigel—it's nice to meet you."

And just like that, first contact had been made. It was arguably the most important moment in the history of the planet, and it flew past Ralph before he realized what had happened.

THIS IS OFTEN HOW it is with the great moments in life—we don't notice them until they have passed. For example, when I was eight years old, and on an Amtrak train to Florida, I had French toast, which turned out to be the best French toast I have had in my life so far. Of course, at the time I did not know this. I just knew it was excellent French toast. It was only after years of eating more pedestrian French toast that I realized in retrospect how extraordinary the breakfast on the train had been. Had I known at the time this would be the French-toast-of-my-life, I might have savored the look and taste. But no one told me it was going to be an exceptional breakfast so I ate it at the normal speed. Other people may have had similar experiences with exceptional sexual partners or particularly comfortable footwear.

AFTER A FEW MOMENTS, Ralph processed what had happened. He stopped searching the heavens and quickly extended his hand.

"Please excuse me," Ralph said. "I am so sorry. I didn't realize it was you."

Ned smiled and shook Ralph's hand. "You were expecting a hideous monster."

"I didn't know what to expect. I have to admit I wasn't expecting someone who looked quite so . . ."

"Human," Ned suggested.

"Human," Ralph agreed, though "young" also would have been a suitable choice.

"My species is a bit like your chameleon. We have an evolved ability to change our shape and faces to blend into an environment. It is part of the reason we are so effective at reaching out to new planets." Ned smiled. "I hope my humanness is not a disappointment for you."

"Of course not," Ralph said. "You have to forgive me. I don't have much practice with this."

"There's nothing to forgive. Besides, I don't offend easily."

Ralph immediately liked Ned.

"You speak English? Is that part of your adaptability?"

"We are definitely more adept at learning languages than the average species, and it gets easier the more you do it, but it still takes some work. I learned English in a few weeks. I think I have it down okay, except for the 'ough' words. I can't see how you get 'thru' from 'through' and the 'i before e except after c' thing is confusing. Otherwise it's no problem. How's my accent?"

"Perfect," Ralph said. "You could fit in without any problem."

"And the clothes?"

"Totally inconspicuous. You could pass for a congressional staffer. Where did you get them? J. Crew?"

"Urban Outfitters."

Ralph pointed to the logo on the shirt. "That's a good band."

"Thanks," Ned said. "It was either this or a Björk T-shirt."

"Excellent choice. Then people might have suspected you were an alien."

Ned laughed.

"How do you know the music?"

"I always do my best to familiarize myself with the culture. I've listened to a lot of your music over the past several weeks. We absorb things pretty quickly."

"Who do you like?"

"I'm not sure you can beat Green Day or the Police. I love Sting, and the Beatles too."

"Outstanding choices," Ralph said.

Now he really liked Ned.

"I wasn't quite sure what to expect," Ralph said. "Your colleague was dressed quite a bit differently in the video that got sent around."

Ned smiled. "That's just my boss's sense of humor. He's a bit of a character."

"What was the joke?"

Ned shook his head. "It's too complicated to explain. You'd have to be really tuned in to what he thinks is funny in order to get it."

Ralph wondered to himself, though hardly for the first time, whether the White House might be getting some things quite wrong.

WITH A GESTURE, RALPH invited Ned to enter the gate. A Secret Service agent named Brocka met them inside the guardhouse. Gruffly, Agent Brocka ordered Ned to sit down in a chair. His tone would have been problematic under any circumstances, but given who Ned was, and given Ralph's exceedingly amicable experience with him, it struck Ralph as grossly inappropriate. Ralph wished Tom was on duty.

Agent Brocka said, "I need to ask you some security questions before you can proceed onto the grounds."

"That's fine," Ned said.

"What is your full name?"

"My full name is not pronounceable in English."

"Can you translate it?"

"I don't think it is possible to translate a name. A name is a name."

"Well, I need a name."

"Call me Ned Anat-Denarian."

"Do you have any identification?"

"For what purpose?"

"So we can run a background check."

"You understand I am from another galaxy?"

"This is standard procedure. It either has to be done in advance or done now. Since it wasn't done in advance, it has to be done now."

"What sort of identification do you have in mind?"

"Anything with your name and picture on it."

Ned rummaged through his pockets.

"I have my library card."

"Let me see," the agent said as he took the card from Ned. "Where is this from?"

"It's from the Intergalactic Library and Geological Oddity Depository."

Brocka examined the card, turning it over in his hands. "This is no good," he concluded.

"No good? It's the best library in the universe. It has over forty trillion volumes and many uncommonly smooth stones."

The agent returned the card.

"It doesn't have a picture. I need a picture ID," he said sternly.

"I don't have any with me."

"Do you have a driver's license?"

"No."

"You don't drive?" the agent asked skeptically.

"I drive," Ned said, "but my wife was in a car accident a few days ago. I had to send back my license by courier."

"Why would you have to send your license back?"

"Because that's the way things work where I come from."

"Well, sir, I can't clear you without a picture ID."

"Why not?"

"It's policy."

I HAD AN EXPERIENCE similar to Ned's encounter with the surly agent. I expect many people have. I was at Kennedy Airport checking in for a flight to Atlanta to attend the funeral of a friend of mine from college when I realized I had forgotten my driver's license. Long story short, I had changed wallets the day before and my driver's license didn't manage to make it into the new one. When the agent—his name was Hank—asked for picture identification, I offered my ID card from the college where I am a professor. Hank said this wasn't a "valid" picture ID. I asked why. He said "FAA regulations." I explained I was on my way to a funeral and if I didn't make this plane I would miss the funeral and asked whether he could just cut me a break. Hank repeated the phrase "FAA regulations."

At this point, I made the mistake of engaging Hank in logical debate. Think about the point of the regulations, I said. Anybody can get a driver's license—including any fourteen-year-old kid with twenty dollars. The airlines don't even check to see whether the license is valid. It doesn't offer any security. It's just a picture. So if it's just a picture, why is one better than any other? It's clearly me in the picture, I said, and he could even call the college and ask if I really teach there. That should assure him it's actually me. He said, "I'm sorry. It's FAA regulations." "Think for yourself," I demanded, to which he replied, "That's not my job." At this point, I called Hank a clod.

I am not proud of my behavior, nor can I explain it. It may have been the stress of my friend's death, or being tired on account of the early hour, but I expect it was really frustration that Agent Hank had been given the capacity to reason and chose not to exercise it. I found this unfathomable and maddening, but it could just be me. I confess I have had this same frustration with respect to aspects of both American domestic and foreign policy, and in certain restaurants. One diner I used to frequent would not let you substitute mashed potatoes for French fries, even though the mashed potatoes were less expensive à la carte. I am ashamed to say that on the last occasion I ate at this establishment, I engaged in a heated debate about the absurdity of the policy that also ended in my calling the waiter a clod.

I fancy the word.

RALPH PUT HIS HAND on Agent Brocka's shoulder. "Our customary security protocols may not be appropriate here," Ralph said. "Mr. Anat-Denarian poses no threat. I think if we were to call your commander, he would agree it is neither logical nor polite to detain the representative of visitors from another planet because he does not have a driver's license. He arrived by spaceship after all."

Agent Brocka considered Ralph's position. "I suppose you're right," he muttered. "Go on ahead."

Outside, Ralph apologized. "I'm sorry about that," he said. "Everyone is flying by the seat of their pants here."

"It's okay," Ned said. "He's just doing his job."

"It's so absurd. He's asking to see your driver's license and meanwhile you could probably destroy Earth in a matter of seconds."

"That's not even a consideration," Ned said. "We don't win friends by force. We win friends by persuasion. We only use force in self-defense."

"Here," Ralph said, "we defend ourselves by checking people's driver's licenses."

"How is that working out for you?"

"Not so well," Ralph said.

As the two men crossed the White House lawn, Ralph was struck by the familiarity of the scene. It had been a little more than a day and a half since he and Jessica made the same walk. Ralph was still completely full with thoughts of Jessica and that perfect evening. This made him feel all the more welcoming toward his guest.

"Can I offer you a tour of the White House?" Ralph asked.

"Thanks," Ned said, "but honestly, if you've seen one government building you've seen them all."

Ralph said, "So I take it you've done this a few times before."

"You mean made first contact?"

"Yes."

"About ninety times."

"There are ninety inhabited planets in the universe?"

"Oh, there are a lot more than that. I have only visited ninety on business and a few more on vacation. My people know about several thousand more."

"Several thousand?" Ralph was incredulous.

"And those are just the ones we have found. There are many, many more out there waiting to be discovered," Ned said. "The universe is a big place. The more you see of it, the more you realize just how incomprehensibly immense it really is. It's quite humbling."

Ralph nodded. "Does making first contact ever get old?"

"Never," Ned said. "Don't confuse my lack of interest in a government building with disinterest in the people. People are infinitely fascinating. I have the most engaging job anyone could ever ask for. I get to travel all over the universe and meet all kinds of interesting people. The work feels important, and I have an amazing boss. It's just the hours that stink."

"I can relate to that," Ralph said.

"What about you?" Ned asked. "What's your position?"

"I am the attaché to the President."

"I suppose that means you work a hundred hours a week and pick up the President's lunch and dry cleaning?"

Ralph chuckled. "Yeah, that's pretty much it."

Ned smiled. "I've been there," he said. "Do you like what you do? Do you like your boss?"

"He has his moments," Ralph said. "Just like the job."

"Well," Ned said, "one public servant to another: Be patient. It'll get better."

"It already has," Ralph said. Ned already felt like a friend.

"What about family?" Ned asked. "Are you married? Do you have—how do you say it—a significant other?"

"Funny you should ask," Ralph said. "I just met someone. It has only been a couple of days, but I'm pretty sure she's it. That sounds crazy, right?"

"No, not at all. When I met my wife, it was love at first sight. She was ahead of me on the ten-items-or-less line in the supermarket. There was this old lady in front of her at the checkout. She had a coupon for everything, taking forever. I was ready to scream, but Maude, my future wife, stood there and helped the woman sort through all of the coupons. And then the woman wanted to pay in our version of pennies, and Maude helped her count through all of those—eight dollars in pennies; she helped her count all eight hundred. I fell in love with her right then and there. We've been together ever since."

"I guess there is nothing like being young and in love," Ralph said.

"That's true," said Ned, "though I am not as young as you think."

"How old are you?"

"I'm six hundred thirty-five."

"Really?" Ralph asked, taking in another extraordinary fact on this extraordinary day. He smiled and looked at Ned. "You don't look a day over thirty," he said.

"Thank you. I have an excellent moisturizer," Ned said, returning the smile.

"How long have you been married?"

"Twenty years."

"So you didn't get married until you were six hundred fifteen. Is that unusual?"

"Not really," Ned said. "On Rigel-Rigel we have a saying: 'Six hundred is the new five hundred.'"

* * *

HEARING NED'S STORY MAKES me feel a bit better about my own situation. I am forty and not married, though I have a beautiful and loving girlfriend. My friends sometimes kid me about still being single, and I confess to feeling some pressure. On the other hand, it is not as if I have twiddled away the past forty years. Admittedly, I have twiddled away some of that time. I watched every episode of *Beverly Hills 90210*, which got pretty bad at the end, and seven years of *The X Files*, which never really resolved the central conflict. But I also ran a few marathons and wrote some books and developed a nice relationship with a pet parakeet. This may not be much to show for forty years, but it's something, and besides, forty is the new thirty.

"SO I GUESS WHAT you're saying is I still have time," Ralph said.

"Well, we have another saying on Rigel-Rigel that is relevant."

"What's that?"

"It's later than you think."

"Catchy, but what does it mean?"

"I have been thinking about the saying a lot recently. It means different things to different people. I think it means we're supposed to value every moment we get."

"How does that translate into action?"

"I don't know," Ned said. "I wouldn't trust anyone who offered a precise answer to that question. But I think the principle is sound."

Ralph considered Ned's words for a while. Finally, he asked, "May I ask you another question?"

"Shoot," said Ned.

"Do they really have supermarkets in other galaxies? I would have imagined if you have the ability to travel from one planet to another you would have something more sophisticated than a supermarket. Like you would order by computer and the food would be teleported to your home or something like that?"

"No," said Ned. "I think you'll find life is pretty much the same everywhere. Supermarkets, dry cleaners, bait-and-tackle shops— they're all out there. The traffic is just worse."

HEARING THIS REPARTEE ABOUT it being later than we think now makes me feel uncomfortable about my situation. While I feel pretty satisfied with the amount of television I have watched, there is lots more I would like to do. I would like to write a few more books. I would like to get a dog, preferably a beagle. I would like to catch up on the back issues of *The New Yorker* I started saving in 1998. And I would like to go spelunking at least once. I have no special desire to crawl around in caves, but I really like the word and want to use it in conversation. I do a lot of things just to use words I like.

Generally speaking I would like to squeeze all of the juice out of life. I want to write a story of my own life that people will look back on in the end and say, "This was a guy who was happy and productive and really liked words with the letter *k* in them." The rub is that doing this requires a great deal of planning, which is hard to find time to do when one is engaged in the business of actually living one's own life. All of this makes me feel intense pressure, which I can only relieve by telling myself there's still plenty of time. And now here's a reputable source saying it's later than I think, and, as if things could be worse, the traffic situation is never going to improve.

RALPH ESCORTED NED INTO a conference room, offered him a seat and a drink, which Ned declined with a wave of his hand.

"Is your wife okay?" Ralph asked. "You told the agent your wife was in a car accident. How is she?"

"She's fine," Ned said. "Not so much as a scratch. She lost her license, though, as you know, and it looks like we're going to get sued."

"That's no fun."

"No, she's quite upset about it. I am feeling pretty guilty about being away from home."

"My dad used to work a lot."

"So you understand," Ned said. "I'm away from my family for months at a time. On top of everything else, my son has been having problems in school. Saying I am feeling guilty is the understatement of the year."

"I guess things really are pretty much the same everywhere."

"It's true," Ned said. "Wherever you are, whoever you meet, life is always just a question of tradeoffs and priorities."

As Ralph absorbed Ned's words, he had, for at least the third time that day, a feeling of deep affection for Ned and a powerful sense he had much to learn from him and his people.

Apprehensively, Ralph changed the subject to business. "I'm

supposed to feel you out about certain details for the visit from your ambassador," he said. "The White House staff is beginning to make preparations."

"You mean things like what color tie my boss should wear and who should sit on the left or the right at dinner?"

"Yes, that kind of thing. If you tell me whatever concerns you have, we can discuss them, and I'll do my best to make sure they get addressed."

Ned put up his hand. "That isn't necessary," he said.

Ralph said, "I understand. You don't think it's appropriate to have this conversation with someone as junior as me. I think it's strange too. But the President was nice to give me this opportunity, and I just felt so comfortable with you I went ahead and asked. I'll set up a time for you to meet with the chief of staff later."

Ned laughed. "I don't mean it's unnecessary to have the conversation with you. That's not the case at all. My people don't stand on ceremony. I mean it is literally unnecessary."

"I don't understand."

"Whatever you guys want is fine."

"What about seating arrangements for the dinner?"

"Whatever you say is fine."

"How many people will be coming?"

"Two. My boss and I."

"Is there any song you'd like played when you arrive?

"Maybe *Day Tripper*? We both really like the Beatles." Ned smiled. "Or perhaps some Rush?"

"No planetary anthem?"

"No."

"What about a banner for us to display?"

"Don't have one."

"Any sort of flag?"

"No."

"How will you arrive?"

"We'll probably take a cab."

"We can arrange a motorcade."

"That won't be necessary," said Ned.

"You'll need to get into the White House."

"Is it fine if we come in through the gate you and I just walked through?"

"I suppose."

"Well, that's what we'll do then."

"Any suggestions for the menu? Any dietary restrictions?"

"No, whatever you guys put out will be fine. The Ambassador and I have been served just about everything you could imagine. If we don't like it, we'll just grab a sandwich or something later. It's not a big deal."

"So, nothing?" Ralph asked incredulously.

"Nope," Ned said. "Nothing at all. In fact, unless you have something you need from us, I'll let you get back to your job. I'm sure you have plenty to keep you busy."

Ralph hesitated to ask his next question.

"So you don't keep kosher?"

"No," Ned said. He laughed heartily. "My boss would love that, though."

Ralph nodded.

RALPH AND NED WALKED together across the White House front lawn back to the West Gate.

"So it's eight o'clock in the evening, day after tomorrow, right?"

"Right."

"Perfect," Ned said, and offered Ralph his hand. "I look forward to seeing you again. It was a great pleasure to meet you."

Ralph accepted Ned's hand with trepidation, trepidation Ned could sense.

"Relax, Ralph," Ned said. "How do you say it here? It's all good. We just want to get to know you and tell you a little bit about the universe. It'll be totally low-key. You and I have real things to worry about. Women, love, family—these are the things that matter. This is nothing."

"It isn't you I'm worried about," Ralph said. "It's us."

Ned nodded, and Ralph felt confident that, somehow, Ned understood.

"Look," Ned said. "People will surprise you. They are often much more than they appear to be."

"Or less?"

"Sometimes," said Ned, "but this is something only time can sort out."

With this, Ned shook Ralph's hand again and exited through

the gate back onto Pennsylvania Avenue. Ralph watched as he receded into the distance. When he disappeared, Ralph turned away from the first meeting between a human and an extraterrestrial feeling a closer association with the alien than with his own people.

Slowly, he walked into the West Wing and then into Joe Quimble's office. There, in response to Quimble's how-did-it-go look, he said, "I think we may be about to commit the biggest screwup in the history of the universe."

9

LAWYERS IN LOVE

AT THE SAME TIME Ralph was meeting Ned Anat-Denarian, Jessica Love was attending Professor Renier Crabtree's class on torts at the Georgetown Law Center. The class was discussing the very important matter of *Smith v. Rapid Transit, Inc.*, a 1945 case decided by the Supreme Court of Massachusetts. On Earth, law professors often call on students to present the facts of a case under discussion and proceed to ask the student a series of confusing questions until the student has a headache. This is referred to as the Socratic method, in honor of the Greek philosopher Socrates.

SOCRATES EMPLOYED THE SOCRATIC method himself. He used it to answer the big questions. What is knowledge? Must one worship God to be holy? Do poets create through skill or divine intervention? That kind of thing. Socrates did not refer to this as the Socratic method. This would have been an act of *hubris*, which is the Greek word for "egoism." Socrates called it *elenchos*, which is the Greek word for "asking questions."

PROFESSOR CRABTREE RELIED HEAVILY upon the Socratic method, and called on students randomly by referring to a seating chart. He referred to the questioning of a student as "getting the benefit of the method." The students called it getting tagged. As luck would have it, that morning Jessica got tagged.

Jessica's mind was elsewhere. She was love-struck and thinking about Ralph's meeting with the extraterrestrial, but she was a good student and had prepared for class. She knew all about poor Mrs. Smith and her unfortunate case.

WHAT HAPPENED TO MRS. Smith is this: At one o'clock in the morning on February 6, 1941, she was driving on Main Street in Winthrop, Massachusetts, when a bus ran her off the road. Mrs. Smith was an old lady and suffered serious injuries, so she sued the Rapid Transit Bus Company for damages. Trouble was, Mrs. Smith did not see the name on the side of the bus and could not identify any of its distinguishing characteristics. She described it simply as a "great big, long, wide affair," which is really just another way of saying she got hit by a bus.

It was eminently understandable that Mrs. Smith did not see the name on the side of the bus since it was one o'clock in the morning when the bus drove her off the road. The lights of the bus would have blinded her. What's more, there were only two bus companies that operated in Winthrop, Massachusetts, and only one of these two—Rapid Transit, Inc.—operated a route on Main Street. What's more still, Rapid Transit's schedule had a bus leaving Winthrop Highlands for Maverick Square at 12:45 A.M. This would have had it going down Main Street around, surprise, one o'clock.

So basically, it had to have been a Rapid Transit bus that hit Mrs. Smith unless she was lying about the whole thing, which seemed quite unlikely given her age and the damage to her car. Nevertheless, the judge refused to let Mrs. Smith's case go to the jury. The judge said it was not enough that "mathematically the chances somewhat favor the proposition that a bus of the defendant caused the accident." He said the evidence had to be stronger.

The Massachusetts Supreme Court agreed. The issue in class that day was whether the court had been right.

* * *

I TEACH LAW MYSELF and have taught the *Smith* case many times. The students always think the bus company should have compensated Mrs. Smith. Pretty much everyone else with whom I have ever discussed the case thinks the same thing. Only law professors disagree. They are a curious lot.

"SHOULD THERE HAVE BEEN liability?" asked Professor Crabtree.

"Of course," Jessica said.

"Why do you say that so matter-of-factly, Ms. Love?"

"Well, an old lady was injured and we're better than ninety-nine percent certain a Rapid Transit bus caused her injuries."

"Is ninety-nine percent enough?"

"I think so."

"What if we were only ninety percent sure? Would ninety percent be enough?"

This is what law professors call taking the student down the "slippery slope." The professor gets the student to commit to a position and then changes the facts little by little to make the student's position seem more extreme. Like most law students, Jessica hated the slippery slope.

"I don't know if ninety percent is enough," Jessica said. "Or eighty or seventy or whatever you'll ask me next. But Mrs. Smith's case is no different than any other. There is always some uncertainty. We put people in prison every day even though we know many of them are not really guilty."

"So you're saying it's okay to convict innocent people." Sometimes Professor Crabtree would be purposefully obtuse.

"No," Jessica said calmly, "I'm just saying it's not fair to deny Mrs. Smith damages just because she can't say for sure what kind of bus hit her. If we are willing to lock up criminals even though we have doubt as to their guilt, then we should also be willing to compensate victims even though we may have some doubt. That she couldn't identify the bus shouldn't make any difference. Even if she said she was sure, we wouldn't know if she was right. The fact is we are never sure about a verdict. Only God knows the truth. Judges and juries are just making educated guesses. We're never sure about anything, really, but we still have to live life."

"And what would it do for people's confidence in the legal system to know judges and juries were just making educated guesses?" It was clear from the frowning manner in which Professor Crabtree asked this question that he was not being *purely Socratic*, as they say, but that he actually believed it would be very damaging for people to believe that juries merely made guesses.

Professor Crabtree had been an economist before he became a lawyer. Generally speaking, he believed the law existed to create incentives for people to act in a desirable manner. For example, if he supported paying damages to Mrs. Smith, which he did not, he would say the reason to do so was to create incentives for bus drivers to be more careful, not to help out an injured old lady. He referred to this as "bracketing" considerations of fairness. Crabtree thought it was bad for people to think that judges and juries made guesses. As he waited for Jessica's answer, he conveyed this sentiment to the class by making a face not dissimilar to Lois Dundersinger's sourpuss.

"Well," Jessica said, "it might make people think lawyers were more honest."

The class laughed at this.

"But it wouldn't do much to reduce bus accidents, now would it?"

Crabtree always had a comeback ready for even the wittiest and most spontaneous of student comebacks. At this point, the tagged student would generally concede defeat and squirm in his or her chair while Crabtree gloated, generally by rolling his head back and nodding vigorously, until he turned his attention to someone else.

SOME OF THE STUDENTS referred to this as the modified Socratic method, suggesting the vanquishing of a student was not itself part of Socrates' plan. In reality, Socrates was not above the kind of thing that Crabtree did, as evidenced, for example, by his behavior with Euthyphro, a noted religious expert in ancient Athens, whom Socrates nearly reduced to tears. In fact Socrates could be quite arrogant. He also had questionable hygiene. He walked around barefoot, wore the same cloak every day, and rarely took a bath. If you were favorably inclined to Socrates you might characterize his behavior as part of the *noble search for truth*. The reality, though, is that Socrates could be a jerk.

NOW, NORMALLY JESSICA WOULD have abided Crabtree's conduct like all his other victims, but on this day Jessica wanted no part of it. Perhaps this was because she was love-struck, perhaps because aliens had arrived on Earth, or perhaps just because it was a really nice day outside. No one could say. But something snapped. Crabtree had finished gloating and was about to torture another student when Jessica, emboldened by love, current events, or the weather, interrupted.

"May I ask you a question, Professor Crabtree?"

"Of course," he said, ever the gracious victor.

"In your view of the case, does it make any difference whether the driver of the bus struck Mrs. Smith by accident or whether he did it on purpose?"

"No," said Crabtree.

"Does it make any difference whether Mrs. Smith was rich or whether she was some poor old lady who couldn't afford to pay her medical bills?"

"No," Crabtree said again. "I have learned to bracket these irrelevant considerations that tug at our heartstrings. You will too someday."

Right then and there, Jessica Love decided she did not want to be an attorney. She closed her laptop and collected her books, and walked out of the classroom, never to return.

As she left, Crabtree called to her, "Where are you going?"

"Outside," Jessica said simply. "It's a beautiful day."

LIKE JESSICA, I TOO decided I did not want to be an attorney anymore, though my story is less dramatic than hers. One day I was representing a banker who was testifying at a deposition and he lied. He told the other lawyer the opposite of something he had told me. Since he told me this contradictory statement in confidence, no one else would have known his testimony was false. Still, it didn't seem right—my mother always told me it's wrong to lie. At the next break, I called a partner at the law firm where I worked out of a meeting, saying it was an emergency, and explained what had happened. With conspicuous irritation he said, "Don't ever call me out of a meeting again," and hung up the phone. After that, I didn't really want to be a lawyer. So I got a job teaching college and started writing books.

Also like Jessica, I enjoy nice weather and make an effort to get outside whenever I can.

AFTER LEAVING CLASS, JESSICA spent the day walking in Rock Creek Park, which is quite a beautiful spot, particularly in the fall. In her walk through the woods she spotted many birds in the trees, including a colorful one that appeared to be a parrot but could not possibly have been since parrots do not naturally occur in North America. The walk left her feeling refreshed and self-possessed and more confident of her decision than before. She experienced not even a moment of regret.

Later in the afternoon she telephoned Ralph and asked whether they could meet that evening. Ralph, of course, said yes. Chinese food had sort of become their first tradition, so they went to Chinatown and walked up and down H Street looking for a place to eat.

They considered and rejected Golden Palace, Jade Palace, Hunam Garden, Hunan Garden, Szechuan Garden, New Big Wong, Mr. Yung's, and the Great Wall Seafood Restaurant. What made the decision so difficult was that each of the restaurants had pretty much the same food. Even the Great Wall Seafood Restaurant, which sounded like it might be distinctive, had the same menu. After thirty minutes of deliberations, they finally settled upon a place on the Potomac side of the street called Eat Here Now. Eat Here Now was the same as all the other restaurants, just a little bit cheaper.

As they walked into the restaurant, Jessica said, "It's funny how the hardest decisions in life are sometimes easy and the easiest decisions are sometimes hard."

Ralph nodded. Life was giving him a lot to ponder that day.

THE SERVICE WAS QUICK at Eat Here Now. As soon as they sat down, they had a feast of noodles, duck sauce, and hot tea placed before them. Had they eaten at Golden Palace, Jade Palace, Hunam Garden, Hunan Garden, Szechuan Garden, New Big Wong, Mr. Yung's, or the Great Wall Seafood Restaurant they would have been offered the same Chinese noodles and hot tea. In this sense, the choice of restaurant was not a decision of any great moment. When the waiter came over less than a minute later, Ralph ordered vegetable wonton soup, scallion pancakes, and vegetable chow mein, which are the same things he and Jessica would have ordered in any of the other restaurants. One could conclude from this that the universe was steering them in the direction of this meal.

RALPH AND JESSICA SAT in silence for a moment. Ralph looked at Jessica. He thought she looked particularly beautiful that evening, even more beautiful than she looked at the Blimpway and in the Oval Office, and he had thought she looked quite beautiful on those occasions. Contentedly, he snacked on a Chinese noodle while Jessica sipped on her tea.

She asked him about the meeting, and Ralph described the events of the day—how Ralph did not recognize Ned, the churlish Secret Service agent, his and Ned's friendly conversation, Ned's exquisite taste in music, Ralph's sense of excitement over meeting Ned and his trepidation about how the government was reacting to the aliens. Jessica listened intently, nodding and asking several questions of her own. When Ralph finished, Jessica said, "I have some big news myself."

"What is it?"

"I left law school," she said.

Ralph smiled. "Bad day?" he asked.

"I'm serious," Jessica said. "I left for good."

Ralph put down his noodle.

"Why?" he asked. "What happened?"

"Nothing that dramatic," she said. "It just didn't seem important anymore."

THE WAITER ARRIVED WITH the wonton soup, which he set down somewhat recklessly, spilling some broth in the process. The service at Eat Here Now was all in all a bit slapdash. The soup was good, though. It wasn't great, but even average wonton soup is generally pretty good. It is very much like pizza in this regard.

The wonton soup was the only thing Nixon enjoyed during his dinner with Zhou Enlai. He tried everything, including the scary monkey dish, because that's the deal at these state dinners. You have to try everything, even if that means just waving the fork or spoon past your mouth. In the limousine, on their way home from dinner, Nixon had someone call ahead for room service.

"I didn't like the food much," Nixon said to Kissinger, "but the wonton soup was pretty good."

RALPH CONSIDERED JESSICA AND what she had said and realized she was entirely serious.

"So what are you going to do now?" he asked.

"I'm not sure," Jessica said. "I'm thinking about moving to Tibet."

"Tibet?"

"I've had the idea in the back of my mind for a long time."

"What would you do?"

"I think I will teach English in an orphanage."

"Oh," Ralph said.

TIBET IS A BEAUTIFUL country in the foothills of the Himalayas with sweet people and lots of goats and llamas and alpacas, which are themselves sweet and gentle animals. One of the great Tibetan delicacies is mono, a dumpling filled with seasoned meat or vegetables. It is often eaten with yak butter tea, which is really much better than it sounds. Mono is pretty good too. It has the same appeal as the wonton.

The spiritual leader of the country is—or was—a gentleman known as the Dalai Lama, a Tibetan Buddhist. I say "was" because the Chinese invaded Tibet in the 1950s and drove the Dalai Lama into exile. They did this in the name of progress, which is a very important concept to the Chinese. In the case of Tibet, progress included destroying many of the historic Buddhist temples. They have been replaced with important things such as supermarkets and highways.

"IS THIS THE RIGHT time?" Ralph asked. "It'd be a shame to let all the work you have put in go to waste. You could finish law school first and then go teach if it's something that still interests you."

"I suppose," said Jessica.

"It's important to have a career."

"Depending on one's priorities."

"Or you could teach here for a while and make sure teaching is something you like. I mean there's lots of time. It's not like there's any rush to make a decision."

Jessica nodded and chewed on a wonton. "I guess you're right," she said. "But I have been feeling a sense of urgency. I'm starting to think it may be later than we think."

"That's funny," Ralph said.

"What?"

"The ambassador's deputy said the same thing to me when I met him today."

"That's a strange coincidence," Jessica said.

"Sure is."

"Do you think it means something?"

"I have no idea."

THE TIBETANS AND THE Dalai Lama subscribe generally to the teachings of Gautama Buddha, who believed the true nature of reality can only be discovered through years of spiritual cultivation, investigation of existing religious practices, and meditation. So the Buddhists believe in controversial ideas such as peace and love and forgiveness. They believe in acting and speaking in a manner that does not cause harm to other people, in improving oneself ethically and spiritually, and in attempting to view life with a clear mind so as to see things as they really are. They strive to attain Nirvana, the end of all suffering, which can only be achieved by extinguishing all worldly desire. This means, either cruelly or ironically depending on one's view, they have very little use for highways and supermarkets.

"WHY DON'T YOU COME with me?" Jessica asked.

"To where?"

"To Tibet."

"I can't just do that."

"Why not?"

"We have the dinner with the aliens tomorrow and that will create all kinds of work, I'm sure. And the President will have to start thinking about his reelection campaign soon. I can't just leave him in the lurch."

Jessica asked again, "Why not?"

RALPH FELT AT THIS moment a knot in his stomach, which could have been caused by the bowl of greasy Chinese noodles he had devoured but more likely, in fact almost certainly, was due to the irresistible urge he felt to drop everything in his life and fly away with Jessica to work in an orphanage in Tibet. He knew all about Tibet and had fantasized about traveling there and trekking in the shadows of the Himalayas and sipping yak butter tea. In light of this, going to Tibet in the company of a woman with whom he was very much in love seems like it should have been a pleasant thought for Ralph and not the source of stress. But Ralph was self-aware. He understood that he had resisted many such temptations before. What really caused the knot in his stomach was that he knew he would never be able to bring himself to do this thing he really wanted to do.

Ralph was, in this respect, like anyone who does something he knows to be bad for himself—like falling in love with a married person or sticking a Q-tip into one's ear to get wax out knowing it will just make matters worse. More accurately, he was like someone who fails to do something he knows would be good for himself—like going to the gym in the evening instead of watching television or keeping an appointment with the chiropodist to have a bunion filed down. Or traveling somewhere exotic with someone you love.

RALPH SIPPED SOME BROTH.

"I'm not sure," he said. "I have a sense of responsibility. I have duties. Maybe that will be different someday."

The truth was, though, Ralph didn't understand his own reluctance.

"I don't think that will ever be different," Jessica said as she considered his words. "It never gets easier—there is only more and more duty."

Ralph nodded.

"Why can't you live like you said we should on the night we met? Live for the moment. Not just that day, but every day."

Ralph returned his last wonton to the bowl.

"I don't know," he said, and that was the complete truth.

10

IT'S THE END OF THE
WORLD AS WE KNOW IT

As a result of losing her driver's license and the use of her automobile, Maude Anat-Denarian was stuck in her house with lots of time on her hands. Normally she would have used this opportunity to tend to her garden, but Maude believed her ruminations about broccoli had been the cause of the accident outside the Trader Planet. She thought often about the incident, and about the health of Nelson Munt-Zoldarian, for whom she had genuine concern. She even sent him a get-well card. This went against the advice of her attorney, but Maude did not care. She felt quite guilty about the whole thing, so guilty that even the thought of broccoli made her uncomfortable.

Maude was resolved to put this extra time to good use and decided to make her son her project. Once and for all she was going to get to the bottom of his problems in class. She made a point of making breakfast for Todd every morning and being there every day when he got home from school. She would ask him how things had gone and what he had learned. These conversations only confused Maude further because, by all indications, Todd seemed happy and healthy. He interacted politely with Maude and, when he had no other plans, willingly played cards with her in the evening. He looked well and had nice friends and even a young girlfriend, of whom Maude approved. He certainly showed no signs of being involved in drugs or gangs or any of the disreputable temptations that sometimes lead teenagers astray.

With respect to school, Todd said he studied and tried his hardest, but had simply not done well on some of the tests. He did not think a tutor would help the situation. He liked his teachers fine and thought highly of the school. All of this only made the situation more confusing.

One evening, when Todd had gone to dinner at a friend's house, Maude went into Todd's room, opened his schoolbag, and pulled out his notebooks. She felt quite guilty about this. Maude was a good person who respected people's privacy, but these were extraordinary circumstances. Maude collected the notebooks, made herself a pot of tea, and sat down on the sofa for a read. She opened first the notebook, which was labeled "Physics."

Maude was no physicist herself, but she had some sense of what a physics notebook should contain. She expected to see complicated equations and formulas and derivations of theorems. She found very few of these. Mostly what she found were doodles. Some of these were quite elaborate and good. Each was dated. That morning in physics class Todd had sketched a remarkable likeness of a dollowarrie.

A DOLLOWARRIE IS A bird found on Rigel-Rigel that is in every respect indistinguishable from the African gray parrot. Both have four toes on each foot and feed primarily on nuts and fruit. Both have highly developed language skills and a striking capacity for mimicry. Both make excellent pets. The main difference is dollowarries live on Rigel-Rigel while African gray parrots live on Earth.

Such a striking similarity between animals on planets separated by hundreds of light-years may seem like a strange coincidence, but in fact is unremarkable. It is an example of what biologists call convergent evolution. This is the idea that unrelated organisms sometimes acquire similar characteristics while evolving in separate environments.

For example, birds, insects, bats, and pterodactyls all fly—or flew—pretty much the same way, but each evolved its wings separately. Echidnas, porcupines, and hedgehogs developed their spines independently. Lots of animals have evolved a lens for the eye. The reason for all this is there are only so many ways to fly, see, and defend oneself against predators.

This would all seem perfectly natural if we were talking about a mathematical problem instead of a problem of dealing with one's environment. I expect it would surprise no one to learn that both Andrew Wiles and Mort Erev-Dalsarian arrived at the same proof to Fermat's Last Theorem or to learn, as we have, that traffic is a problem throughout the universe. People need to get around and, as they say, there are only so many ways to slice an apple, or a plique, depending whether you live on Earth or Rigel-Rigel.

It's the same thing for animals, just a different kind of problem. African gray parrots evolved their distinctive feet to effectively pick at fruits and nuts. They learned to speak as a way of facilitating cooperative feeding. The same was basically true of dollowarries.

IN AN IDEAL UNIVERSE, I would include here a reproduction of Todd's sketch of the Rigelian dollowarrie. The great Kurt Vonnegut used to include simple sketches with his fiction. Vonnegut wrote about trendy topics such as time travel, free will, and the bombing of Dresden. Sometimes he illustrated these lighthearted discussions with simple drawings, which were pretty lousy but fun. For many teenage boys, viewing the sketch of the "wide open beaver" in *Breakfast of Champions* is a transformative moment in their lives. Unfortunately I do not possess even rudimentary drawing skills. Thus the sketch of the dollowarrie is not included.

WHEN TODD CAME HOME that evening, Maude sat him down for a chat. She explained that she had looked through his notebooks. She apologized profusely for the intrusion into his privacy. It was a bad life lesson, she said, but she thought these were exceptional circumstances. She wanted very much for Todd to succeed and was concerned about his performance in school. She had gone through the notebooks in the hope of getting to the bottom of what was bothering Todd at school.

Todd said he understood and was not mad.

"So why are you doodling in class?"

"I like sketching."

This was the first Maude had ever heard of her son's interest in sketching.

"Why didn't you ever mention this before?"

"I didn't think Dad would approve."

"Why wouldn't your father approve of you drawing?"

"I don't just like to draw as a hobby. I want to be a sketch artist."

Todd was right. His father would not approve.

Maude said, "Oh, I see."

"I'm really good at it," Todd said. "It's what I really want to do."

Maude wished yet again that Ned was home and not off in another part of the universe. This was the kind of challenge to which parents needed to present a united front, but Maude knew her and her husband's initial reactions to the crisis would be quite different. Ned would not approve of drawing as a career. Maude, on the other hand, did not care what her son did so long as he finished school and was happy. She and Ned would agree at least on the importance of finishing school, so this is what she chose to emphasize with her son.

"Well," she said, "it's one thing to want to be an artist and another to fail out of school. Why are you doing this in class? And why in physics? I didn't notice so many drawings in any of your other notebooks."

"It's boring."

"You don't find the subject interesting?"

"Actually the things he teaches us about are pretty interesting. But he's not interested in the ideas. All he's interested in is the math and the formulas."

"What is he teaching you?"

"He's teaching us that the universe is going to end faster than anybody has realized."

Maude said, "Oh."

ON RIGEL-RIGEL, APOCALYPTIC PREDICTIONS are almost unheard of. This is part of the reason for Maude's reaction. On Earth, however, they are as much a part of life as the World Series and the Running of the Bulls. They can be traced back as far as the second century, when Montanus prophesied the end of days. Several are currently pending.

Generally speaking, these predictions have been incorrect. Charles Taze Russell, founder of a group of Bible students who later became known as Jehovah's Witnesses, boldly predicted the world would end in 1874. Russell and his followers later revised this prediction to 1881, 1914, 1915, 1918, 1920, 1941, 1975, and finally 1994. Their current position is that they don't know when the end will come, but that it is certainly coming soon.

In 1974, astrophysicists John Gribbin and Stephen Plagemann caused a stir by noting that all nine planets of the solar system would align on March 10, 1982. They predicted this would increase gravitational pull and cause an increase in solar flares and earthquakes. The world did not end as feared, but Gribbin and Plagemann were right about the solar flares and earthquakes and the resulting increase in gravitational pull. The March 10 high tide was approximately 0.04 millimeters higher than usual.

A Korean group called the Mission for the Coming Days predicted the world would end on October 28, 1992. They had no apparent basis for this prediction, but thousands of Koreans nevertheless sold homes, quit jobs, and had abortions to prepare for the day on which 144,000 believers around the world would be lifted into heaven (so long, apparently, as they were not homeowners, employed, or heavy with child).

And, of course, the most famous prognosticator of all time, Nostradamus, foretold, hundreds of years earlier, that Armageddon would occur in July 1999. History did not prove Nostradamus to be a competent sooth, but he was, by all accounts, a fine apothecary.

LATER THAT EVENING, MAUDE did something stupid and called Helen Argo-Lipschutzian, the president of the Rigel Prep Parent-Teacher Association. After the conversation with Todd she needed to talk with someone. Maude would have preferred, of course, to discuss the matter with Ned, but she had already spoken with Ned several times that week about the car accident so the roaming charges were mounting, and she knew he was about to make an important first contact; in fact he could have been in the middle of it right then. So she called Helen. Helen was a nice woman, but she had a tendency to take things too far. She had lots of money and lots of time on her hands and liked to take things on as projects. She was also a bit of a gossip.

The Anat-Denarians and Argo-Lipschutzians socialized, so Helen already knew Todd had been having trouble in school. Maude explained that Todd wanted to be an artist and that he had been sketching in physics class because he was bored. He found the idea that the universe is going to end faster than anyone realizes interesting, but all those formulas and equations just weren't for him. Frankly, Maude confessed, math hadn't been for her when she had been in school either and she could understand where the boy was coming from. No one should be forced to learn anything they really didn't like. And, besides, who really needed physics anyway? You didn't need to understand quantum mechanics to clean out the filter on the cold-fusion generator. But Ned would never buy it. He would be upset. And Ned was away and she didn't want to upset him in the middle of a mission but this upset her and what was she going to do? All of this left Maude a bit breathless.

"Wait, wait, wait," Helen said. "What did you say the teacher said?"

"Well, that's not really the point of the story."

"But did you say the teacher was telling them the universe is going to end faster than anyone realizes?"

"Yes."

"When?"

"About eighteen months from now."

"That's decidedly inconvenient," Helen said. "We just bought a summer time-share. It includes use of a cabana and free fruit."

"Well, maybe it's a few weeks longer, give or take," said Maude. "But it's certainly a lot shorter than the prevailing guess, which I think is fourteen billion years."

"Who does this teacher think he is?" Helen asked, more agitated now. "What right does he have to tell our children the universe is about to end?"

"Todd said the better math students thought the proof was pretty solid."

Helen would have none of it. "No wonder Todd is failing," she said. "No wonder he's doodling in class. Do you know how upsetting it would be to a young man to be told the universe is about to end?"

"Actually, Todd said the teacher is pretty good. Todd just doesn't like physics."

Helen still would have none of it. "This is outrageous," she said, her voice rising. "This teacher has absolutely no right to be filling our children's head with this kind of nonsense. He's going to have to answer for this."

"Really," Maude said, "I just wanted to talk about Todd."

But Helen had already decided.

"I'm going to take care of this," she said. "We're going to make an example of this professor and show the school they can't teach our kids whatever they want without fear of repercussions. You just relax, Maude."

Helen hung up the phone then, but Maude did not relax. She suspected, correctly, she had just made a very bad mistake.

ALL AROUND THE UNIVERSE, PTAs are a disruptive force. They are filled with nice people with good intentions but too much time on their hands. When people with too much time on their hands get together, they cause nothing but trouble. This is another example of convergent evolution.

11

I LOVE WOODY ALLEN AND
WALKING IN THE SNOW

THE PRESIDENT OF THE United States and the First Lady stood on the North Portico awaiting the arrival of the Ambassador of the Intergalactic Union with a small measure of anticipation and a large measure of concern. The same could be said of the entire White House staff, which had assembled on the porch to form a ceremonial receiving line. Each staff member was eager and concerned, though for quite different reasons.

For example, Lucian Trundle, the chief butler, was anxious that all of the preparations had been adequate. The tables in the East Room had been set with Eisenhower gold base plates. Later the Franklin Delano Roosevelt china would be used for service. Kennedy Morgantown crystal and vermeil flatware had been set on soft gold damask tablecloths. Gold tapers adorned the crystal candelabra centerpieces, which were surrounded by an assortment of roses and snowberries. The menu was traditional Israeli. Trundle worried, among other things, that it would have been better to set the table with the Woodrow Wilson base plates instead of the Eisenhower base plates and that the matzoh ball soup would be too salty.

Len Carlson hoped the state dinner for aliens would be enough to turn around the President's fortunes. The President's numbers had been sinking at the polls. The dinner could reestablish his credibility on national security and solidify support for his position on the Middle East. It could be just the thing to help the President turn the corner, but everything would have to go perfectly.

The President was thinking more or less the same thing.

The First Lady worried that she would explode out of her dress. Since the earliest days of the presidential campaign, her husband's advisors had been urging the First Lady to lose weight. It was not so much that she was overweight as it was that the President was underweight. The press had poked fun at the President for his obsessive attention to fitness, which became more conspicuous when juxtaposed against his more robust wife. With the arrival of the aliens, the state dinner would draw more attention than any dinners that had come before, and, in turn, the relative waistlines of the President and his wife would be subject to the most exacting scrutiny. So the First Lady had basically starved herself for a week and gotten down from a size twelve to a ten and then squeezed herself into an eight. She could barely breathe.

Joe Quimble worried the whole thing had been a terrible mistake. So much depended on the premise the aliens were Jewish, a premise that was highly questionable to say the least. Ralph and David Prince also worried a terrible mistake had been made, but at the same time felt a breathless excitement at the prospect of Earth being welcomed into the community of the universe.

Chaim Muscovitz, director of the klezmer band that had been engaged to provide the evening's entertainment, worried whether his group would be a hit. This was a huge deal for the Heavy Shtetl Klezmer Band. Other than this, their most important gig had been at Moishe Yosin's Yiddish Festival in 1999, the year Shecky Greene headlined.

As with all things, it was a matter of perspective.

NED AND THE AMBASSADOR exited from a cab on Pennsylvania Avenue. Ned was dressed smartly, in a blue oxford button-down shirt and khaki pants. As promised, the Ambassador was dressed like a rabbi. He looked not unlike Menachem Mendel Schneerson, the beloved and recently deceased rebbe of the Chabad-Lubavitch sect of Judaism.

The fare from the hotel to the White House was seven dollars, but Ned gave the driver a twenty and told him to keep the change.

People on Rigel-Rigel tip big.

The President waited nervously as the Ambassador, trailed by Ned, crossed the White House lawn. It seemed to take forever. Finally, the Ambassador ascended the steps to the North Portico. Solemnly, he turned to the President and addressed him in a commanding voice for all to hear: "People of Earth, we enslave you in the name of the Galactic Union. This planet will become a massive dry cleaner's. The people of our home world have a wedding to attend next week. We are going to leave you four billion pairs of pants. Have them cleaned and pressed for next Thursday. We will return then to pick them up."

At this point, the President of the United States peed in his underwear. He was quite upset about this since it was his only remaining comfortable pair that was clean.

After letting the President twist in the wind for a few seconds, the Ambassador slapped the President on the back and said he was kidding. Laughter broke out on the receiving line, although it was the nervous titter of relief and not the robust laughter of appreciation. The staff of the White House were universally pleased they would not be conscripted into service as dry cleaners. Len Carlson was particularly pleased since he was allergic to perchloroethylene.

Only the Ambassador adequately enjoyed his own joke. He howled long after the nervous laughter had subsided and at one point appeared unable to breathe. When the Ambassador finally calmed himself, the President softly said, "I don't get it."

"What's that?"

"The joke. I don't get the joke."

"Oh, it's an old Woody Allen routine," the Ambassador said, straightening himself. "Haven't you heard it? These aliens arrive and put everyone on Earth into a deep trance. The humans wake up and find out they have all been turned into tailors. The aliens give them pants to alter. 'Can you have them by Friday?' the aliens ask. 'How about Monday?' say the humans. The aliens say, 'We have a wedding to attend and really need them for the weekend.' The humans agree and the aliens return on Friday, but the joke is on them because they travel a hundred million light-years and forget their ticket."

The President offered a halfhearted effort at a smile. "You must be a great fan of Mr. Allen's," he said.

"We particularly enjoy his early, funny movies," the Ambassador replied.

He then began to work himself into hysterics again. "I just love the idea," the Ambassador said to himself, "of these aliens landing and demanding that their dry cleaning be done. We just had to do it. I told my associate Ned here it was the funniest thing I had ever heard in my life."

The President nodded politely.

Ned, who had taken a position at Ralph's side, leaned over and said, "I told him no one would get it."

THE PRESIDENT OF THE United States may not have found the Woody Allen routine funny, but I find it to be quite brilliant. If I had been on the receiving line, I would have shared a hearty laugh with the Ambassador and like to believe the two of us would have become fast friends.

IT WOULD BE INACCURATE to say the President disliked Woody Allen. He had simply never seen a Woody Allen movie and had no idea Allen had ever been a stand-up comedian. Len Carlson, on the other hand, actively disliked Allen. Carlson knew of Woody Allen's stand-up career because he had seen exactly one Woody Allen movie, *Annie Hall*. More accurately, Carlson had seen half of one Woody Allen movie because he walked out halfway through.

Annie Hall is about Alvy Singer, a neurotic stand-up comedian and his relationship with the title character, played by Diane Keaton. At one point in the movie, Singer and Annie Hall are waiting in line to see a movie behind an insufferable blowhard who is pontificating about the philosopher and literary critic Marshall McLuhan. Allen steps out of character and, speaking as himself, gets into an argument with the gasbag about the correct interpretation of McLuhan's work. To bolster his argument Mr.

Allen, or more accurately Mr. Singer-as-Allen, produces Professor McLuhan himself, who takes Woody's side and puts the arrogant ticket holder in his place.

This was the point in the film where Len Carlson walked out. Carlson liked action movies with strong main characters and clear messages. He particularly liked Charles Bronson movies, especially *Death Wish*, *Death Wish II*, and *Death Wish 3*. Carlson found the whole idea of an actor stepping in and out of his character silly and off-putting. Carlson believed in a fundamental principle of performance art: the "fourth wall" should not be broken. This is the idea that people in a play or a movie should pretend the things happening on the stage or the screen are real and the audience is not there.

This is sometimes hard to do. At Broadway shows, for example, you can often hear the warning beep of a backward-moving truck or someone opening the wrapper to a sucking candy. I am not personally inclined toward violence, but one time at a play someone took almost five minutes to open a sucking candy, and I wanted to kill the person. It is particularly maddening behavior given one can buy cough drops or Life Savers, which do not come wrapped in plastic and are quite delicious. Anyway, distractions such as these do make it hard to suspend one's disbelief, as they say in the story-telling biz.

Suspending one's disbelief may be difficult, but Len Carlson, like many others, thought one must try and that it was incumbent upon the director or artist to help us along in this difficult process. So he didn't like Woody Allen. But although neither Len Carlson nor the President liked Mr. Allen, they were nevertheless pleased the Ambassador was fond of the director. This was because Carlson and the President believed the only fans of Woody Allen were Jewish.

THIS CLAIM—THAT ONLY Jews like Woody Allen—is patently untrue. Allen's films are enormously popular in France, despite the reputation of the French as anti-Semitic. They are also popular in Italy and Argentina. They are also popular in many other galaxies, including the galaxy in which Rigel-Rigel is located. Because of Earth's previous isolation from the intergalactic community, no residuals have been paid in connection with the extraterrestrial screening of these movies. This is a matter for Mr. Allen's attorneys.

AFTER THE AMBASSADOR MET the First Lady, Len Carlson, Joe Quimble, and the rest of the White House executive staff, the President ushered him into the East Room, where the Eisenhower base plates had been set upon the tables. The President gestured for everyone to sit, which they did. He then made an effort at small talk, which is obligatory at such events. For example, Nixon and Mao spent several minutes discussing luggage.

The President turned to familiar terrain. "Have you had a chance to explore Washington?" he asked.

"A little bit," the Ambassador said.

"Have you enjoyed our beautiful fall weather? I think it is the nicest time of year here in the capital."

"Yes," said the Ambassador. "Ned and I enjoy weather very much."

Nonplussed, the President nodded politely and tried another tack. "We have prepared a fine meal in your honor this evening. I hope you are hungry."

"Yes," said the Ambassador. "And I see the visage of Dwight Eisenhower adorns our dinnerware?"

"You know Eisenhower?" the President asked.

"We are fascinated by history. Eisenhower was a remarkable man."

"Yes, he was a great general and led our nation to victory in World War II," said the President. "He was not an outstanding athlete, but by all accounts an enthusiastic, if not gifted, golfer. I understand as a young man he was a fair runner. I like to think that in his younger years he could have offered me a fair race, but I expect I ultimately would have beaten him."

The Ambassador nodded politely.

"We do not have war where I come from," the Ambassador said.

"Surely you must have disputes or conflicts," the President said incredulously.

"Of course we have conflicts."

"Then how do you resolve them?"

"We resolve them through indefatigable negotiation. One time we had a dispute with a neighbor over ownership of a comet that regularly passed between our planets. The negotiations lasted more than six hundred years."

"And when negotiation fails?"

"We will fight only when it is absolutely necessary."

"Then you do have war."

"Not exactly. Your word has a connotation that does not apply to our concept. We do not see our conflicts as battles between good and evil. If someone attacks us, we will defend ourselves. But we respond with precisely proportionate force. And we take life only when absolutely necessary."

"What if it's a race of hideous insect creatures?"

"We treat all life with respect."

"Well, perhaps you do not view your conflicts as being between good and evil, but surely at least between right and wrong."

"Not even this," the Ambassador said. "The universe is a big place. We understand people's interests will sometimes come into conflict with one another, and sometimes the peaceable resolution of these conflicts is not possible."

"But sometimes people are just evil and must be dealt with."

"Like your Hitler," the Ambassador said, to which the President nodded vigorously.

"We view acts as evil and respond to these acts proportionately," the Ambassador said, "but we do not judge people. We understand people are to a large extent a product of their environment. Born into one set of life circumstances, they may do things that would horrify them if they had lived under another set of conditions. We understand also that some component of evil is relative. For example, many planets in the universe regard the farming and slaughter of animals for food as mass murder. We have found it is best not to be moralistic about these things."

Eager to change the topic, the President made a second effort at small talk. "Have you had a long trip?" he asked.

"Quite long," said the Ambassador. "We traveled approximately fifty thousand light-years to get here."

"You must have quite a case of jet lag."

"We don't travel in a jet per se. It's a luxury intergalactic cruiser capable of traveling more than ten times the speed of light."

"All the same," the President said, "traveling long distances can be brutal even under the best of conditions."

"It is not so bad," the Ambassador said. "If we had to fly the entire way it would be tough. But there are wormholes scattered around the universe, which cut down the trip. Fortunately, there is one near my home planet and another on the far side of your sun."

The Ambassador smiled.

"If you time things right," he said, "it is possible to arrive before you leave."

The President nodded politely.

DURING A LULL IN the awkward small talk, a waiter collected the Eisenhower base plates and set down the FDR china in their place.

"Why did they do that?" the Ambassador asked. "We haven't yet had our first course."

"We don't eat off of those plates," the President explained.

"Why not?"

"They're just placeholders."

"But you do eat off of *these* plates?"

"Actually, they'll take these plates away when the soup comes."

"So these are just placeholders too?"

"Yes."

"I have visited almost two hundred different planets in fifteen different galaxies," the Ambassador said, "but this is the oddest dining ritual I have ever seen."

Shortly thereafter, the waiters presented a tureen of soup to the table and ladled its contents into bowls. The chicken broth contained *lokshen*, which is the Jewish word for noodles, *kreplekh*, which are Jewish dumplings not dissimilar from the wonton, and *kneydlekh*, which are unleavened balls.

When the Ambassador inquired as to the contents of the soup, the President was surprised but he nevertheless endeavored to explain. He had rehearsed the names of all of the dishes to be served that evening. Nevertheless, he mangled the words badly. He called the noodles "lotion," and the dumplings "crap lock," as in a thing to secure waste matter. David Prince, the only Jew within earshot, cringed. The Ambassador did not cringe because he had never heard these words before. He did not know whether they had been pronounced elegantly or tortured.

The President said, "But I don't need to tell you. I am sure you have had Jewish soup many times before."

"No," said the Ambassador. "Why would you think that?"

"We presumed you were Jewish."

The Ambassador laughed heartily, again to the point of not being able to breathe.

When he caught his breath, he asked, "Is it because of the beard?"

"In part," the President said, nonplussed again.

At this point, the Ambassador removed the beard and his *peyes* and slipped out of his black overcoat to reveal a white Brooks Brothers oxford shirt. Without the beard and the earlocks, the ambassador looked like a WASP.

"I told you it would work," the Ambassador said, smiling and pointing in the direction of Ned, as he began to howl again in glee.

"I don't understand," the President said.

"You know the Woody Allen movie *Bananas*. You have seen it, yes?"

"No," said the President.

"It's brilliant. This consumer-products tester named Fielding Mellish becomes infatuated with a beautiful political activist. To win her love he travels to the fictitious country of San Marcos, joins the rebels, and eventually becomes president of the country. There's this great scene where Mellish calls for foreign aid. A plane lands and out comes this stream of Hasidic rabbis in *peyes* and tallises. Mellish says, 'I said call the UN not the UJA.'"

The Ambassador yet again worked himself into a state of hysteria.

"I just love the idea of these rabbis coming out of the plane to assist with the war," he said, wiping his forehead with a napkin, "and I thought, wouldn't it be great to re-create that scene, only this time it is alien rabbis coming to render assistance to the planet Earth. What do you think? Isn't that great?"

Ned, seated next to Ralph at the dinner table, leaned over and said, "I told him no one would get it."

IT WAS AT THIS point the President of the United States formed the operative hypothesis that the Ambassador was a pain in the ass. The President didn't get the jokes. This was part of it. More, though, it was the President's rapidly developing impression that the Ambassador was not someone with whom he could be friends. Most of the President's friends liked to golf or hunt or fish, or golf and hunt, or hunt and fish, or golf and fish. None liked Woody Allen movies and definitely none liked staging elaborate practical jokes that involved dressing up as Orthodox Jews. The President suspected, correctly, that the Ambassador liked neither golfing nor hunting nor fishing nor any combination thereof.

WHILE THE AMBASSADOR HAD not gotten off on the right foot with the President, the reaction in the rest of the room was more favorable. Ralph could take Woody Allen or leave him, but he was impressed with the Ambassador's spirit and enthusiasm, which was infectious. David Prince, the former history professor, was a huge fan of Woody Allen. He found the idea of Orthodox aliens hilarious and expected the great director himself would have approved. Joe Quimble was disappointed from a political standpoint that contact with the aliens could not be used to bolster the President's standing in the Jewish community, but he liked the Ambassador nevertheless. In the Ambassador's position, the temptation would be nearly irresistible to demonstrate the superiority of one's power. Quimble felt the Ambassador's efforts at good humor sent a very positive alternative message: We want to be friends.

Len Carlson, on the other hand, was right with the President. He thought the Ambassador was a pain in the ass.

"SO YOU'RE NOT JEWISH," the President said.

"No," said the Ambassador. "We are not particularly invested in the belief in a God or supreme being either one way or the other."

"Do you keep kosher?"

"No."

The President nodded.

"So you've never had crap lock soup before," he said.

"No," said the Ambassador with a smile that suggested a large appetite. "But I'm sure it's wonderful."

HERE, THE PRESIDENT SUMMONED over the chief butler. "Tell the chef to bring me up a plate of macaroni and cheese," he said, "and not that gemelli-pancetta crap either—just the Kraft straight out of the box." As Lucian Trundle started to turn away, the President added, "And tell the band they can go home."

Thus the historic occasion of first contact between humans and extraterrestrials ended in great disappointment for Chaim Muscovitz and the Heavy Shtetl Klezmer Band.

12

IT'S LATER THAN
YOU THINK

THE AMBASSADOR'S STATEMENT THAT he was not particularly invested in the belief in God was no trivial matter for the President. The President believed in God, very much. He had been raised a Baptist, which is a sect of Christianity with more than forty million followers in the United States. Christianity has a host of different denominations, including Lutheran, Presbyterian, Anglican, Assyrian, Baptist, Anabaptist, Pentecostal, Mennonite, Fundamentalist, Scandinavian Pietist, and Christian Scientist—just to name a few. These are pretty much like the restaurants on H Street in Chinatown; they serve more or less the same thing. The Baptists' major innovation is drinking nonalcoholic grape juice instead of wine to represent the blood of their Savior, a practice they adopted in the 1920s in deference to Prohibition. They believe wholeheartedly in baptism and communion, which are the duck sauce and noodles of Christianity.

NEEDLESS TO SAY, THE President would not have appreciated the irreverent manner in which I have presented his belief system. Even though Baptists do not adhere to the doctrine of transubstantiation, the President would have resented the suggestion that Chinese noodles could substitute for the body of Christ.

RELIGION HAD BEEN AN integral part of the President's life since his childhood. He had served as a choirboy, played in the church little league, and participated to acclaim in various roles in the Christmas Nativity. Religion was one of the few vehicles through which he bonded with his father, a quiet man of few words. On Sundays, when he returned with his mother from church, he would find his father sitting on the couch watching football or baseball, depending on the season.

His father would say, "How was church?"

The President would say, "Fine."

This was their way of staying in touch.

(It may be obvious, though it merits mention, that during his childhood the President's parents did not refer to him as "the president.")

Religion continued to play a role in the President's adult life. He still attended church religiously, and counted several ministers among his closest golf, hunting, and fishing partners. He often turned to prayer during national crises. The President considered himself *born again*, which meant he had undertaken to be baptized as an adult when he could volitionally accept the teachings of Christ. Though he had been trained to say otherwise in public life, the President privately believed he was going to heaven and that many, many people, including the Jews, Muslims, Hindus, Confucians, and Scientologists with whom he conducted affairs of state on a regular basis, were going to hell.

The Ambassador's lack of belief was strike two against him.

"SO YOU'RE AN ATHEIST?" the President asked.

"Well," the Ambassador said, "my mother was an atheist and my father agnostic, so they didn't know what religion not to raise me."

The President nodded.

"That's another Woody Allen line," the Ambassador said.

The President smiled weakly.

"I suppose I would be more of an agnostic," the Ambassador confessed.

"I've never really understood the difference."

"It isn't so much that we believe God does not exist as we believe that God's existence has not been proven."

"Do you expect such proof to be found?"

"At this point, it does not seem likely."

"Then I really do not see the difference," the President said.

"I suppose it is an academic point."

"It is strange to me," said the President, "you believe as you do given your occupation."

"How do you mean?"

"I would presume in your profession you travel extensively and see many things."

"I do," said the Ambassador. "I have been to hundreds of planets in dozens of galaxies. I have seen supernovas, black holes, and nebulae of unimaginable splendor. I have seen life in every imaginable form, from telepathic snails to peanut-butter-and-jelly fish, from turtles that age backward to chipmunks that shift in time when they are being chased. I have seen soaring birds of such magnificence they would make your hawks and eagles seem mundane. I have seen nature in all of its glory, and it is glorious indeed."

"In all of this," said the President, "you must find evidence of a higher power. Surely all of this could not have arisen by chance."

"Life is miraculous, Mr. President, but there are no miracles."

"Well," the President said, "I have not seen as much as you have seen, but I have seen far too much to dismiss it all as the product of chance. I draw the opposite conclusion as you do."

"I know," said the Ambassador. "That is, in large part, what my associate and I have come to speak with you about."

After this statement, all conversation around the dinner table stopped. The dialogue between the Ambassador and the President had been the focus of everyone around the table, but there had also been some small talk and side conversations. These all ended. Needless to say, this was the subject everyone was most eager to hear discussed.

AT THIS POINT, THE gefilte fish arrived. Gefilte fish is ground, deboned, rolled into small balls, and served with a sauce of horseradish and vinegar. The fish used is generally carp, which is a prolific fresh-water fish closely related to the common goldfish. Whitefish or pike is sometimes used as a substitute. Gefilte fish has a bland, vaguely bilious flavor, and the consistency of organ meat. The Ambassador may not believe in such things, but it is surely a miracle that anybody eats it.

"THIS IS WHAT WE are all curious about," said the President. "Why are you here? And why are you here now?"

"To warn you about the consequences of your choices," said the Ambassador, addressing everyone at the table. "You see, Mr. President, Ned and I are sociologists by training. Our organization has studied and continues to study tens of thousands of planets throughout the universe. Most of the time we make no contact . and the inhabitants are blissfully unaware of our presence, as you humans have been for thousands of years. Some of the planets have primitive life with which we could not possibly interact. Others are hopelessly bellicose. But sometimes we are compelled to intervene, as we are now."

"And the reason for this has something to do with religion?" the President asked skeptically.

"You are a strikingly theistic people. You have a great deal of belief and great diversity among your beliefs."

"The United States has a proud history of religious tolerance."

"I don't mean Americans," the Ambassador said. "I mean humans. Human beings are strikingly theistic."

"And I suppose you go around the galaxy preaching atheism."

"An intergalactic anti-Crusade," Len Carlson chimed in.

The Ambassador waved his hand. "No," he said. "We do not care at all about what you believe. Like the United States, my planet also has a proud history of religious tolerance. We are deeply respectful of people's personal beliefs."

"Then what is the cause for concern?" asked the President.

The Ambassador paused for a moment, searching for the right words. Finally, he said, "You understand we are scientists, yes? To a scientist, belief in religion is not good or bad, right or wrong, it is simply a fact. A field researcher examining a species simply checks a box, 'Believes in God,' just as he might, as appropriate, check a box that says 'Bipedal' or 'Endothermic.' He does not care about his subject's religious beliefs any more than he cares whether it is cold-blooded or warm-blooded. Do you understand this?"

"Somewhat," said the President.

"We have effectively checked these boxes for all of the tens of thousands of planets we have visited around the universe. In other words, we have a lot of data. One consequence, or benefit if you will, of having all of this data is we can make certain predictions about the ramifications of particular choices for the long-term health of a species or a planet. Of course, that's not to say we can predict anything with certainty. Only God can do that."

The Ambassador broke into a big toothy grin. "That's a good one," he said softly. This time the President did not muster even a thin smile.

"Anyway," the Ambassador continued, "it turns out religious belief, generally speaking, is a significant risk factor. Belief in religion isn't itself problematic, but it is closely tied to other factors that are: likelihood of war or genocide, an inability to respond open-mindedly to new threats, things such as this."

"So you're here to tell us that religion is bad."

"No, no, no. Not good or bad. That would be a value judgment. We're scientists. We just talk about data. In any case, the concern here isn't just about religion. We would never have come just over that. It's really all of the various risk factors taken together. The reason we came is that on our aggregate scale humanity has passed a certain critical stage, a tipping point you might say."

"And what is that?"

The Ambassador paused for effect.

"It is more likely than not humanity will destroy itself."

PRESENTLY, THE BRISKET ARRIVED. The meat had been marinated for two days in a cabernet reduction and was so tender it could dissolve on the tongue without chewing. The First Lady eyed it longingly. Even more than the brisket, she craved the potato latkes, which were being served as a side. To lose the weight she needed to lose, or felt she needed to lose, the First Lady had gone on a diet that tricked her body into thinking it was starving. She could eat all of the meat and fish she wanted, but no carbohydrates, and absolutely no potatoes. She knew if she ate just one of those delicious lightly fried latkes she would undo all of her hard work over the preceding week.

She would explode out of her dress right there in front of the Ambassador. She thought this would be embarrassing for her and the President. On the other hand, if the world was going to end, what could be the harm?

NEITHER THE PRESIDENT NOR the Ambassador touched his main course. The President did not eat because he found the kosher food repugnant and because he was saving room for macaroni and cheese. The Ambassador did not eat because he found the idea of killing and eating sentient creatures abhorrent. He was tempted to try to influence the President on this point, but as they say on Rigel-Rigel, "one fish at a time." What they actually say on Rigel-Rigel is "one floshbecarran at a time," but the idea is the same.

The President was having a hard enough time with the idea that humans were teetering on the verge of extinction without having to deal also with the argument that it is immoral to kill self-aware species for food. This would have been a particularly tough sell with the President since he liked nothing better after a day of hunting or golf than to tear into a juicy 22-ounce rib eye.

"So," the President asked skeptically, "you believe that religion will cause the destruction of humanity?"

"No," the Ambassador said. "It isn't a causal thing. A high level of religious belief is just a risk factor. And, as I said, it is just one among many factors that humanity displays."

"What are the others?"

"Well, destruction of the environment is a big one. For long-term survival, a species needs to reach equilibrium with its environment. Humanity is exhausting Earth's natural resources. You have caused a massive extinction of species over the past hundred years. Deforestation and carbon dioxide emissions have set in motion planetary warming, which will be extremely difficult to reverse."

"And this will be the end of life on the planet?"

"Not all life," the Ambassador said. "Just human beings and most mammals. Plants and insects can adapt effectively to changes in the atmosphere. People are not so evolutionarily nimble."

The President said, "Our scientists are studying global warming. Many have expressed skepticism about the phenomenon. Our approach has been to wait and see."

The Ambassador smiled. "Wait and see is fine," he said. "But we have an expression on my planet, Mr. President, that we often use whenever someone says that."

"What's that?"

"It's later than you think."

SOME INTERESTING SYNERGIES PRESENT themselves here. On Rigel-Rigel, the saying is as old as the hills. Like most sayings, it falls in and out of favor over time. The expression has also been around on Earth for some time. It was popularized in the 1950s by Guy Lombardo in a song by Carl Sigman and Herb Magidson called "Enjoy Yourself (It's Later Than You Think)." It goes:

> Enjoy yourself, it's later than you think
> Enjoy yourself while you're still in the pink
> The years go by as quickly as a wink
> Enjoy yourself, enjoy yourself, it's later than you think.

It has a catchy tune. In the 1990s, Woody Allen, seeing irony in the song, used it in his musical postcard to Paris, *Everyone Says I Love You*. The relevant scene in the movie takes place in a funeral parlor after the death of the grandfather of the main character Djuna, played by Natasha Lyonne. All of a sudden the corpses jump out of their coffins and start to sing, "Enjoy yourself, it's later than you think." It's quite funny. The movie did not do especially well in the United States, but was enormously popular in France and on Rigel-Rigel, where it sparked a renaissance of the old expression.

Of course, the President had not seen the movie. Even if he liked Woody Allen he still would not have seen it since more than anything else, more than Ivy League graduates and fancy food, the President hated the French.

THE AMBASSADOR ASKED, "WHAT if we could prove to you, Mr. President, that global warming is man-made and catastrophic to the future of the planet?"

"How could you do that?"

"Ned." The Ambassador nodded in the direction of his assistant. Out of a bag he had stored under the table, Ned pulled a massive document, which he handed to the Ambassador, who in turn handed it to the President.

"This is a hundred-thousand-year-long longitudinal study of two thousand three hundred seventy-five planets. It examines the effect of environmental destruction on the long-term viability of indigenous sentient species. In other words, it examines what happens when intelligent creatures purposefully destroy their environment. In short, it demonstrates that where a balance is not achieved with the environment, the offending species is thirty times more likely to become extinct itself."

The President grudgingly accepted the document. "How do I know this is reliable?"

"It's peer reviewed," the Ambassador said.

The President rifled the pages of the mammoth document.

"This is quite impressive," the President said with gravitas. Those associated with the President had seen him thumb the pages of many other research and advocacy documents and comment in the same manner. Generally speaking, he did not like to read anything longer than a page.

"Of course," the President said, "even if this research were true, it would not prove the same thing would happen here."

"That's true," the Ambassador said.

"And we all know the problems with peer review," the President said. "It's just a bunch of professors helping one another get tenure."

Even the Ambassador could not deny the truth of this.

"I APPRECIATE YOUR COMING here," the President said. "I really do."

He really did not.

"But I think we're going to just have to make our own mistakes and figure things out for ourselves. I have faith in mankind. We have proven ourselves quite resourceful. We'll find a way to manage our environment, and I'm sure we'll find a way to somehow resolve all of our religious differences too."

The Ambassador nodded. "I understand," he said.

He really did not.

"Let me ask you a question, Mr. President."

"Okay."

"What is the fundamental tenet of your religious beliefs?"

The President thought about this for a moment.

"I suppose," he said, "it is that God created man and Earth."

"What if I could disprove that to you?"

The President smiled. "How could you possibly do that?"

"Ned." The Ambassador again nodded in the direction of his assistant.

Ned reached into his bag once more, this time producing a spiffy handheld holographic video projector.

"Human beings were the product of a genetic experiment," the Ambassador explained. "The Aurorans were a race from a star system near this one. They had begun to tinker with modifying DNA and they set out to see whether they could introduce genes for sophisticated speech and written expression to primitive primates. This is a video record of the experiment. It is in Auroran with English subtitles."

The Ambassador nodded to Ned. "Go ahead," he said.

The footage had been filmed in front of what was unmistakably the Great Pyramid of Giza. Standing in front of the pyramid was a two-legged gecko in a white lab coat, apparently an Auroran scientist, holding what appeared to be a human infant. Text of subtitles follows:

"Is this working? Is this working? Are you sure? I don't want to have to do this again. The microphone doesn't feel like it's attached right. Okay. You're sure? Okay. Testing. Testing. Arnold Lusterberger has left the building. Arnold Lusterberger has left the building. One, two, three. The sound is okay? Good. Are you sure? Okay, good. This is Humbert Wollongong standing in front of the remote laboratory on Sol Three. We have just delivered the first genetically modified chimpanzee. We have altered the genetic code of this native primate to enhance memory and capacity for expression. The mother is nursing the infant, which appears to be healthy and fertile. This is a pivotal moment in the history of this planet and our own. I must confess I feel a bit like God. You're kidding me? That wasn't working? Oh, you did get it. Are you sure? One hundred percent? Okay, good. Should we double-check? No? Okay, good. What a schlep."

THE STORY OF THE Aurorans' demise is a sad one. They were a sweet, fun-loving people who enjoyed Chinese checkers and jelly beans.

They had a generous philosophy of life, were nice to children, and possessed great intellectual curiosity. On top of it all, they were long-lived and physically robust. Their thick exoskeletons rendered them impervious to injury by flying coconuts and other dangerous projectiles. They had only one Achilles' heel, which in the case of Achilles was his Achilles' heel: they were allergic to nuts.

They never saw the end coming. When the meteor approached Aurora, they confidently proclaimed it would destroy itself in the atmosphere, which it did, splintering into a million little pieces, and how could they have known, even with their spectacularly sophisticated technology, that the offending asteroid, which had traveled millions of light-years across the galaxies, came from a planet made of pralines?

"WAIT A MINUTE, WAIT a minute," the President said. "These Aurorans believed in God?"

"Not the same god as you," the Ambassador said. "They worshipped a different god, a guy named Bert. But the concept was the same. The word 'god' is simply the best translation available."

"And these Aurorans built the pyramids themselves?"

"Yes."

"And created humans?"

"Yes."

"What happened to them? Why haven't we heard from them?"

"They are extinct now."

"So the beings that created man are themselves extinct."

"Right."

"Because they believed in God?"

"No, it was an allergy to nuts, but that's not the point."

"And you're telling us the name of the scientist was Humbert Wollongong?"

"Names are so difficult. It is again the best available translation."

"How do you expect us to believe that?" the President asked, his voice rising slightly. "We have no idea what Professor Wollongong is saying. How are we supposed to know these subtitles are accurate?"

The Ambassador, doing his best to suppress his glee, said, "You'll just have to take that on faith."

"This is too much to handle," the President said. "I cannot accept any of this."

"You're skeptical," the Ambassador said, "because you need to believe in a higher power. You need to believe things happen for a reason."

"We *choose* to believe."

"No, you *need* to believe."

"Don't we have a right to believe as we want to believe?"

"You do. But we believe we have an obligation to tell you the consequences of your beliefs."

"So you're telling me your people think things happen by chance. You're telling me you believe life in the universe arose randomly. You believe our meeting here today is just an accident."

"The universe is a very big place, Mr. President. Lots and lots of things happen. So many things happen, many of these things are bound to appear coincidental. The appearance of meaning is just an illusion."

"And you're telling me it doesn't bother your people to believe things just happen by chance?"

"Not at all. On the contrary, we find great humor in the rich, varied ways that life unfolds. You would too, if you were programmed a bit differently."

"I doubt it."

"I could prove it to you."

"How could you possibly do that?"

"Why don't we discuss that over dessert?"

AFTER THE DINNER PLATES were cleared, the Ambassador gestured to Ned, who produced from his seemingly bottomless bag an oversized Bundt cake. Ned handed this to the Ambassador, who in turn handed the cake over to the President with an air of formality.

"I present this to you in the name of all of the people of the universe, Mr. President," the Ambassador said. Then with less formality, he added, "I always like to bring a cake when I visit people for the first time. It's sort of a welcome-to-the-neighborhood thing."

A BUNDT CAKE IS the name for a dessert cake cooked in a Bundt pan, which was the creation of David Dalquist, the founder of Nordic Ware. He invented the pan at the request of the Hadassah Society of Minneapolis. They wanted a pan that could be used to make *kugel*, a Jewish dessert. The pan became popular after a Bundt cake won second place in the 1966 Pillsbury Bake-off. Dalquist knew this, and it pleased him greatly. What he did not know was that the Bundt cake, together with Woody Allen movies, Police albums, and Sour Patch Kids would become one of the handful of products of human culture that were popular throughout the universe.

THE CAKE WAS THE first plus on the Ambassador's ledger. The President was far more pleased to receive it than he had been to receive the immense peer-reviewed study setting out the data on environmental destruction and the decline of sentient species. The President was a great fan of cake and considered himself an expert on the subject.

In the President's opinion, the key to a good cake was moistness. This was what separated, for example, Devil Dogs from Ring Dings. Each was a Drake's product, and each was chocolate cake filled with cream, but the Ring Ding was infinitely better than the Devil Dog, which was a dry cake. Ring Dings were moist and delicious. But too moist was no good either. Hostess Cup Cakes, for example, were too moist. The Bundt was a simple choice, and though not especially popular in the twenty-first century, could be wonderful if prepared just right. It so happened the Ambassador had brought a fine Bundt. After the President sampled the cake and judged it worthy he ordered the Bundt be sliced and shared with all members of the party.

For many who had not enjoyed the kosher state dinner it was welcome nourishment. For the First Lady, however, it was just more torture.

13

WE DON'T NEED NO
THOUGHT CONTROL

AS ARNOLD NENE-ZINKELREEN RANG the bell of Professor Fendle-Frinkle's front door, he thought to himself that the house could use some work. The architecture had some inherent charm, and the home must have been nice in its day, but it had lapsed into a state of disrepair. The garage door had a hole in it. Ivy had crept up the side of the house and was wearing away the mortar. The gutter system had collapsed, leading water to drip down the side of the house, dislodging chunks of brick and stone in the process.

The lawn was an absolute disaster, years past the point where it could even be called a lawn. The weeds had vanquished the grass and established a flourishing empire. These weeds were rich in their diversity—some had flowers, some had spines, one had a cylindrical protuberance that discharged toxic pollen. This all stood in sharp contrast to the other homes in the subdivision with their finely manicured yards.

The front porch was littered with a peculiar mélange of garbage—some traditional suburban fare such as empty diet soda cans and pizza boxes and, incongruously, the wrappers of organic energy bars and spent containers of homeopathic remedies. The deck had fallen through in two places. A pair of orange cones warned visitors of the danger. Even the doormat was in tatters and had split down the middle. Divided in this way, the Rigel-Rigel word for welcome could have been construed as a sexual reference.

Arnie wondered about the owners of the house. His potential client, the Professor, seemed nice enough when Arnie had called after reading about the brewing controversy at Rigel Prep. But he asked few questions about the nature of Arnie's work and seemed shockingly disinterested in his own potential demise. After seeing the house, his apathy seemed somewhat less shocking.

A gentleman answered the door in an old flannel shirt and wrinkled corduroys. He seemed in every respect a part of the house.

"Can I help you?" he asked.

"I'm Arnie Nene-Zinkelreen," said the attorney. "I'm here from the Intergalactic Civil Liberties Union."

"Of course," said the Professor. "Everyone knows the good works of the ICLU. My wife is a longstanding member."

IN FACT, ANYONE CAN join the ICLU for the eminently reasonable fee of twenty-five dollars or its equivalent in the unit of intergalactic exchange, the Iuro. The ICLU puts this money to work protecting the rights of oppressed people throughout the universe. In addition to supporting important litigious causes, such as the rights of teachers to teach what they want to teach, upon payment of annual dues, members receive three sheets of self-adhesive return-address labels. Given the reality of faster-than-light-speed travel and object teleportation, mail is not a popular method of communication, but the labels enjoy a strange, ongoing vestigial popularity among civil libertarians.

"PLEASE," SAID THE PROFESSOR, beckoning the attorney to enter. "Let's go down to my study. It'll be easier for us to chat."

Arnie followed the Professor downstairs. There appeared to be a pleasant living room up just a few stairs, with a nice couch and loveseat, but the Professor bypassed this room and led Arnie instead to the basement, where he offered Arnie a seat on a bridge chair, just in front of the hot-water tank. The Professor sat at his desk, which was really just a sheet of plywood suspended between the washer and the dryer. The desk was cluttered with papers containing elaborate calculations, unmatched socks, and underwear that had been marked in red ink. The attorney became conscious of his own underwear, which was all of a sudden bunching uncomfortably.

"So what can I do for you?" the Professor asked.

"It's what I can do for you," Arnie said. "The ICLU has been monitoring your situation. We want to offer our help."

"What is my situation?" the Professor asked. Some water dripped on the Professor's forehead from an overhanging pipe. He did not flinch.

"The Rigel Prep PTA is irate over your lesson about the contraction of the universe. They are demanding your dismissal."

"I see," said the Professor.

"The ICLU believes this is an issue of *academic freedom*." Arnie said these last words slowly, with emphasis, as if it were a novel and important concept. "As a teacher," he continued, "we believe you have the right to control the content of what occurs in your classroom."

"I see," said the Professor.

"We believe this is the start of a *slippery slope*." The attorney said the words "slippery slope" with emphasis, as if it too were a novel and important concept. "The school board is trying to characterize this as a question of values," he continued. "Once the board controls the contents of a physics lecture it is only a matter of time before it dictates what books are read and what philosophies are taught."

"I see," said the Professor.

ON RIGEL-RIGEL, CENSORSHIP IS almost unheard of. This is part of the reason for the Professor's reaction. On Earth, however, it is as much a part of life as the Labor Day parade or the Iditarod. Attempts at banning books can be traced as far back as the third century B.C., when Qin Shi Huang, first ruler of the Qin dynasty, burned all copies of the *Analects of Confucius*, and ordered that followers of Confucius be buried alive. Confucius's philosophy emphasized personal and governmental morality, correctness of social relationships, justice, and sincerity.

Religious tracts have been a common target for censorship. The Spanish suppressed the Koran in the sixteenth century. The Catholic Church spent much of the Middle Ages attempting to suppress the Talmud. Pope Innocent XI ordered King Louis XIV of France to burn all copies. In 1536, William Tyndale was burned at the stake for translating the Bible into English. Tyndale believed, heretically, that the word of God should be known even to common people.

Some targets seem obvious. Darwin's *The Origin of Species* was banned in Tennessee, which, for half of the twentieth century, prohibited teaching evolution. Others seem counterintuitive. Children's books, for example, have met surprising resistance. Laytonville, California, banned Dr. Seuss's *The Lorax* because it criminalized the foresting industry. A Colorado librarian removed Roald Dahl's *Charlie and the Chocolate Factory* from the shelves because she believed it espoused a poor philosophy of life. The Alabama State Textbook Committee rejected Anne Frank's diary because, they said, it was a "real downer."

But no genre has met greater disapprobation than science fiction novels, which rival religious tracts in the frequency with which they have been the object of censorship. Past targets include:

Kurt Vonnegut's *Slaughterhouse Five* by Owensboro High School in Kentucky because of the sentence: "The gun made a ripping sound like the opening of the fly of the God Almighty."

Madeleine L'Engle's *A Wrinkle in Time*, by a Florida elementary school, for grouping Jesus with scientists and philosophers who defend Earth against evil.

C. S. Lewis's Christian allegory, *The Chronicles of Narnia*, by the Howard County, Maryland, school system, because it failed to adhere to "good Christian values."

Orwell's *1984* for being pro-communist.

Huxley's *Brave New World* for focusing on "negative activity."

And, finally, Ray Bradbury's *Fahrenheit 451*, a book about censorship.

BY CONTRAST, THE PEOPLE of Rigel-Rigel had the broadest possible conception of civil liberties. The Rigel-Rigel constitution protected freedom of speech and freedom of association and freedom of religion. It also protected the right of privacy, construed in the broadest possible sense. This meant that people were free to do whatever they wanted in their homes and free to do whatever they wanted with their bodies so long as these activities did not harm other people. A person could drink alcohol or smoke or take any of the vast array of drugs available for consumption with impunity. One could have sex with whomever one liked—man, woman, alien—so long as it was consensual. Not only could they have sex with whomever they liked, the constitution assured that the law would treat the relationship in the same manner as the traditional relationship between a man and a woman.

This tolerance was a source of pride for the citizens of Rigel-Rigel, who respected even the most eclectic of preferences. For example, the Rigelian press celebrated the strange case of Rothlorian, a decorated army veteran who married a plant. It was a highly evolved plant, with a conspicuously succulent leaf, but a plant all the same. Nevertheless Rigel-Rigel law protected the relationship to the fullest. When Rothlorian died, the plant collected the residual of his pension.

IN LIGHT OF THIS cultural predisposition, the question is why the parent-teacher association of Rigel Prep would have felt comfortable attacking the civil liberties of Professor Fendle-Frinkle. The answer is that Helen Argo-Lipschutzian and the rest of the PTA did not see this as an issue of civil liberties. Helen believed it to be about a much bigger issue: how a hypothesis passes from tentative conjecture to accepted fact, and which among the many hypotheses scientists develop should be presented as truth.

This is really an epistemological question. It is a question about whether we really know anything and, if we do, how we know it, and how we can differentiate among the things we are sure we know, the things we know we don't know, and the times we are just guessing.

Helen would have put it differently. She would have said teachers should not teach anything about which they are not certain, particularly when it is something likely to be upsetting to children.

Helen also believed another crucial issue to be at stake, which did not affect civil liberties in any manner: asserting the power of PTAs.

FROM THE DISTANT TOP floor of the house, a shrill voice screamed, "Tissues! We need more tissues upstairs!" The Professor waved his hand in front of his face, urging the attorney to go on.

"You see," Nene-Zinkelreen continued, "this is just the latest attempt by the emerging conservative element in our society to erode our civil liberties. They are frustrated by the rights granted to our citizens by the Intergalactic Constitution, rights that have been protected for millennia. They want to teach their values in the classroom, but the line they are trying to cross is sacred. We cannot surrender so much as an inch. If we relent, the battle will be lost for all time. Professor, these people do not have the right to keep you from teaching what you believe to be true."

"Kleenex!" screamed the Professor's wife, but he dismissed her again with another wave of his hand. (Of course, she did not scream "Kleenex." It is merely the best translation available.)

"Why not?" asked the Professor.

"How's that?"

"Why can't they stop me from teaching this?"

"How can you even ask that?"

"Well, what difference does it make?"

"It's the difference between teaching science and teaching fiction."

"They're not telling me what to teach. They're trying to stop me from teaching something."

"But by not teaching that something you're denying a basic reality."

"So what if they want to believe a fiction?"

"I can't believe of all people you, a man of science, would say such a thing."

"Well, it seems quite important to them," the Professor said.

"But this is school," said the lawyer. "Parents can teach their children whatever they want in their homes, but the government does not have the right to teach fiction in the schools."

"They teach novels in school."

"That's totally different."

"How?"

Arnie stumbled on this for a moment, but he was a fine attorney and he had an answer to all questions.

"The existence of the novel is fact. The teaching of it doesn't endorse the message of the book. A school does not, however, have the right to rewrite a novel or to censor one or to pretend novels don't exist."

"I see," said the Professor. "That's an interesting distinction."

Arnie felt bolder now.

"We're going to go to all of the major newspapers with this.

We're going to make sure the whole galaxy knows what is being done to you here on Rigel-Rigel. And you, Professor Fendle-Frinkle, are going to go down as one of the great defenders of freedom of thought in the history of the universe."

The Professor said, "I see."

ARNIE COULD SEE FROM the Professor's nonplussed, less-than-enthusiastic reaction that he did not particularly want to go down as one of the great defenders of freedom in the history of the universe. In fact, Arnie had some sympathy for this position. Originally, Arnie had not wanted to be an attorney. He had wanted to be a jazz musician. As a child, Arnie had excelled at playing the cocleteen, the horn of a ramlike animal, which is blown, atonally, on the first day of a new year. He dreamed of someday playing professionally.

One day, after a particularly bad class, Arnie dropped out of law school and resolved to play the cocleteen in a jazz band. He didn't succeed. It is hard enough to make it as a jazz musician if you play a popular instrument such as the saxophone or the trumpet. Jazz bands have hardly any demand for cocleteen players. Furthermore, as soon as he left school, Arnie's mother began a relentless campaign of guilt, morning, noon, and night. She had always dreamed her son would grow up to be an attorney, and Arnie ultimately succumbed to her pressure.

So Arnie returned to his studies, reluctantly at first, but over time more willingly, until finally he fully embraced his role and fancied himself a young Clarence Darrow. More accurately, he fancied himself a young Lionel Hut-Zanderian, the great Rigel-Rigelian attorney. Arnie believed, given time, the Professor would overcome his reservations and similarly embrace his role in life.

IN FACT THE PROFESSOR was not thinking about any of this. Since the universe was going to end, the issue, which was not the sort of thing that resonated with him to begin with, seemed particularly unimportant. He could not see any point to going down in history for anything. What he was thinking, as he had been thinking throughout the entire conversation, was that he would like to have a piece of pie.

This is how it often is with celebrity: some people choose it, while others have it thrust upon them.

14

A SLEEP TRANCE, A DREAM DANCE, A SHAPED ROMANCE, SYNCHRONICITY

THE AMBASSADOR NEGLECTED, WHEN he presented the moist Bundt, to inform the President that the cake contained a chemical substance that temporarily suppressed the expression of certain genes. Specifically, it suppressed the expression of the genes that coded for characteristics such as ambition and ego, which incline a human being to believe life has a greater purpose, and that this purpose somehow involves him.

None of the guests at the dinner knew this, of course. They just knew it was particularly good cake, so good as to border on addictive. For Ralph, the cake evoked pleasant memories of college brownies, and he wondered whether this cake had been prepared in a similar fashion. This would have been fine with him.

"This is particularly good cake," the President said, his mouth half full.

"I am glad you like it," the Ambassador said. "Please enjoy."

What followed is known in certain countercultural movements as a moment—or moments—of lucidity.

FOR EXAMPLE, DAVID PRINCE realized his life had gone astray. He had been seduced from academia into politics by the allure of power and the grand hope of effecting social change. But he saw in his altered state that none of these things mattered. Life was ephemeral, far too short to worry about line items in the federal budget. What mattered was to find satisfaction in one's life in whatever way possible. For David, that had been teaching and research. He resolved in that moment to return to his passion, his magnum opus, the definitive biography of President Millard Fillmore.

AT THE SAME MOMENT, Ralph Bailey doubted the path of his own life. He had sat in the Chinese restaurant and questioned Jessica about her decision to leave law school. That had been a projection of his own anxiety about accomplishment and prestige. In fact he envied the freedom of Jessica's spirit. In further fact, the happiest moment of his own life had been when he forgot about convention and responsibility and audaciously proposed to Jessica that they camp out on the carpet of the Oval Office on their very first date. He longed to see her and to recapture the carefree spirit of that evening.

He also realized he liked Chinese food more than he cared to admit and should eat it more often.

LEN CARLSON REALIZED HE had been petulant and unprincipled in his politics, and should give Woody Allen a second chance.

THE PRESIDENT OF THE United States felt strangely empty, not entirely unlike a man who has fallen out of love. He remembers the fact that he was in love, and remembers that at one time he could not imagine life without this person, but cannot for the life of him remember why he felt this way in the first place. The President knew that not five minutes ago, God had been important, but now he could not say why. He could not even recall the sensation of faith. It struck the President as bizarre, perhaps even ironic, that this crisis should occur while eating a delicious Bundt cake. All the same, he took stock of his own life. Looking at it with dispassion, the President concluded that his obsessive pursuit of success in politics had been a reaction to his father's failure to give him attention. Looking at it with the same dispassion, the President further concluded that his father had been an asshole. He also noticed his underwear was feeling quite comfortable.

THE FIRST LADY REALIZED that the idealized image of the emaciated woman with enormous breasts was a social construct without validity. What was beautiful was whatever we perceived to be beautiful and whatever gave us pleasure. This realization emboldened the First Lady to have another piece of cake. This in turn solidified her hormone-free conclusion about the subjectivity of beauty, which in turn emboldened her to have one of the latkes. It was, depending upon one's perspective, either a vicious or a virtuous cycle.

NED ANAT-DENARIAN HAD HIS own moment of lucidity. He realized that while he had devoted his life to reaching out to new worlds and making the lives of others better, he had neglected his own family. His son was growing up without him. He had placed too much of a burden on his wife. In short, he had been away for too long. It was time to go home.

Ned's was a true epiphany. While the humans' experience had epiphanic qualities, theirs was qualitatively different from Ned's own. This was because the people of Earth and the people of Rigel-Rigel had quite different physiologies. The transformative compound in the cake had no known effect on Rigelians. In fact Ned ate it only because the gefilte fish had given him indigestion and he thought the Bundt might settle his stomach.

So his epiphany was spontaneous, a long time in the making but spontaneous. That it happened at the same time the humans experienced their cake-induced revelations could have been an example of the sort of convergent behavior people sometimes exhibit, such as when people who spend a lot of time around one another start to speak in the same manner. Or it might have just been a coincidence.

THESE WERE NOT THE only epiphanies occurring at that moment in the universe.

STANLEY SMITHERS, THE DEPUTY manager with responsibility for dried foods at the Kraft manufacturing plant in Worcester, Massachusetts, was having a very bad day. The machine that desiccated and granulated the cheese had broken a spring and sprayed powdered cheddar all over the factory floor, covering the employees in dried cheese and sending several home with severe irritation of their sinuses. It had taken more than six hours to repair the apparatus and in the process Stanley split the pants of his best suit, a Nino Cerutti, which he had just purchased at the Men's Wholesale Outlet. The jacket was covered in cheese speckles.

It had been a very bad day indeed. But on his way out, Stanley's spirits were buoyed, first by a coffee cake, which he bought from the vending machine, and then by a poster hanging on the wall by the time punch. It had been patterned on the World War II poster of Rosie the Riveter. It said:

Kraft Salutes Its Patriotic Employees

And under that:

Kraft Macaroni & Cheese
The Presidential Dinner of Choice

In the dried-cheese food business, the hours could be brutal, and a short circuit in the granulator could dampen even the most resilient of spirits. Stanley was exhausted and at the end of his patience, but he was a great patriot, and he knew of the historic events transpiring in Washington. The notion that Stanley's product might be served at the White House or might help sustain the President during a time of national need made all of it, even the pants-splitting granulator, seem worthwhile.

AT LAKE HOUSE, HIS home in Wiltshire, England, Sting found himself at home for the evening with nothing to do—no tour, no album marinating in the studio, even the wife and kids were out for the evening. It was the kind of evening that invited quiet reflection. He built a fire, cut himself a slice of Sara Lee pound cake, and sat in his favorite chair by his favorite window. Looking out over the verdant countryside, he thought about how much larger the universe had become over the past week. For a moment, he became anxious. Would there be in this new cosmos a place for the music of Sting? He took a bite of cake and wondered. Then, with a sudden sense of calm, he realized that the making of the music had been an end in itself.

PROFESSOR CRABTREE WAS OUT at dinner with a group of fellow tort professors. For dessert, he ordered a cup of coffee and a slice of chocolate chip loaf cake. He sat and listened as his colleagues debated the minutiae of jurisprudence. For the first time, he saw the absurdity of it. Right then and there, he decided he had been wasting his life studying and teaching tort law. As of that day he would pursue his life's dream: studying and teaching contract law.

AT THE SAME TIME as all of this, in a distant galaxy, on an as yet unmentioned planet not unlike Earth, a mother brought her son milk and cookies and sat down to read him a bedtime story. They were reading from a novel titled *First Contact—Or, It's Later Than You Think (Parrot Sketch Excluded)*. In the book, aliens reach out to this planet called Earth with the best of intentions, but the President of the biggest nation on the planet is implausibly dim and screws everything up. Boy and mother had just reached the point in the novel where several people on Earth were eating dessert at more or less the same time and all thinking about the meaning of their lives. The boy did not like the book.

"I don't like this book," he said.

"It seems okay to me," his mother replied. "I think it's kind of funny."

Of course, this conversation took place in the native language of this unnamed planet in the distant galaxy. What is set out here is simply the best translation available.

"The themes of the book are pedestrian and trite," the boy said. "I think what the author is trying to say is that the desire to find meaning in things is just an evolved response that leads some species to work harder and accomplish things they otherwise would not. The belief in meaning is ultimately a fiction, and a potentially destructive one when people become too passionate about the myths in which they believe."

This may seem like sophisticated speech for a two-year-old, but the boy was precocious.

"The author's argument is internally contradictory," he expounded. "By attempting to convince the humans that the search for meaning is destructive, the aliens are themselves buying into the search for meaning. If nothing means anything, what difference does it make whether people on some planet believe things matter and some others do not? So what if a planet destroys itself? It only matters if things matter. And of course all this is going on while the universe is about to end, so nothing really matters at all."

The boy stopped and waved his hand. "It's old existential stuff," he said, "handled quite clumsily really. He bludgeons people over the head with all of it. And the exposition is heavy-handed. He might as well have one of the characters just come out and articulate the themes of the book."

"I just thought he was trying to be funny," the mother said. "I really like that the President is obsessed with his underwear."

The boy paid his mother no heed and continued, more animated than he had been before. "The book has all kinds of contradictions," he said. "For example, the people of Rigel-Rigel are capable of faster than light travel, but the Professor has an ancient washer and dryer and leaky pipes in the basement."

"I thought the Professor's basement was funny," the mother said. "I liked that his wife circled the holes in his underwear."

"The use of language is confusing," the boy continued. "The aliens have a Bundt cake on their planet? How could that possibly be? And why in that chapter where he is talking about the Professor's neighborhood does he translate Rashukabia as "Dutch"? That's just a gratuitous shot against a perfectly nice people. You can't translate a proper name."

"He could be commenting on the ambiguity of language."

"Sometimes he seems to be saying there is no meaning," the boy continued. "At other points he suggests there is meaning. All of these coincidences occur, but they don't lead anywhere."

"Perhaps that's intentional," said the mother.

"What about the video of the Aurorans? How absurd is that? These aliens have the ability to travel to another planet and genetically modify a species, but they only have a handheld video camera."

"Maybe they were making a home movie."

"Why does Sting keep coming up? It's so random. Is he really using him as a substitute for Jung? Is it really philosophy lite?"

"Well, everybody likes Sting," said the mother.

"Sometimes stories are factual, sometimes they're made up. Sometimes product names are real, sometimes they're fake."

"Perhaps there were legal issues."

"And for God's sake, from a literary standpoint, pick a main character. Is the book about Ralph and Jessica or the Anat-Denarians or the dim-witted president of the United States? As if anyone that dumb could get to be president of a country. And what does the subtitle, 'Parrot Sketch Excluded,' mean? At the very least, the title of a book should make some sense."

The mother offered no further answers to her son's questions. Rather she waited to see whether he had finished his rant. Children of her son's age could get this way sometimes. On her planet, they referred to it as the "terrible twos." When the child threw a fit, sometimes the parent simply had to let it go on until the child had expended its energy. Her son now appeared to be spent.

"Well, should we finish the book?" she asked in a gentle tone.

"I suppose," her son said, calmer now. "It isn't completely hopeless." He gestured to his mother with his hand and said, "Read on."

The mother said, "'Well, should we finish the book?'"

The boy said, "I already said read on."

"No," said the mother. "That's what it says in the book. It says, '"Well, should we finish the book?" she asked in a gentle tone.' Now it says, 'The boy said, "I already said read on."' The text is changing as we speak. The punctuation is very confusing."

She looked up. "That's what it says in the book."

"They're called recursively nested quotation marks," the boy said.

"Now it says, 'They're called recursively nested quotation marks.'" Her eyes showed concern. "Try saying something else," she said.

The boy said, "I like macaroni and cheese."

"It says you say, 'I like macaroni and cheese,'" the mother said. "It's getting quicker too. The first time it took a second for the words to appear in the book after you said them. That time it was almost instantaneous."

All of these words appeared in front of the mother as she spoke.

"We're trapped in a recursion," said the boy.

The mother said, "That time it said, 'We're trapped in a recursion' before you even said it. Now it says I am going to ask you what a recursion is."

"It's like a paradox," said the boy.

"That's what it said you would say," said the mother, anxiously. "And that's what it said I would say."

"This is most unsettling," said the boy. "If the words anticipate our actions, then we do not have free will. The author is depriving us of our free will."

"But why?" asked the mother. "Why is this happening?"

"It's spite," said the boy, his voice rising. "This is spite, pure and simple. We're not even characters in the book. This is so absurd. He's just angry because I said I didn't like the book. Well, he is no better than the characters in his book. He is worse. He thinks the entire universe revolves around him. He cannot tolerate the idea that someone would find what he writes to be anything less than brilliant. It is a low and mean-spirited thing for a writer to do this to his readers."

All of these words had already appeared on the page.

I INJECTED MYSELF AS a character in this book in the hopes that I might grow from the experience. Some of the characters in this book do not grow. These include some peripheral characters such as Stanley Smithers, the manager at the Kraft factory, Nelson Munt-Zoldarian, the con artist who makes his living being rear-ended by cars traveling near the speed of light, and as will be evident in a few pages, some central characters including, quite maddeningly, the President of the United States. I knew all of this before writing the book. On the other hand, some of the characters, including Ned Anat-Denarian, Ralph Bailey, and the wonderful Jessica Love, evolve substantially. I also knew this before writing the book. I did not know where I would fit in, but I hoped that I might be among the characters experiencing personal growth.

I am tempted to refer to Ned and Ralph and Jessica as the "sympathetic" characters in the book. But I decline to do so because this would suggest, incorrectly in my view, that each of the characters who does not experience growth is unsympathetic. Perhaps this is a self-interested view on my part.

I feel I could stand to grow a bit as a person. I have some nice qualities. I am gentle with children and animals, especially dogs and birds, but I can be sarcastic and oversensitive to criticism. These childish qualities are substantial personal liabilities. Thus, I threw myself into the book and hoped that some of the positive perspective that several of the characters acquire would rub off on me.

Alas, sadly, everything the precocious two-year-old said in the preceding section is entirely true. I did write him and his mother into a recursion. And I did it for the reasons he said. I did it because the boy said snide things about my book, some of which hit a bit too close to home. I would like to be above such criticism, and I feel regretful about doing this to the mother, who seemed like a delightful person with a nice sense of humor, but I am who I am, and truth be told the boy was a genuine pain in the ass.

In Manhattan, Kansas, Margaret and Allan Stoopler settled into bed for the evening. She was reading a short novel ostensibly about an inept president who bungled the first interaction between humans and extraterrestrials. He was working on a Sudoku puzzle in the *Manhattan Mercury*.

"This is terrible," Margaret said.

"What's that?" asked Allan, not looking up from the puzzle. The puzzle had been rated "medium" difficulty, though Allan questioned the validity of the classification system. He found them all difficult. Sometimes when he needed to sleep he would just give up and read the comics. He particularly liked *The Wizard of Id*.

"In this book I'm reading," Margaret said, "the author just did something I really hate."

"What's that?" Allan still did not look up. He was having trouble placing a 9.

"He just injected himself as a character in the book."

"Injected," said Allan. "Is that the right word?"

"The plot is going along fine and then the author introduces these characters who comment on what he has written. Then he reacts to their reaction. It's quite bizarre. It breaks the fourth wall. That's taboo, you know. It's like one of those old Monty Python sketches where they're in the middle of a bit and then all of a sudden one of them steps out of character and apologizes for the scene and what has been going on."

Allan perked up. "You're reading a Monty Python book?"

"No, it's supposed to be a science fiction book, I think, though there really isn't much science fiction in it, and most of it is quite silly."

"Monty Python was great," Allan said. "I love the parrot sketch. That thing is hilarious. This guy buys a dead parrot and brings it back to the store, but the store owner won't admit it's dead. He insists the parrot is just resting. 'He's pinin' for the fjords,' he says. How great is that? 'He's pinin' for the fjords.' I love those guys."

"It's not a Monty Python book," Margaret repeated, but her husband did not hear. Communication in the Stoopler home was less than ideal.

"Do they have the parrot sketch in there?" Allan asked.

"No," Margaret said, exasperated. "The parrot sketch is not included."

15

I WANT A NEW DRUG

BUNDT CAKE CAN MAKE people thirsty, but the moment had been prepared for. The Ambassador gestured to Ned, who produced from his magical bag a large jug of what appeared to be, and in fact was, fruit punch, which the Ambassador presented to the President of the United States. The Ambassador said, "Whenever we meet new people, we like to provide cake and punch."

This was the second plus on the Ambassador's ledger. Like everyone else at the dinner, the President needed something to wet his whistle. It so happened the President also considered himself to be a great expert on punch. He particularly enjoyed Hawaiian Punch—Fruit Juicy Red flavor. Because of his extensive travel, the President knew Hawaiians don't much like Hawaiian Punch. He knew they prefer a blend of papaya, orange, and guava juice, which they refer to as "POG" or, sometimes, punch. But this did not trouble the President. He still liked it. He accepted the Ambassador's offering with his customary gravitas and took a sip. It was fine fruit punch. The President pronounced it so and ordered it distributed to the guests.

Ralph and Joe Quimble and everyone else, with the exception of Ned and the Ambassador, dutifully consumed the beverage. Like the others, Ralph felt his head clear. It was as if he were coming down from a bad trip, though it would be a mistake to call the cake-induced state of heightened awareness a bad trip, since it was not at all unpleasant. Suffice it to say he felt different.

At this point, the Ambassador announced the perpetration of a canard. "I have a confession to make," he said. "That was not ordinary cake and punch you just consumed, Mr. President." He explained, "The cake was altered to suppress the expression of certain genes that contribute to the desire or need, if you will, to believe in a guiding process. It suppresses traits such as ego and motivation, that sort of thing. The punch reverses the process. You are all exactly as you were before, except you have now had the experience of seeing the world through, shall we say, an untinted lens. I hope you have a new perspective from which you can make a more reasoned, dispassionate judgment about your situation. I hope you have learned and grown from the experience."

INDEED, MOST OF THEM had learned and grown from the experience. Moreover, much of this heightened self-awareness, and the resolve it produced, persisted even after the punch counteracted the effect of the cake. Ralph remained determined to spend more time with Jessica and to eat more Chinese food. David Prince already had a well-formed plan for tackling the biography of Millard Fillmore. The First Lady was going to find a recipe for potato latkes.

But the President of the United States had not changed at all. He synthesized the experience of the cake and punch in a peculiar way. He recalled the feeling of faithlessness, but it did not cause him to question his religious belief. In fact, his faith was so strong the President concluded the cake had been the work—or baking—of the devil. He felt more devoted to his god than ever before, completely invested in his political career, and confident about the upcoming reelection campaign. The President even reconstructed his image of his father as a quiet and mis-understood man who loved his son in his own manner. Wistfully, he remembered their quiet conversations on Sunday afternoons.

NOW THE PRESIDENT UNDERSTOOD he could not very well come out and accuse the Ambassador of doing the work of the devil, just as he could not tell all of the Jews, Muslims, Hindus, Confucians, and Scientologists with whom he met on a regular basis that they were going to hell. Instead he presented quite a clever argument. It was really an argument about prayer in school but it applied with equal force to the Ambassador's somewhat patronizing statements about the desired effects of the cake.

Publicly, the President supported the separation of church and state. Privately, however, he thought prayer in school could do American children a world of good. He thought kids could do with a bit less sex, fewer video games, and a bit more fear of God and Hell. In conversations with friends, he had heard the argument advanced that opponents of prayer in school were really preaching their own brand of religion, a sect that might be called secular humanism. By arguing against the teaching of religion in school, they were sending the message to children that God did not really exist.

Opponents of prayer in school would say they weren't saying anything at all about the existence of God. School was for facts, not theories. They just wanted the issue discussed at home and not at school. The fact was, though, that if your parents told you that two plus two equals four and then you went to school and asked the teacher whether this were true and the teacher responded that she could not discuss the issue because of a directive from the school board, this could send a very confusing message to a young person about the reliability of addition.

The President made a similar argument to the Ambassador. The President said, "I thought you denied earlier that you are preaching atheism."

"I do deny it," the Ambassador said. "We are not advocating any set of beliefs."

"Then why did you refer to our nonbelieving, Bundt-cake-influenced condition as the 'untinted lens'?"

"What do you mean?"

"You might just as easily have referred to the believing state as the untinted lens."

"I suppose that is true," said the Ambassador.

"Who is to say what the baseline is here?"

"I assure you, Mr. President, we are not making any value judgments."

"But you're here to advocate that we change our way of life."

"We are here to educate you about the consequences of certain choices and to offer our assistance to change paths should you choose to do so."

"Because we will destroy ourselves otherwise."

"The probabilities suggest this."

"And you think it would be better for us to live your way than to die our own."

"I suppose that's true."

"So then you are making a value judgment."

EACH PERSON IN THE room reacted differently to the President's argument. Joe Quimble worried the President was squandering an historic opportunity. Len Carlson didn't like the Ambassador and silently cheered as the President gave him heck. David Prince maintained the dispassion of a historian. Ralph Bailey reacted with surprise. He did not know the President could offer such a cogent argument. Up until that point, most of their discussions had been about physical fitness, sandwich meat, and underwear.

THE AMBASSADOR, OF COURSE, had heard it all before.

"I was warned you might react this way," he said.

"How is that?"

"The French suggested you would be less than receptive to this argument about belief. They are a bit more existentialist than you, quite receptive really to the relativity of good and evil."

"You met with the French?"

"Yes," said the Ambassador. He tapped the President on the shoulder. "Do you know what they call French toast in France?"

"What?"

"Toast."

The Ambassador laughed heartily, rolled his head back, and said, "That's a good one." The President offered not even a cursory smile.

"When did you meet with the French?" the President asked.

"We've made the rounds over the past twenty-four hours," the Ambassador said. "We've met with the Indians and the Chinese, your European leaders, and most of the parties in your very intriguing Middle Eastern conflict."

"That's quite a day," said the President.

"It's amazing what one can accomplish when it's possible to travel faster than the speed of light."

The President was peeved on at least three levels. First, he was peeved the Ambassador had not visited the United States before all other nations. Second, he was peeved he had not been told until that moment that the Ambassador had not visited the United States first. Third, and most substantially, he was peeved the Ambassador had mentioned the French in any sort of positive manner.

"So you met with all of these people?" the President asked quizzically. "Many of these nations are quite hostile to one another."

"We are equal-opportunity distributors of enlightenment," the Ambassador said with a smile.

"I see," said the President, with gravitas. Then he asked, "What did you think of the French?"

"Lovely people," the Ambassador said. "Delicious wine."

This was strike three against the Ambassador.

BY NOW, THE AMBASSADOR, who had made first contact with hundreds of planets, knew the whole thing had gone quite poorly. And the President, who for his part had met hundreds of national leaders, knew the Ambassador knew. But this is not the kind of thing that heads of state acknowledge in polite company. It is better to find some common ground and emphasize a positive aspect of the experience. Food is always safe ground.

Thus, when the Ambassador and Ned took leave of the President and the First Lady, the Ambassador said, "Thank you, Mr. President. Thank you for your gracious hospitality and for the delicious dinner. We particularly enjoyed the outstanding potato latkes. We look forward to our new friendship and a successful future partnership."

The President said, "Thank you, Mr. Ambassador. Thank you for your wisdom and your kind offers of assistance. Most especially, thank you for the delicious Bundt cake."

This is similar to the exchange between Premier Zhou Enlai and President Nixon upon Nixon's departure from Beijing.

Zhou said, "Thanks for coming to China."

Nixon said, "Thanks for the delicious dinner. Do you think I could have another one of those fortune cookies for the road? Pat is especially fond of them."

Zhou said, "Of course. Please take two."

In truth, neither Nixon nor his wife liked fortune cookies and once aboard Air Force One, Nixon gave the cookies to Kissinger.

THE AMBASSADOR AND NED departed, as they had arrived, through the West Gate, hailed a cab, and headed back to their hotel. Through the rear window, they could see the President retreat into the White House with an air of what could only be described as good riddance.

"Well, that didn't go well," Ned said.

"No," the Ambassador said. "No, it didn't. And the gefilte fish was terrible, just terrible."

A PECULIAR POSTSCRIPT TO this historic dinner between the American head of state and the representatives of Rigel-Rigel: Later that evening, after everyone had gone home, S. K. Wellington, the chief White House custodian, supervised the cleanup of the East Room. Willie, as he was known to his friends, always carried several plastic storage bags and a Thermos, which he used to take home the more appealing leftovers from these functions. In this way, Willie had consumed in the privacy of his simple home some of the finest meals any human being had ever enjoyed.

Since Willie did not care for Jewish food, he sampled only the dessert offerings, a Bundt cake and some fruit punch. Willie had no inkling, of course, that the cake and punch had been prepared several galaxies away. When he got home after work, at a little past midnight, Willie microwaved a TV dinner of Salisbury steak and mashed potatoes. When he finished, he cut himself a slice of cake and poured a glass of punch from the Thermos. Willie ate in the fashion most people eat dessert: he took a bite or two of cake then washed it down with a splash of punch. This system works well with peach pie and coffee or with Oreos and milk. It is less well suited to cake and punch that respectively suppresses and reactivates the expression of certain genes.

That evening, after his Salisbury steak dinner, S. K. Wellington, who considered himself, and by all accounts was, a God-fearing man, experienced what could only be described as an existential yo-yo, alternating with each bite of cake and sip of punch between euphoric joy in the ultimate meaning of life and utter despair.

Willie made a mental note to tell the White House chef that the dessert had turned.

16

TEACH YOUR
CHILDREN WELL

At approximately the same time the White House state dinner ended, the meeting of the Rigel Prep Parent-Teacher Association was set to begin. A controversy brewed, and not just over whether Professor Fendle-Frinkle should be allowed to teach his students about the impending demise of the universe: there was a problem with the refreshments.

"Where is the punch and pie?" Edith Dradel-Hanukean asked Helen Argo-Lipschutzian. Edith was a past president of the PTA and she had made it clear in many passive-aggressive ways that she did not approve of the manner in which Helen handled the office that had been bequeathed to her. Helen, in turn, quite disliked Edith.

"We're having a problem with the vendor," Helen said.

"I fail to see what is so difficult about setting out punch and pie."

"We had a bit of a miscommunication," Helen replied. "The

vendor thought the special meeting had been set for tomorrow instead of today, and now it's too late to arrange something else."

"Well," Edith said, "I cannot see why a vendor needed to be involved in the first place. Back in my day all of the mothers used to bring things from home. It would be potluck."

"The PTA is a lot bigger than it once was. Besides, people don't bake like they used to."

"That's true," Edith said. "But the PTA can't get through the meeting without something to eat. And I'll die of thirst if I don't get a drink soon."

"How about I send someone out to get you a cola?"

"Diet cola," Edith said. "I can't have sugar."

"I'll make sure it's unsweetened," Helen said.

This appeared to satisfy Edith.

"What are we meeting about anyway?"

"We're here to debate whether a professor can teach his students that the universe is going to end in eighteen months."

Edith nodded.

She said, "For this it would be nice to have some pie."

AS SOON AS THE dinner at the White House ended, Ned Anat-Denarian telephoned his wife, who was on her way to the PTA meeting. Because her license was still under suspension, Maude had taken a car service. Maude insisted the driver stay in the right-hand lane and drive under the speed limit. She and Todd were thus running a bit late. When the phone rang and Maude saw it was Ned, she handed the phone to her son.

He answered, "Hi, Dad."

"Hi, son."

"What are you doing?"

"I just finished dinner with the people of a planet called Earth."

"What's the time difference where you are?"

"About eight hundred twenty-seven years and three hours."

"So where you are, I haven't been born yet."

"That's true. For that matter, I haven't been born yet either."

"That's pretty weird."

"I don't understand it myself," Ned said.

They considered this for a moment.

"What are you doing tonight, son?"

"Mom and I are on our way to the PTA meeting."

"How do you feel about this thing?"

"I like Professor Fendle-Frinkle. He's a nice man. I just don't like physics."

"Your mother tells me you want to be an artist."

"Yeah, kind of."

"How come you never mentioned it to me?"

"I thought you wouldn't approve. Anyway, you're not around so much."

"Well, that's going to change. And as for whether I approve, I want you to do whatever makes you happy. Okay, son?"

This struck Todd as a substantial change in his father's attitude, and he could not guess what sparked the transformation. Yet Todd did not say or ask anything about it. What he said was, "Thanks, Dad. Do you want to talk to Mom?"

Sometimes between fathers and sons it is best to leave the most important things unsaid.

Todd handed Maude the phone. Before her husband could speak, Maude said, "Ned, this is going to cost a fortune. These are peak intergalactic hours."

"It's okay, Maude. I needed to talk to you."

"Is everything okay?"

"Everything is fine, but I've been doing some thinking. There's a job posting for someone to do follow-up on first contacts. Instead of doing all the advance work and participating in the initial outreach, I would continue observation and see how the contacted planets progress. I would still have to do a little bit of traveling, but it's basically an office job. I could be home a lot more."

"I don't know what to say."

"You don't have to say anything."

"What caused this change of heart?"

"I got a bit of clarity about what's really important. It's time I got things right. It's like I tell people I meet: 'It's later than we think.' I want to be home with you and Todd. Maybe we can even think about having another child."

Maude was so overwhelmed she could not find words.

Ned continued, "I have substantial reservations about this PTA meeting tonight. I don't think this physics teacher means any harm. It would be wrong for the board to fire him."

"I have substantial reservations too," Maude said. This was true. She had been having second thoughts from the very moment she called Helen Argo-Lipschutzian. But there wasn't much that could be done at that point. "Unfortunately, it's out of our hands now," Maude told Ned. "This thing has gotten pretty big."

BIG WAS AN UNDERSTATEMENT. All of the major intergalactic news networks had sent reporters to cover the Rigel PTA meeting. Some of the top personalities in the universe were on hand, including Kent Cato-Brockerian, the dean of Space News Network, SNN. To prepare for what he had called the Trial of the Eon, Cato-Brockerian spent two hours in makeup. Most of the people on his team endeavored to avoid him. He was in a foul mood over the absence of refreshment.

THE RIGEL PREP PTA and the Intergalactic Civil Liberties Union agreed to structure the meeting as a debate, followed by a short period of public comment, followed finally by a vote. Under the agreed-upon rules, Helen Argo-Lipschutzian had the first word.

"Thank you all for coming," she said. "I want to apologize for the absence of refreshment."

"It is very hot," said one parent in the crowd.

"We could use something to drink," said another.

"I am truly sorry," Helen said. "We have been having problems with the vendor."

"Perhaps we could have some pizza delivered," said a third parent.

"And some soda," said a fourth.

"Dr Pepper is the best," said a fifth.

"I don't think it would be practical to order out at this point," Helen said.

"What is Dr Pepper?" asked a sixth parent.

"It is a drink from a planet called Earth," replied the fifth.

"Is it good?"

"It is quite good. Better even than cream soda."

"I quite like cream."

"As do I. Yet this Dr Pepper is even better still."

At this point, Arnold Nene-Zinkelreen, the young would-be Clarence Darrow, stepped forward and said, "Perhaps we should make do and press forward with the debate."

The people grumbled, but matters proceeded all the same.

SEVERAL QUESTIONS PRESENT THEMSELVES at this point. One, how did the people of Rigel-Rigel know about Dr Pepper? Answer: The people of Rigel-Rigel were curious and absorbed the best of all cultures, whether contact had been established with the planet or not. In the case of Earth this included Dr Pepper and, as established, Woody Allen movies and the albums of the Police. Second, why is there no period in Dr Pepper? Answer: There was a period, originally, but it was dropped in the 1950s for reasons that are not clear. Third, was there Dr Pepper at the historic Scopes trial? Answer: Unclear. The historical record on this is sketchy. The timing certainly works. Dr Pepper (then Dr. Pepper) exploded (pardon) at the 1904 World Expo in St. Louis, which was attended by more than twenty million people. This was also the first time frankfurters and hamburgers were served on buns. The Scopes trial occurred more than twenty years later. So it is possible. What we do know is that it was hot at the trial, and William Jennings Bryan, who represented the state of Tennessee, had a prodigious appetite. So I like to think they drank cold Dr. Peppers during breaks in the trial, even though this is not depicted in *Inherit the Wind*. I expect this is because the movie predates product placements.

NO PROMOTIONAL FEES OF any kind have been paid in connection with this book.

THE MEETING WAS AGAIN called to order. Helen Argo-Lipschutzian began with a simple argument. "I do not understand why there is such a big brouhaha over all of this," she said. "This is, first of all, an untested theory. We can't just allow our teachers to race into the classroom anytime they have some half-baked idea about how the universe works. We don't teach diet fads in our health classes or journalism in our history courses. We need to wait until an idea passes into accepted wisdom before it is taught in our classrooms.

"More important, though, the idea the universe is going to end in eighteen months is something that will be very upsetting to the students. We have a responsibility to protect our children from hurtful or dangerous messages. Even if this nonsense about the universe ending were not merely speculation, which it is, it would not be necessary or appropriate to teach our students about it."

General rumbles of approval.

MAUDE AND TODD ARRIVED in the middle of Helen Argo-Lipschutzian's opening remarks. As soon as they walked in the door, Edith Dradel-Hanukean buttonholed Maude. Maude could tell from Edith's expression that something at the meeting had gone horribly wrong.

"What is it?" Maude asked. "What's the matter?"

"The situation is dire," Edith explained. "There has been a problem with the vendor and there is nothing to eat or drink."

As it happened, Maude had a solution to offer. Maude always liked to have something to drink with her. She carried around a bottle of water and powdered drink mix, which she would prepare as the need arose. Her drink of choice was a preparation that tasted like a combination of tree bark and Worcestershire sauce, which may not sound appealing, but is regarded as a delicacy on Rigel-Rigel. Earlier that week, though, she ran out of her preferred drink mix and, because of the loss of her license, had been unable to shop for several days. Still, she wanted something to drink. That evening, before leaving for the meeting, she took from the basement several packages of a dehydrated fruit punch Ned sometimes used for work. Maude explained all this to Edith and suggested they prepare the fruit punch and offer it to the meeting. Edith agreed that this would be a wonderful idea.

Maude did not know the fruit punch contained a chemical substance that reactivated in humans the expression of genetic characteristics that could be suppressed by Bundt cake. Nor did she know that on Rigelians the substance acted in the opposite manner.

Ned tried very hard not to bring his work home with him.

ARNOLD NENE-ZINKELREEN, THE ICLU attorney, spoke next, and quite eloquently. "It is a noble idea to protect children," he said, "but an even more noble principle is at stake here: the integrity of the truth. Notably, no one has questioned the reliability of the Professor's methodology or the accuracy of his conclusion. It is surely important to make our children feel safe and secure, but it is just as surely more important to inform them about the realities of their universe."

"But this is only a theory," Helen Argo-Lipschutzian said.

"It was also once merely a theory that faster-than-light-speed travel was possible," Nene-Zinkelreen replied. "It was also once merely a theory that life evolved through natural selection instead of at the hand of an all-powerful creator. It was also once merely a theory that chewing gum could retain its flavor for more than six hours."

Helen interjected, "It was also once a theory that the Rigelians were the only intelligent species in the universe."

Murmurs of agreement—"touché, touché" and "well done."

Arnold could not deny that a debating point had been scored against him. Thinking strategically, he pulled out his ace in the hole. He stepped out from behind his podium and faced the crowd with open hands, a gesture of supplication. "So now we get to the heart of the matter," he said. "This is the dilemma for civil libertarians. We support freedom of thought. This means we support your right to criticize the governor and your right to worship a canine God and your right to marry a geranium. It also means we support your right to say mean and hateful things and to believe facts every scientist in the universe says are false. Civil libertarians believe—I believe—this is the lesser evil. Better to allow all ideas to be discussed than for the government to pick and choose among them, lest it chooses incorrectly. Falsehoods may have their day in the sun, but ultimately, inevitably, the truth emerges.

"While it's true some invidious theories have been advanced throughout our history, the benefits of allowing scientific exploration and discourse to continue unfettered far outweigh the costs. For every despicable, unfounded theory, a hundred others have been advanced by honest, public-minded citizens. Many of these have immeasurably improved our way of life.

"To attempt to distinguish between ideas that are worthy of exploration and others that should be rejected out of hand is to embark on a path fraught with peril. It is the most slippery of slopes. It invests the government with the power to decide what we should think about and what we should not. Too often, the government will be wrong. We must reject this course without fear of consequence. History has demonstrated time and again that useful theories will be confirmed and hateful hypotheses disgraced. Ultimately, the truth will prevail."

Rumbles of approval.

IT WAS QUITE CLEAR Attorney Nene-Zinkelreen had regained the upper hand. He accepted, with gratitude, a glass of fruit punch that was offered to him, as had been to everyone in the audience, and returned to his place behind the podium. He took a sip of the punch, and thought it tasted a bit off.

HELEN ARGO-LIPSCHUTZIAN WAS DOWN, but not out. As her adversary had done, she stepped out from behind her lectern. "Mr. Nene-Zinkelreen would like to make truth the issue, but truth is not the issue here. We do not propose to suppress the truth. Professor Fendle-Frinkle is free to research and write about anything he wants. The question here is what he should teach our children. Of course we should teach them the truth. But not every truth!

"Imagine a lion lives outside my home and every evening it waits in the bushes ready to lay siege and eat my children. Every evening I stay awake to defend my home. Sometimes I have vicious life-and-death battles with the lion. Even the nights when the lion does not attack leave me exhausted. I never sleep soundly. I understand the consequences of any lapse in vigilance.

"If all of this were the case, it would certainly be true that a lion was trying to eat my children, but I still would not tell them because I would want them to feel safe and secure. That is what I want here, to make our children feel safe and secure. For this I make no apologies."

At this point, Helen also accepted a glass of punch that was offered to her. The presence of the beverage annoyed her. It appeared Edith Dradel-Hanukean had arranged the drink, which thus became, in Helen's mind, another example of Edith butting in and criticizing her presidency in a passive-aggressive way.

OF COURSE, HELEN ARGO-LIPSCHUTZIAN did not use the word "lion" since there are no lions on Rigel-Rigel. She used the example of a tongolarish, which is a menacing, catlike creature with a voracious appetite and the annoying habit of killing large creatures, gorging on their entrails, and then leaving the carcass in the most inconvenient of places.

It was somewhat disingenuous for Helen to make this argument. The Argo-Lipschutzians lived in a swanky suburb. The prospect of a tongolarish lying in wait in the backyard of their home was as implausible as the idea of a lion lurking in an American suburb. But the notion, however far-fetched, would be equally disturbing to a child on either planet.

* * *

THERE ARE SOME OBVIOUS similarities between the Rigel Prep PTA meeting and the debate over the teaching of evolution in public schools, which came famously to a head during the aforementioned trial of twenty-four-year-old science teacher John Scopes in Rhea County, Tennessee in 1925, with the notable difference that no one on Rigel-Rigel believes in God.

I like to think if I had been around at the time of the Scopes trial that I would have been on the side of the evolutionists. I must confess, though, I have considerable sympathy for Helen's argument. Evolution is a young theory, and was even younger at the time of the Scopes trial. It's not young by the measure of a human life, but measured against the enormity of the universe, it is a mere infant. It certainly seems better than any of the competing crackpot ideas, but we have to at least acknowledge, I think, that one hundred fifty years may not be adequate time to conclusively demonstrate the validity of any idea. And with respect to evolution specifically, one can hardly deny that in the time since Darwin first advanced his theory, many people have not evolved at all.

I also have some sympathy for Helen's instinct to protect children. Like Helen, I live in a fairly nice suburb, so it's unlikely I shall ever see a lion or a tongolarish in my backyard, but if I did, I would not tell my children. All in all, I think it is better for kids to have a sense of security, even if it is false.

For many children, this sense of security comes from belief in the existence of a gentle and benevolent God. When I was a kid, I did not believe in God and hence used to worry about all kinds of things, including my parents' death, my own death, nuclear war, and dust mites. Sometimes, I would step out of time and view human life as the universe sees it. From the subjective perspective of a human being, things often appear to move quite slowly. When you're waiting on line at the Department of Motor Vehicles, for example, life moves at the pace of a snail. But from the standpoint of the universe that time in line is just a blip; our lives are nothing more than a flickering light. The universe views our lives in the same way we might see the life of an amoeba or a nematode. This may all be true, but these kinds of thoughts aren't exactly the recipe for a happy childhood, or adulthood for that matter.

As a result of this gestalt I obsessed about the meaning of life.

FIRST CONTACT 163

My imagination fixated on obscure and macabre aspects of growing older. For example, I wrote a short story about a middle-aged Jewish vampire named Nosferatu Rabinowitz. Nosferatu Rabinowitz is immortal, which is nice, but has problems with his prostate and needs to go to the bathroom three times a day. Since he cannot leave the coffin in which he sleeps he is forced to pee into an apple juice bottle. Several of these themes, including the many problems associated with underwear, have disturbingly recurred in my writing, which makes me wonder whether things would have turned out better if I had just believed in God as a child.

BACK AT THE MEETING, Maude sat in the rear of the room, prepared to speak up in defense of Professor Fendle-Frinkle. But no one rumbled in approval after Helen finished her analogy to the tongolarish. Maude sensed a change in the tenor of the meeting. Everyone seemed to be more subdued.

Arnold had a response to Helen's argument, but all of a sudden he didn't feel the importance of becoming a young Lionel Hut-Zanderian. For her part, Helen no longer believed in the importance of PTAs. Everyone just sat for a while in silence, sipping their punch, until finally Helen asked whether anyone had anything else to say.

Only Professor Fendle-Frinkle did, and he stepped forward and took the podium. One peculiar fact in this strange story is that neither Arnold Nene-Zinkelreen nor Helen Argo-Lipschutzian nor anyone else had ever asked Professor Fendle-Frinkle what he thought about the situation. These remarks by the Professor were his first public comments on the issue.

What he said was this: "I'll teach something else. It's no big deal."

NOW, YOU ARE PROBABLY thinking the Professor's comments were the product of the punch, but he had not had anything to drink at the meeting. He had eaten dinner at home. Specifically, he had eaten a TV dinner and had a Dr Pepper to drink. He ate in the basement under the dripping pipe because his wife was having a Tupperware party upstairs.

NEEDLESS TO SAY, THE product was not called Tupperware.

***

THIS SENTIMENT—THAT IT wasn't a big deal—resonated with the assembly. They were satisfied with the Professor's answer and inclined to drop the matter at that, though they might also have been satisfied with allowing him to continue to speak. Everyone at the PTA meeting just felt less energized about everything. It was as if the air had been let out of the room. This is how it is sometimes with PTAs. They get all agitated about something and then, just as quickly, they can't remember what it was they were agitated about in the first place.

The parents began to filter quietly out of the auditorium. Several felt, strangely, a craving for pound cake.

17

I LOST MY FAITH IN
SCIENCE AND PROGRESS

THE MORNING AFTER THE dinner with the Ambassador, the President convened a meeting of the senior staff in the Roosevelt Room. Ralph knew it was serious because the President also invited to the meeting the National Security Advisor and the Joint Chiefs of Staff. Even the breakfast was on the grim side: miniature cheese Danish and decaffeinated coffee. Strangest of all, the President arrived on time. He entered the room, gestured for everyone to remain seated, and solemnly said, "I want to develop some military options for responding to the alien threat."

This comment took Ralph, David Prince, Joe Quimble, and Martha Jones each by surprise. They were not expecting to hear words like "military" and "threat." They were expecting to hear words and phrases like "cooperation," "good fortune," and "historic opportunity."

The disconnect between what they had expected to be said and what was said was so great the group was stunned into silence. And they all knew the President could be quite obstinate once he made up his mind about something, as it appeared from his resolute expression he had on this issue. So the group sat quietly for a while, all a bit uncomfortable, except for Len Carlson, who seemed not to be bothered at all.

Finally, timidly, Joe Quimble asked why military options were being developed. "These people seem quite nice," he said.

"These people are our enemies," the President said direly.

Quimble said, "They have done nothing to suggest they pose any danger to us or that they mean any harm."

"These aliens are evil."

"How can you say that?"

"I believe it to be true," said the President. "I slept on it last night, and I know it to be true."

"But what evidence is there for this?"

"I do not need evidence," he said derisively. "I prayed on this and God told me the aliens are evil and a threat to humanity."

David Prince, who rarely spoke at these meetings, spoke next. He said, "There's a certain irony here, Mr. President. One of the lessons the Ambassador tried to share with us is the danger of relying on faith over empiricism. Is it wise or even permissible to make policy on the basis of prayer and messages from God?"

"Should I ignore something I believe to be true and authentic?"

"Even you must admit, sir, this is a substantial leap of faith."

The President frowned. He said, "Let me ask you a question, David."

"Sir."

"You were a history professor before you came to work for me, weren't you?"

"Yes, Mr. President."

"Do you know much about physics?"

"No, sir," David said. "Nothing at all."

"And have you ever flown in an airplane?"

"Of course, sir, many times."

"If you don't know anything about physics then I don't suppose you have any idea how airplanes work, do you?"

David thought about it briefly. "Only in the vaguest sense," he said.

"For example, you don't know anything about jet engines, do you?"

"No."

"And you don't know anything either about the principles of aerodynamics, do you?"

"No, sir."

"And yet you fly in airplanes?"

"Yes, sir."

"That sounds like a substantial leap of faith to me, son."

THIS BECAME THE SECOND time in as many days that the President impressed Ralph and David Prince with the quality of his argument. It seemed as if the President's rhetorical powers improved when the discussion touched upon matters close to his heart. Nevertheless, Ralph believed a distinction could be drawn between the leap of faith involved when one boarded an airplane and the leap the President had made regarding the true nature of the Ambassador and his people. Even if one does not understand engine mechanics or aerodynamics, lots of evidence suggests airplanes work. People fly in airplanes all the time and arrive quickly and unharmed in fun places such as Bali and Seattle. On the other hand, the President had no evidence from which to conclude the Ambassador meant humans harm.

But the President may have been onto something about the necessity of belief. It is not as if no basis exists to believe in God. The world is improbable and fantastic in all sorts of ways. And, besides, life would be difficult to manage if a person required complete understanding of everything he or she did or verification of the safety of every product used. Like many people, Ralph had no idea how almonds, which are naturally poisonous, had become safe to eat. But he liked them all the same and would have been sad to lose them as a snacking option.

EVEN THE FIERCELY LOYAL Martha Jones challenged the President on this course of reasoning. "Sir," she said, "we don't have any evidence the Ambassador is, as you put it, evil."

"Don't we?" the President asked. "The Ambassador acknowledged that he met with the leaders of many different nations around the world. This clearly implies he met with many of our enemies.

He may also have met with the heads of terrorist organizations. He tricked us into consuming a mind-altering substance. And he showed a lack of respect, if not disdain, for our beliefs. You may question whether that's evil, but it sure isn't good."

"This is a tenuous conclusion at best," she replied. "Shouldn't we wait until we're sure about the aliens' intent?"

"I am not willing to have an academic debate about whether these people are our friends or not. I am not a fence-sitter. I recognize evil when I see it. When I do, I act swiftly."

"But, sir," Joe Quimble said, "even if you do question their motives, what reason do we have to think they have the capacity or the desire to destroy us?"

"Well, I don't think capacity is a question," the President said. "I presume if these people have the means to gallivant about the universe with their peculiar desserts then they also have the means to destroy our puny planet. As for whether or not they intend to use their weapons against us, I don't intend to wait around and find out. I don't believe I have any obligation to let my enemy strike me before I defend myself, particularly when that enemy is grossly stronger. We're going to get them before they get us."

"But, sir," Joe Quimble interjected again, with the aim of saying more.

The President waved him off. "This is what a leader does, son," he said. "He acts on his best judgment. This is my best judgment. The American people and, indirectly, the people of Earth have put their faith in me. I am going to protect them from what I know in my heart to be a danger."

THE PRESIDENT'S STATEMENT PRESENTS the interesting philosophical question whether one has the right to hit someone whom he thinks has the inclination to hit him before the person actually hits him first. The people of Rigel-Rigel believed the contrary. They only used force when force was used upon them, and then only the minimal amount of force necessary. I am inclined toward that position, but once again feel some ambivalence, in part because of a personal experience.

The incident in question occurred in Great Barrington, Massachusetts, the heart of the Berkshires, at a diner that serves some very nice pie. I was eating lunch and began to fancy a piece of apple crumb, which happens to be the house specialty. Normally I would have waited to finish lunch to order the pie since it is a bit strange to order dessert while still in the middle of a tuna melt and crinkle cuts, but I had noticed that only one piece of the apple crumb remained. The diner has many kinds of pies, including a more than decent strawberry rhubarb, but none are on par with the apple crumb, and they were out of rhubarb anyway. Even still, I ordinarily would have waited and taken my chances the apple crumb would be there when I finished lunch.

On this day, though, I noticed a man sitting at the lunch counter eyeing the apple crumb with what could only be described as a lean and hungry look about him. I could not prove he was eyeing the apple crumb specifically, of course. He might have been looking at the peach pie, or the Boston cream, or any of the dozens of others. He might just have liked looking at the pie carousel in general, watching its mesmerizing perpetual slow turn. But in my heart I knew he wanted that last piece of apple crumb, and I did not take any chances. I may not have had the moral right to act first or on the basis of a faith-based belief, but nevertheless I launched a preemptive strike. I did not even wait for the waiter. I got up from my table, went over to the carousel, and took that last piece of pie.

I ALSO BELIEVE, WITHOUT any supporting evidence, that cats are evil.

I FURTHER BELIEVE DOGS are intrinsically good. While I cannot present an overwhelming empirical case in support of this conviction, I can at least offer a story I saw on *Animal Planet* about a sweet beagle who ran two miles to get help for his owner, who was having a heart attack. This may not be much to go on, but it is surely more than any cat would ever do.

THE MILITARY HAD ONLY had a few hours to prepare for the meeting with the President, but the Joint Chiefs of Staff presented him with a surprisingly appealing option. For decades, the military had been preparing contingencies for dealing with the threat of an approaching asteroid. One of these options involved orbital Jell-O. A more promising option involved the use of nuclear warheads. This plan could be modified to combat an attacking spaceship or a hostile planet.

The problem was that it ordinarily would have taken Earth's fastest spaceship approximately 28 million years to reach Rigel-Rigel. In military terms this would be analogous to loading ICBMs onto the back of elephants. Such daunting transportation challenges were a large part of the reason the military had developed few options for countering alien threats. But the wormhole, which the Ambassador mentioned at dinner, changed everything. Knowing more precisely where to look, astronomers had already confirmed its existence on the far side of the sun. While it would have taken millions of years to get to Rigel-Rigel directly, a spaceship could get to the wormhole in a week and thus to Rigel-Rigel inside a month.

The chairman of the Joint Chiefs told the President an experimental long-range spaceship could be outfitted with nuclear weapons and ready for launch in forty-eight hours. The chairman believed it would have the capacity to get to Rigel-Rigel and, as they say in the war biz, deliver the package.

The President said, "Authorized," and that was that.

THESE MAY SEEM LIKE unsatisfying orders, but that's how it goes when it comes to delivering weapons of mass destruction. On July 23, 1945, Assistant Secretary of War George Harrison telegraphed Harry Truman, then in Potsdam, that the atomic bomb was available for release.

Truman wrote his reply with a lead pencil in large, clear letters on the pink message delivered to him by Lieutenant George Elsey, Princeton graduate and witness to one of the defining moments in human history.

It said: "Suggestion approved. Release when ready."

THE GENERALS DID NOT address the wisdom or morality of the attack ordered by the President. They regarded this matter as outside of their jurisdiction. Most military types do. This is analogous to lawyers bracketing considerations of fairness, as Professor Crabtree encouraged his students to do, and motivated by the same reasoning: it is difficult to perform one's job if one has to think about all the consequences of one's actions, particularly if one's job is to deliver bombs or lawsuits.

This idea sounds objectionable, but generally speaking we don't demand that soldiers have dormitory-style debates about the ultimate justness of the causes they are called upon to defend. No one asked TR whether the Cubans really deserved what they got on San Juan Hill. Certainly no American asked Paul Tibbets, the air force colonel who dropped the first atomic bomb on Hiroshima, whether the tens of thousands of people killed instantly by the blast deserved to die, or the larger question whether the use of weapons of mass destruction against civilians is ever morally justified. Dropping the bomb was his job and he did it.

This makes all the more sense when one considers the highly impractical alternative. It would be debilitating, for example, if we required a doctor to explore a patient's moral character prior to treatment. And we might not be happy with the results. I, for one, might never have gotten that flare-up of psoriasis to subside.

SADLY, NO ONE THINKS very much either about the toll exacted on the soldiers whose moral judgment is suspended. Surprisingly, Paul Tibbets experienced none. Asked fifty years later how he would act in the same situation, Tibbets said, "If you give me the same circumstances, hell yeah, I'd do it again."

Claude Eatherly wasn't so lucky. He was tormented for the remainder of his life by recurring feelings of guilt. He sent many of his paychecks to Hiroshima and attempted to undermine his status as a war hero, which he felt was undeserved, by committing pointless crimes, such as robbing a bank but taking no money.

Eatherly piloted the *Straight Flush*, a B–29 that performed weather reconnaissance an hour before the *Enola Gay* went in. When dropping atomic bombs it is important to have precisely the right sort of weather.

TO THE EXTENT THE generals allowed their minds to wander, they ruminated over the similarity between the mission the President had ordered and two big-budget motion pictures about the attempted destruction of asteroids headed toward Earth. The crux of the debate within the military focused on who made the better commander: Bruce Willis, who headed the destroy-the-asteroid mission in *Armageddon*, or Robert Duvall, who led the team in *Deep Impact*.

To a man, the generals chose Willis.

For my money, I'd take Bobby D.

THE PRESIDENT COULD SAY whatever he wanted to his staff about the Ambassador's contact with the leaders of hostile nations and about his questionable decision to spike the punch, but the fact remained the President didn't like the Ambassador for two much more basic reasons: One, the President didn't like the French and didn't like that the Ambassador liked the French. Two, and this was really the nub of it, the President didn't like that the Ambassador rejected his god. One could sugarcoat it if so inclined, and say it was really about the Ambassador's lack of respect for the President's beliefs rather than about his actual beliefs, but the plain truth was the President thought the Ambassador was a heathen.

So the real question here is why did the President believe so absolutely that God exists and reject all those who did not? It was true, as the President told the Ambassador, he believed life was too complex and wonderful to be explained by mere chance. There were simply too many coincidences to believe things happened randomly.

But one coincidence, above all others, made the President believe in the existence of God. As with everything with people, it went back to his childhood. As you know, the President's father was not an especially talkative man. He did not possess any of the interests, such as fishing and hunting and golfing, which fathers sometimes share with their sons. Aside from the occasional chat after church, father and son hardly spoke at all. So far as the boy could tell, his father's only interest was reading biographies. He appeared to particularly admire Dwight Eisenhower and had read several accounts of Eisenhower's time as a general and later as president. So, as a young boy, the President prayed he would one day grow up to become president himself. He did, of course, and did not see how this could be attributed to anything other than the existence of a just and attentive God.

HARRY TRUMAN BELIEVED IN God too, though not with quite the same fervor. During his courtship of Bessie Wallace, he confessed that one Sunday "he made a start for church, but landed at the Shubert." Still, on the Sunday before he ordered the release of the bomb, he attended church twice: a Protestant service in the morning and a Catholic mass in the afternoon. A Baptist by birth, Truman nevertheless thought it important to cover all the bases.

"I guess I should stand in good with the Almighty for the coming week," Truman wrote Bess from Germany, "and my, how I'll need it."

THE CURRENT PRESIDENT, ON the other hand, experienced no such moral quandary. He went about his business as usual, meeting with various constituencies, and dining in the evening on macaroni and cheese, straight from the box, delivered to him, as always, by Lucian Trundle, his faithful butler and occasional confidante.

"I ordered a nuclear strike today on those aliens," the President said.

"Very good, sir," said Lucian Trundle. "Their table manners were deplorable."

18

I'M NOT THE MAN THEY
THINK I AM AT HOME

AFTER THE FENDLE-FRINKLE CONTROVERSY fizzled out, life for
Maude Anat-Deñarian got much better. Most important, Maude
felt better about her son's direction. Todd would complete the year
at Rigel Prep, but they had begun looking into art schools where
he might finish his education. Ned was on his way home from the
mission to Earth and had accepted the position in the follow-up
division of the first-contact bureau. This would have him away
from home much less. Really the only problem was the lawsuit
stemming from the car accident.

Now Maude was the kind of person who needed a project, and
with the rest of her life in decent order she had almost no choice
but to obsess about the accident. The more she thought about it, the
more it bothered her. Perhaps she had been distracted by the discussion of broccoli on the radio, but it could not have been for more

than a second, and she was such a cautious driver there was just no way she could have missed a car stopped in the middle of the road.

So she sat down one morning to do some research on the Intergalacticnet. The connection was slow because Ned refused to pay extra for warp-speed satellite access. It could be maddening waiting two seconds for a screen to upload, and twice it bumped Maude off while she was in the middle of a search, but it was okay—Maude had time.

She first did some searches on Nelson Munt-Zoldarian and found nothing particularly interesting. He once had a job in the waste management industry, but had stopped working many years ago after suffering an injury on the job. He regularly attended Mason meetings and was an avid birder, serious enough to have published two articles in *Interstellar Ornithology*.

Then, on a whim, Maude tried another tack. She searched for news articles about people being rear-ended in car accidents. From this she discovered something odd. A man named Nelson Mint-Zoldarian had been struck from behind on the Transorion Freeway. A man named Abner Munt-Zoldareen had been struck from behind in the HOV lane of the Andromeda Motorway. A man named Niles Mant-Soldareen had been struck from behind on the famous speed-limitless Spaceshipbahn in the Runnymede Solar System, built by the guilt-ridden Runnymedians as peculiar penance for their ancestors' war crimes.

Maude found seventeen examples of a person with a name similar to Munt-Zoldarian being struck in the rear end of his car. Each occurred on a highway under similar circumstances: in the late afternoon on a high-speed motorway, and in each case the driver of the offending car never saw the car in front of him. Maude could only conclude it was the same person, and realized for the first time she might have been the victim of a fraud. Then she did what anyone would do under these circumstances: she called a lawyer.

SPECIFICALLY, MAUDE CALLED ARNOLD Nene-Zinkelreen, who had quite impressed her at the PTA debate, before he and everyone else petered out at the end of the meeting. She expected to get a secretary or a voice mail, but Nene-Zinkelreen answered the phone himself. Maude explained that she had thought well of the attorney at the meeting. She explained further what had happened to her,

her suspicions about Munt-Zoldarian, and asked whether Nene-Zin-kelreen might be able to refer her to an attorney who could handle the matter.

"I'll handle it myself," he said.

"That would be fine with me," Maude said, "but if you don't mind my saying so, it seems to me you have all of the makings of a young Lionel Hut-Zanderian. I had the impression you were excited by much larger issues than a car accident."

"I was," the attorney explained. "But I got over that."

"The PTA meeting was only a few days ago."

"I had something of an epiphany," he said.

"Is that right?"

"It is," he said quietly, and added, "You seem like a nice woman."

"Thank you," said Maude.

"And what this man did doesn't seem very nice."

"That's true."

"Well, I could get excited about something like that."

WHEN YOU ARE A lawyer, you look for just about any hook on which to hang your hat. My students ask me all the time whether I ever defended a person whom I knew to be guilty. I did, and tell them so, and they always ask how it felt. The truth is it felt fine. When I defended a criminal, I could get emotionally invested in the gross disparity of power between government prosecutors and defendants. The prosecutors' targets were, by and large, indigent and impotent, and got railroaded through the system on a regular basis.

Defending even a guilty person against the government machine seems like a moral crusade when compared to the civil cases that make up the bread and butter of an attorney's work diet. I spent the last two years of my career as an attorney representing a man worth $1.2 billion in a lawsuit brought by a man worth $400 million over who was entitled to $40 million earned by a business they once had together. They each spent approximately a decade and $5 million litigating this question.

That was tough to get excited about.

SO ARNOLD NENE-ZINKELREEN TOOK the case. In a matter of hours he moved to dismiss Munt-Zoldarian's lawsuit against Maude, brought a retaliatory lawsuit against Munt-Zoldarian on Maude's behalf, and notified the attorneys for all of the other victims of Munt-Zoldarian's frauds. By the end of the day, Joseph Caratzo-Gambarian, the attorney for Munt-Zoldarian, had been served with five lawsuits and received phone calls from eleven other attorneys regarding Munt-Zoldarian. Late in the day, he called his client on the phone.

"What is it?" Nelson asked.

"They're on to you. The heat is being turned up pretty good."

"What gave?"

"I think it was that last woman. I think she figured it out."

"How much time do I have?"

"A few hours. Tomorrow morning at the latest."

Nelson was disappointed, but not surprised. He had always known this day would come.

"I know what to do," he said

"Okay then," his attorney said.

"Okay then," Nelson repeated. "Have a good life."

THE CONTINGENCY PLAN THAT had been prepared in the case of this precise eventuality was for Nelson to disappear. If the victims couldn't find Nelson, they would be unable to get so much as a thin ditron out of him. That was the law. Caratzo-Gambarian had deposited some money in an account on Tchwitts, a planet with secure tax-free accounts, a history of neutrality in interplanetary wars, and an outstanding reputation for the manufacture of fine chocolate, cheese, and clocks. Nelson had enough money set aside to live out the remainder of his years in a remote quadrant of the universe and indulge without restraint in his three favorite hobbies: lying on the beach, watching birds (not necessarily on the beach), and having sex with prostitutes.

Nelson's friends did not believe Nelson could be happy retired. They thought he would get bored. But Nelson kept his different sets of friends separate, and none of his friends knew all of his interests. For example, Nelson did not tell his friends from his days in organized crime about his interest in ornithology, largely out of fear they would kill him if they found out. Specifically, Nelson's friends from his days in organized crime knew only of his interest in prostitutes. Nelson's friends from the birding community knew only about his interest in birding. His friends at the Mason lodge knew only that he planned to retire to a beach. Moreover, no one knew the entire story—his birding and Mason friends believed Nelson was a mortgage broker. Nevertheless, all of his friends shared the common belief that Nelson was too active to spend the remainder of his days lolling around, on the beach or wherever.

Nelson, on the other hand, believed he would be perfectly content in retirement. He expressed this sentiment differently to his different groups of friends. For example, when his friends in the intergalactic Mafia, who regarded his rear-ending scheme as high-risk, asked what he would do if he had to take it on the lam, Nelson would say sarcastically, "Like I'm really going to get tired of banging broads." When his birding friends raised the same question, he would ask rhetorically, without sarcasm, "Could one ever possibly tire of watching dollowarries scavenge for nuts?" To his friends in the Mason lodge, he would say, "Is it conceivable I could get tired of watching the sunset?" Indeed, as he packed his things to flee the jurisdiction, Nelson had beach, birds, and prostitutes on his mind.

GIVEN THE CONSTRAINTS OF time, it was only possible for Nelson to pack a few things. It is an instructive exercise to list the things you would bring if you were being sent, say, to a desert island. If I were confined to three things, I would bring the memory of my first kiss (Huey Lewis's "Power of Love" playing in the background), the memory of my father jumping up and down like a kid when a horse we bet on came in at 45 to 1, and a giant thing of sunscreen. If I were restricted to tangible items, I would take my stuffed bunny rabbit, a sharp knife, and a giant thing of sunscreen. The speaker at my college graduation really impressed upon me the importance of sunscreen. It now strikes me as invaluable.

Like many thought experiments, however, the answers one offers are not especially meaningful. For example, I ask students all the time whether a person has a moral obligation to save a young child drowning in a lake, even if saving the child involves no risk to the rescuer. Everyone always says yes. When I probe they all say further that they would unhesitatingly jump in the water if they were confronted with the situation in real life. But the fact of the matter is I see very few people jumping into lakes to save children.

This is the problem with all hypotheticals. What really matters is not what people say they would do, but what they really do, or, in the case of What Three Things Would You Bring with You to a Desert Island, not what the people say they would take, but what they actually do take. To his own exile, Nelson Munt-Zoldarian brought: a copy of *The History of Masonry in the Known Universe* (Unabridged), a pair of field glasses, and an industrial-sized box of condoms. This says all you need to know about him.

AS IT TURNED OUT, though, the beach and birds did not keep Nelson occupied for long, not even for a day. He puttered around his beach house a bit and took a swim. But what he found himself thinking about more than the sand and the women and the dollowarries was that he would never be in another car accident. Rather than make him happy, this made him quite sad. In fact, he began to wistfully yearn for his halcyon days on the highways of the universe. The thought had never occurred to him before but, he realized while watching the sunset, more than birds or beautiful women, what he truly, genuinely enjoyed best of all was his work.

IT MUST SOUND DECIDEDLY strange that Nelson's epiphany occurred without the aid of any cake or fruit punch. It must sound stranger still that his moment of lucidity led him to conclude that stopping short in front of cars was not just his vocation but also his avocation. The fact is, though, many people have unusual avocations. I have one friend who collects the trucks Hess stations sell each Christmas. Another has a complete collection of the covers of *Cosmopolitan*, each autographed by the cover model. A third has a rather peculiar collection of eggshells. Every time he eats an egg, he saves the shell, which he then rinses, shellacs, and displays in a wooden case in his living room. He finds the distinctiveness of the cracks interesting and beautiful.

I personally have several utterly pointless hobbies. I like to play cards, which is a mostly useless endeavor, and golf, which is the epitome of a useless endeavor.

None of these activities are particularly harmful, though, so the analogy to Nelson's car crashing may not be apt. Still, there are people who hunt animals for sport and others who drive motorcycles and Hummers even though they contribute to greenhouse gas emissions. I daresay these people find their pursuits satisfying if not important.

At a certain level of abstraction, it is very difficult to draw a distinction between the class of pursuits that might be deemed worthwhile and those that would not. If someone's pastime were, say, feeding soup to the homeless, this would certainly strike me at first blush as more important than contriving interstellar car accidents. But if one looks at things with the kind of angst-ridden, metaphysically paralyzed what-does-any-of-it-mean sensibility that underlies this book, then nothing really matters. I mean, we're all going to die anyway, perhaps as soon as eighteen months if Fendle-Frinkle is right, and many homeless people don't even like soup. From this perspective, none of these choices make one bean of a difference.

Besides, it isn't true that the first category of pursuits is harmless. The eggshell guy actively injures no one, but causes harm by omission. He could just as easily devote his time to working on a cold-fusion generator or something else to benefit mankind. The friend who collects Hess trucks could be out curing cancer. I don't ordinarily hurt anyone playing golf, though I could certainly use the greens fees to help feed the poor or buy up some rain forest.

Either we take the leap that altruism is morally required of people or we can draw no distinction among people's many diversions. If this is the case, whatever makes a person happy is valid, and, much as we might dislike it, Nelson Munt-Zoldarian has to be cut some slack.

ANYWAY, NELSON MADE A dramatic change in his life plans. He abandoned retirement on the beach, twenty years in the planning, and decided instead to continue his career. He would have to do it on a smaller scale, of course, on a pre-lightspeed planet, one out of the intergalactic loop. And he would have to start from scratch since such a planet would be unlikely to accept wire transfers from Tchwitts. But the pioneer spirit in him found all of this exciting. He did some searching and finally settled on a quaint little spot in a remote corner of the Milky Way, a little planet called Earth, which, by all accounts, had lots of highways and many speeding drivers.

BOMBS AWAY,
BUT WE'RE O.K.

GIVEN THE GLOBAL IMPORTANCE of the mission against Rigel-Rigel, the President desired that a multinational crew be assembled for the voyage. Trouble was, few other nations supported the undertaking. The Germans, Mexicans, Russians, Lithuanians, Canadians, Bulgarians, Australians, Peruvians, Norwegians, Swedish, Danish, Spanish, Chinese, Burmese, Senegalese, and Dutch, among many others, all declined the invitation to participate in what the President termed an "intergalactic peacekeeping mission."

The prime minister of Tuvalu, a nation of nine coral atolls and a population of 9,700, asked the President how this could be called a peacekeeping mission, given that the aliens had neither attacked Earth nor threatened to attack Earth.

"Sometimes you need to attack first in order to prevent a war," the President explained.

"I don't follow," the Tuvalese prime minister said. "Though I wish your people safe voyage."

Other national leaders were not so polite. The prime minister of the archipelago nation of Seychelles protested vigorously. "This is not an appropriate military action," he said. "By all accounts, these are a kind and generous people. They brought the most extraordinary cake when they visited. I have not had such a fine Bundt since my uni days at Oxford."

The president of the mountain nation of Andorra, population 64,000, went a step further still, suggesting the mission was an unjustified act of violence against not only the people of Rigel-Rigel but also the people of Earth. "The Rigelians have explained very clearly their principle of self-defense," he said. "They respond to violence with equivalent counterforce. You are bringing harm upon the people of our planet." The president of France, who co-governs Andorra with Spain's Bishop of Urgel, was on the conference call. He said, "You murder your steak with ketchup so why should this be any different?"

It was in fact true the President liked ketchup on his steak.

In total, the leaders of 173 nations rejected the President's invitation to join the intergalactic peacekeeping mission. In addition, as noted, most of the President's staff opposed the idea. One might think the unanimous and passionate rejection of his planned attack would have dissuaded the President of the United States from his mission. To the contrary, the opposition, particularly of the French, only solidified his confidence. The President was a true believer in this cause of his own creation. After consultation, he was convinced, more firmly than ever, that attacking Rigel-Rigel was the right thing to do.

So the mission went on, although the resulting coalition was a bit on the smallish side. The Intergalactic Peacekeeping Force consisted of the following nations, ranked by population:

United States of America
Balta
Nauru

It should be noted, though, in point of fact neither Nauru nor Balta actually supported the mission.

THE PACIFIC ISLAND NATION of Nauru, formerly known as Pleasant Island and independent since 1968, is home to ten thousand people, making it the least populous member of the United Nations. Nauru's economy revolves almost entirely around the mining of phosphorous. Unfortunately the phosphorous is running out and a century of mining has degraded the environment of the tiny island. Life on Nauru is tough. Monsoons pelt the island four months a year. Humidity is almost always near one hundred percent. Yet, ironically, the Naurese have little fresh water. They depend almost entirely on an antiquated desalination plant. The Naurese national motto is "God's Will First."

In the late 1990s, the United States made Nauru an offer it could not refuse. America was looking at the time for a place to store its strategic petroleum jelly reserve. In exchange for use of the island, the United States offered to relocate the Naurese when their resources ran out once and for all. Specifically, the Americans proposed to relocate the Naurese to Kalaupapa, a stunning peninsula on the Hawaiian island of Molokai. Kalaupapa is currently home to a colony of lepers, but with leprosy under control, most of the former residents have left to lead normal lives. The remaining population of lepers is aging and expected to die out with splendid timing to accommodate the Naurese, who eagerly accepted the American offer. Over the following years, they came to speak of Kalaupapa in mystical terms, as if it were a Shangri-La, and looked forward to their collective retirement.

When the President called his Naurese counterpart to ask whether he might be interested in participating in the intergalactic peacekeeping mission, the Naurese president politely said no. It was at this point the President mentioned that several offers had been made for Kalaupapa, including one from a Japanese consortium that wanted to develop a golf course and condominiums on the peninsula. Resisting these lucrative deals would be difficult and politically feasible only to aid a close ally. One way of demonstrating the strength of the relationship between Nauru and the United States would be to participate in the peacekeeping mission.

The Naurese president asked, "If these real estate offers are accepted, to where will you relocate my people?"

"Fairbanks," said the President.

It thus seems fair to say by way of summary that the participation of the Naurese involved a bit of arm-twisting.

BY CONTRAST, THE MEDITERRANEAN island nation of Balta, population 362,000, joined the coalition because of a football bet. The bet was placed by the chancellor of the exchequer, who had a bit of gambling problem. This was the scandalous dirty secret of the Baltese central government. It was whispered about at the right kind of cocktail parties but by and large unknown to the masses until his Right Excellency staked the entirety of the national reserve on the 2005 Super Bowl. Unfortunately, he bet on the Philadelphia Eagles. Had he bet on the New England Patriots he would have been praised for producing a hundred-percent annual return on national investment.

Now, losing the entire national currency reserve on a wager can do bad things for an economy. Not the least of these was that the government was unable to meet its foreign obligations, including a substantial debt to the United States, and to pay government employees. So Balta did what any good nation does when things get tight: it printed money.

Printing money paid the bills, but inflation in Balta began to creep up. Specifically, it crept up 800 percent per hour. To put this into perspective, the price of a gallon of milk on the morning of February 6, 2005, was $2.79. By the end of the business day it was $29,371.33. People quickly grew tired of this hyperinflation, though not because of the rapidly increasing price of milk. The government and businesses increased salaries to keep pace with inflation. The real problem was one needed a wheelbarrow of money in order to buy a gallon of milk. Even this wouldn't have bothered the Baltese so much, but for the shortage of wheelbarrows, the price of which really got out of control. One needed thirty or so wheelbarrows full of money to buy a wheelbarrow. So you can see the problem.

After a week or so, the United States came to the rescue. The Americans offered to forgive the national debt. In exchange, the U.S. asked for the exclusive license to export wheelbarrows to Balta, and the unspoken understanding that amnesty for the debt was a chit that the President could, and in this time of great international need did, call in.

* * *

NAURU HAD NO SPACE program of which to speak. Hence its designee to the intergalactic peacekeeping mission was chosen randomly by a national draw of straws.

Balta had a small space program, consisting of four toy rockets owned as a hobby by a tile grouter in Balleta, the capital city. On alternate Sundays, he launched the rockets in Independence Park, and thereby became something of a Pied Piper celebrity to the ten-year-old boys who gathered in the park to watch the launches. Because of his expertise in rocketeering, he became the Baltese designee to the mission.

BALTA IS A FICTITIOUS place. I made it up. Of course, I made up everything here, except the true things. What I mean by this is that I made it up and not the President. Within the context of the book it would be entirely plausible for the President to have created a fictitious ally, but this is not the case. In the President's world, Balta is as real as Wisconsin.

Truth is, I could just as easily have used the real island nation of Malta. Malta is also in the Mediterranean (just south of Sicily) and also has a population of 362,000. Both Balta and Malta gained independence from the United Kingdom in 1964. Malta is similar in every respect to Balta with two notable exceptions. One, no movie called the *Baltese Falcon* was ever produced. This is a sore spot with the Baltese government, which offered substantial tax incentives to both Bogart and the movie's producers. Two, if you were to take a flight to Balta, you would end up getting quite wet.

So why not just use Malta? Sometimes writers create a slightly altered reality in order to make a point about real life. This is called allegory, and it is a powerful literary device. I do not happen to have any point to make about Malta or any Mediterranean island, but if I did, inventing the neighboring island of Balta would be an effective and subtle way of getting that point across.

Nauru, on the other hand, is a real place with rapidly diminishing phosphate reserves.

SO THE PRINCIPALS ON the multinational intergalactic peacekeeping mission were: Armando Tanzarian, mission commander, twenty-year NASA officer and veteran of four space shuttle flights; Tex McBain, an Air Force major, decorated veteran of three foreign wars and a nuclear ballistics expert; Hanukapi Puli, a Naurese phosphorous miner and amateur pool player, nicknamed Minnesota because of his resemblance—in body shape only—to the famous pool player; and toy-missile enthusiast Sinclair Lewis, a Baltese tile grouter.

THE MISSION GOT OFF to a good start. *Earth's Hope* launched without a hitch, broke free from Earth's gravity, and set off on its course to the wormhole. This seamless start was something of a surprise to NASA, which rushed the spaceship onto the launching pad at the behest of the military. NASA felt the ship was years away from being ready.

The trouble started four days later when the toilet clogged. *Earth's Hope* wasn't all that big and when the ventilation system blew, the resulting stench was overwhelming. Remonstrations abounded aboard the ship, which soon became an interstellar tinder box. The situation was rendered all the more incendiary because of the preexisting tension among the international crew. In the case of Tanzarian and McBain, this stemmed from a jingoistic mistrust of foreigners. In the case of Puli and Lewis, it stemmed from the fact that they didn't want to be there in the first place.

Most of the finger-pointing focused on Puli, in large part because on the first day of the voyage he ate the entire supply of Chocodiles, which were supposed to last for three months. This would make even a child with the sweetest of sweet tooths sick, and Puli spent several hours on the toilet. The crew also insultingly (and incorrectly) presumed they did not have plumbing on the island of Nauru and that Puli didn't know how to use the latrine properly. None of this would have mattered, but for the fact that in the haste to get the mission under way, NASA had forgotten to pack a plunger.

As the stink worsened, pressure mounted to return home to collect proper plumbing supplies. Halfway around the sun, the ship was out of radio contact with Earth. The decision thus fell to Commander Tanzarian. Given the unique nature of the mission and the risks involved, Tanzarian decided it would be appropriate to poll the crew as to whether the mission should continue. Applying his knowledge of parliamentary procedure, Lewis called for a roll call ballot. Hanukapi Puli was designated secretary of the meeting and the votes were recorded as follows:

<u>Aye (Continue Mission)</u>

McBain
Tanzarian

<u>Nay (Suspend Mission)</u>

Lewis
Puli

Whereupon ensued a discussion of the consequence of a tie ballot. Commander Tanzarian argued that in the absence of a majority, the proper course of action was to pursue the status quo. Sinclair Lewis argued this invested the status quo with a false authority. For example, he asked what if a mighty intergalactic wind had begun blowing *Earth's Hope* in the direction of home. Then, according to Tanzarian's reasoning, the 2-to-2 vote should mean that the ship continue to Earth. Or what if they had quite reasonably stopped the ship while the vote was taken? Then what would a tie vote mean? Would the ship then drift aimlessly in space until a majority could be formed, even though this was no voter's preference? Tanzarian disagreed, but acknowledged Lewis had a fine argument, and agreed to put to a vote the significance of a tie vote. Once again, Lewis demanded a roll call. The questions were presented and votes were recorded as follows:

<u>Aye (Tie Suggests Status Quo Be Preserved and
Hence Mission Continued)</u>

McBain
Tanzarian

<u>Nay (Status Quo Is of No Consequence and
Burden Should Be on Party Proposing to Continue Voyage
Through Space with Faulty Toilet)</u>

Lewis
Puli

Whereupon ensued a discussion of the consequence of a tie vote on this corollary question. The heated discussion continued for several hours, with no progress toward a final solution. Finally, Commander Tanzarian exercised his authority and unilaterally declared the mission would go on. He had only modest confidence in his chosen course of action, but firm conviction that democracy cannot function with an even number of people.

OF COURSE, MOST SPACESHIPS do not have flush toilets. I would like to tell you *Earth's Hope* represented a substantial advance in interplanetary travel or that I invented the space toilet to serve some storytelling purpose, but in fact the reason was greed. Loomis Loos, a leading manufacturer of commodes, had a well-placed mole inside the Department of Defense. When the company learned about the mission, the board decided it would be good for business to have a Loomis Loo aboard the ship that saved Earth. Thereafter, Loomis's lobbyist took the DoD procurement officer out for a night on the town during which the lobbyist explained how enthusiastic Loomis would be about having one of its toilets aboard the ship. It would be an avant-garde product placement. The Department of Defense representative explained the difficulty of operating a toilet in space, but saw the light after the evening's entertainment.

The evening's entertainment consisted of a steak dinner at Morton's, complete with a two-hundred-dollar bottle of wine, pleasant conversation with representatives of Loomis's Young Executive Program in the Champagne Room of the Capital City Playhouse Club, and concluded with the rather unfortunate loss by some sap of the keys to a brand new BMW convertible. By remarkable coincidence, call it synchronicity if you will, the owner of the BMW had the same exact name and social security number as our man in the DoD.

The next morning, Loomis corporate headquarters received a miraculous and wonderful call from the Department of Defense. A toilet was needed aboard *Earth's Hope*, which was scheduled to launch in three days. Loomis hopped to it, but time was short. They also skimped a bit on materials, using hard plastic instead of porcelain, in part to save money and in part because weight restrictions limited the allowable size of the toilet to three pounds. Thus the real reason the toilet backed up on *Earth's Hope* was not because of Hanukapi "Minnesota" Puli's gluttony, but rather because when the manufacturer installed the toilet, it did, pardon, a crappy job.

SO THE MISSION CONTINUED. Surprisingly, *Earth's Hope* arrived at the wormhole about ninety seconds ahead of schedule.
Commander Tanzarian said, "We made terrific time."
Major McBain said, "Maybe the universe is shrinking."
They both laughed heartily. Tanzarian said, "That's a good one."

EARTH'S HOPE EMERGED FROM the wormhole onto the Intergalactic Highway System. The crew saw the sign for Rigel-Rigel, but made a wrong turn. This seemed strange to them, when they realized their mistake three days later, because the sign had appeared to be in English. In fact the letters used by the Intergalactic Sign Commission were the same as in English, and much of the grammar identical, but the meaning of many of the words was the opposite. Thus the crew went left when it should have gone right.

ONCE AGAIN THE BLAME focused on Hanukapi Puli. No one articulated this, but it was clearly conveyed through dirty looks, sour pusses, and periods of silent treatment. Blaming Puli was absurd for a variety of reasons, not the least of which was that at the moment when *Earth's Hope* emerged from the wormhole, and Commander Tanzarian and Major McBain made the decision to turn left instead of right, Hanukapi Puli was sitting in the back of the ship reading an article about Scarlett Johansson in *Maxstuff* magazine. The ship had been stocked with an ample supply of magazines, including not only *Maxstuff* but also the most recent *New Jerseyan* and several back issues of *Sports Explicated*.

Puli had never heard of *Maxstuff* magazine or Scarlett Johansson before the voyage. He was fascinated by each and quite absorbed in the article at the time the ship's brain trust made the wrong turn. Even had Puli been paying attention, he could not have contributed much of value since he had never driven a car before, let alone a spaceship. But Tanzarian and McBain blamed Puli nevertheless, reasoning that the smell from the toilet had impaired their otherwise impeccable decision-making abilities.

* * *

THE NEED TO BLAME others is a conspicuous aspect of the human condition. It is another way of finding meaning in the universe. People search for causal connections, sometimes crediting the most attenuated and implausible chain of events, rather than accept that random bad things sometimes happen.

Once, when I was living in Manhattan, a seven-year-old kid was eaten by a mountain lion. This was exceedingly strange for a variety of reasons, not the least of which is that there is no natural mountain-lion habitat within a thousand miles of Manhattan. The parents of the devoured child told the newspapers the accident had been the work of the devil. What really happened was the lion escaped from the circus, hid in some bushes near a playground, and ate the child for breakfast.

The notion of a lion escaping from the circus in New York is less improbable than it might seem at first blush. To get the animals into the city, the circus walks them all, including quite famously and spectacularly the elephants, through the Lincoln Tunnel late at night. If you are ever in Manhattan when it happens, you should make a point of checking it out. It is surreal and wonderful.

AT THE SAME TIME, if you have children, you should probably not tell them the story about the lion escaping from the circus and eating the little boy. This is the sort of thing that can be very upsetting to a child. For that matter, it would probably be best not to tell them the universe is ending either.

THOUGH THE WRONG TURN delayed the mission of *Earth's Hope*, the error gave the crew time to forgive Puli and an important opportunity to bond with one another. Such coming together is a common experience during wartime. Two sorts of bonding are possible. The first sort is closeness deriving from shared commitment to the cause. For example, during World War II, a young farm boy from Kansas might have said to his battalion mate, "We are united together against a common evil—a genocidal maniac. I love you as a brother for your commitment to this grand cause." The second sort is intimacy stemming from the plight of participating in the conflict. For example, during the Vietnam War, another Kansas farm boy lying in a muddy mosquito-infested swamp with shells flying overhead might have said to his battalion mate, "I was drafted into this conflict, the purpose of which I do not understand. My sinuses are highly sensitive to humidity and I am allergic to bee stings. I understand that you are in the same situation, but for the allergy to bee stings, and because of our shared plight, I regard you as a brother."

Each of these sentiments is often translated loosely as "War is hell."

In the case of *Earth's Hope*, bonding of the first sort, over shared commitment to the cause, was not in the cards. One night over dinner, Hanukapi Puli asked why they were traveling across the universe to bomb the people of Rigel-Rigel. Major McBain shrugged his shoulders and looked to Commander Tanzarian who in turn said, "Damned if I know." Sinclair Lewis said he had not realized until that very moment it was a military mission. He had been told they were attending an interplanetary grouting convention.

But the crew bonded quite nicely in the second manner. Over a bottle of fine scotch whiskey, each man revealed he had a wife and children whom he missed more than he could bear. This was only partially true. In fact the men could bear the separation from their wives and children. But each had an additional partner whom he missed more than words. For Commander Tanzarian, it was his housekeeper. For Major McBain, it was a twenty-year-old air force private. For Hanukapi Puli, it was the local baker. For Sinclair Lewis it was a special sheep from the meadows of Balta. The resulting empathy each crewmember developed for one another was thus based on false premises, but sincere all the same.

Furthermore, each man offered a wistful sentiment about Earth. Armando Tanzarian said he missed arena football. Major McBain said he missed fly-fishing in the fall. Sinclair Lewis said he missed the sight of toy rockets soaring through the clear, blue sky. Hanukapi Puli said he missed Chocodiles and expressed regret and contrition for having eaten them all on the first day of the voyage.

Commander Tanzarian said, "War is hell."

He spoke for the entire crew.

WHEN THE SHIP NEARED Rigel-Rigel, Commander Tanzarian ordered the armaments be made ready. Military specifications dictated that *Earth's Hope* be outfitted with two nuclear missiles, each of which represented the most powerful weapon ever created by man. To put the power of these weapons into context, consider by contrast the atomic weapons used by the United States against Japan at the close of World War II. *Little Boy*, the uranium-based atomic bomb dropped by Paul Tibbets and the *Enola Gay* on Hiroshima, had an explosive yield of thirteen kilotons of TNT and killed approximately a hundred forty thousand people. The nuclear warheads designed for *Earth's Hope* each had an output of fifty megatons, meaning they were about four thousand times more powerful than their predecessors. While *Little Boy* did a pretty good number on Hiroshima, one of these bombs could have done a pretty good number on all of Japan, most of the Korean Peninsula, and a good part of eastern China and Mongolia. This is an example of scientific progress.

QUESTIONS HAVE BEEN RAISED about the role of American scientists in the development of the atomic bomb. Some of these same questions might be asked about the work of Professor Fendle-Frinkle. The central question is whether scientists have an obligation to consider the larger implications of their work. Those who answer this question in the affirmative say, for example, that J. Robert Oppenheimer and his colleagues should have taken more seriously the negative consequences of nuclear weapons for the people of Germany and Japan specifically and the future of warfare and diplomacy generally. With respect to Professor Fendle-Frinkle, the argument would be that he has a duty not to use theoretical physics just as an escape from his unhappy home life, but must try to stop the universe from contracting or at least to slow it down. The scientist should not bracket considerations of morality, so the argument goes.

I think it would have been funny if the scientists on the Manhattan Project had spent their time in Alamogordo, New Mexico, playing bid whist and backgammon instead of working on the atomic bomb. One day, President Truman would have called Oppenheimer in for a report. "Show me what you have produced and how it works," President Truman would have said.

At this point, Oppenheimer could have pulled a small orb of granite from his pocket. "You see, Mr. President," he would have said, "what one does is grasp this projectile in his hand, recoil his arm, and then thrust the arm forward, releasing the spheroid in the same motion."

Truman, knowing tens of millions of dollars had been wagered on the Manhattan Project as well as the best hopes of an American victory, would not have understood at first, and perhaps thought the scientist was speaking metaphorically. But he would get it eventually and ask, incredulously, "You're telling me how to throw a rock?"

The historical record suggests Truman would not have been amused. A strong thrower with good aim could have taken out an important official, such as the mayor of Hiroshima, but Truman had his hopes pinned on having at his disposal the most powerful weapon in the history of mankind.

At this point, Oppenheimer would have explained the ethical duty of the scientist.

UPON EXECUTING TANZARIAN'S CALL to battle stations, the crew discovered things had not gone as planned. Unfortunately, or fortunately depending on one's perspective, the Air Force had failed to load one of the nuclear warheads. This is not as unusual as it may seem. The military is a big organization with diffuse responsibilities. Sometimes things get forgotten, particularly when it is pot pie night at the mess.

The military successfully loaded the second warhead, but it was not in good condition. Here the fault rested with Loomis, which installed the toilet above the armaments chamber. Upon examination, it became evident the overflow from the commode had leaked onto the warhead, eroding the casing of the weapon and shorting its fuse. The bomb had been rendered useless and the crew exposed to lethal doses of radiation.

As if matters could be worse, the crew also discovered a stowaway raccoon, now deceased. Before expiring, the raccoon had eaten through the lining of the crew's spacesuits, the wiring of the release mechanism for the bombs, and six heretofore undiscovered boxes of Chocodiles, which had mistakenly been stored in the armaments chamber instead of the galley. The crew could not determine whether the raccoon had died from gorging itself on snacks or from exposure to the nuclear warhead. They stood at silent attention before the body of the irradiated, bloated raccoon. Commander Tanzarian broke the quiet. He again spoke for everyone when he said, "War is hell."

THIS IS THE KIND of situation that could make any crew despair, but the men of *Earth's Hope* rose above themselves. Sinclair Lewis repaired the outer casing of the warhead with some water and spackle, which he always carried with him. Hanukapi Puli created a makeshift fuse from some phosphorous shavings he had in his pocket. The automatic release mechanism had been damaged beyond repair, but Commander Tanzarian jerry-rigged a manual trigger. Unfortunately, releasing the bomb in this manner required two men to open the bay doors and two men to sit on the missile and release it from its moorings. Tanzarian explained these unfortunate facts to the group.

"But we don't have any spacesuits," said Hanukapi Puli. "If we release the bomb manually then we'll all be sucked into space and die."

"That's true," said Commander Tanzarian.

"We're all going to die anyway from the radiation," said Sinclair Lewis.

"That's also true," Tanzarian said.

"Well, then we may as well take some commies with us," said Tex McBain. Though they had never heard of commies before, Puli and Lewis nodded their heads in agreement. It seemed like the thing to do. For his part, Commander Tanzarian did not know much about the enemy, but was reasonably sure they were not communists. Nevertheless, he said nothing. As a lifelong military man, Tanzarian understood the power of symbolism.

One by one the members of the crew of *Earth's Hope* thrust their hands into the middle of the circle they had formed around the dead raccoon.

"I'm in," said Sinclair Lewis of Balta.

"I'm in," said Hanukapi Puli of Nauru.

"I'm in," said Tex McBain of Narragansett, Rhode Island.

And finally, Armando Tanzarian of Ocala, Florida, said, "I'm in," and concluded the pact.

Thus the crew of the *Earth's Hope* came together and displayed the determined best of humanity in the face of a certain crisis and in the name of an uncertain cause. Upon achieving orbit around Rigel-Rigel, the men took their positions. On Tanzarian's command, Lewis and Puli pulled the handles of the makeshift release mechanism and were thereafter sucked into the vacuum of space. McBain and Tanzarian released the clamps, rode the missile out of the launching bay, and died in a manner similar to Major

T. J. "King" Kong in Stanley Kubrick's classic *Dr. Strangelove or: How I Learned to Stop Worrying and Love the Bomb*. A huge fan of Kubrick, Major McBain recognized the similarity to *Strangelove* and attempted to scream "woo-hoo" in the same manner as Slim Pickens, but could not because of the absence of air. Commander Tanzarian did not attempt to scream. He had never seen *Dr. Strangelove*, was not especially jingoistic, and did not understand the point of his own death.

PROBABLY FOR THE BEST, the crew of *Earth's Hope* did not survive to see what became of its efforts. It was not much, really. What happened was the nuclear warhead struck the Rigel-Rigel orbital defenses, which were like a giant plastic shell around the planet. It created a pathetic, sickening thud, not unlike the sound made by striking a spoon against a Tupperware bowl. The defensive shell disarmed the warhead and deflected it into space where it drifted feebly until a gizmo that looked like a giant ball-peen hammer smashed it into flotsam and a second gizmo, which resembled a giant broom, swept it up, and a third gizmo, which looked a bit like a Greenpeace volunteer, separated out the recyclables and deposited the debris in the appropriate bins. The unmanned spacecraft met a similar fate.

All that survived was the flight recorder, contained inside a miniature ship resembling a homing pigeon. After the destruction of the ship, the tiny craft made its way back to Earth with news of the demise of *Earth's Hope* and its crew. The trip from the wormhole to Earth took approximately nine minutes less than the outbound journey.

The recorder contained most of the pertinent information about the doomed journey, but excluded the unfortunate misplacement of the Chocodiles and their ultimate consumption by the engorged, irradiated raccoon who, together with Armando Tanzarian, Tex McBain, Hanukapi Puli, and Sinclair Lewis, died in service of his planet.

These facts were, sadly, lost to history.

War is hell.

BAD NEWS ON THE
DOORSTEP

SIX WEEKS TO THE day after *Earth's Hope* set off as the last, best hope of mankind, the interstellar homing pigeon returned with news of the journey, all of it bad. The crew was dead, the sole nuclear weapon aboard the ship failed to penetrate the Tupperware shield of Rigel-Rigel, and the toilet had overflowed.

The chairman of the Joint Chiefs of Staff announced this in the Roosevelt Room at a morning meeting of the President's senior staff. Each person present recalled what the Ambassador had said at the White House dinner regarding the Rigelian policy on use of force.

Len Carlson spoke for everyone gathered when he said, "Uh-oh."

IN LIGHT OF THE possibility of a counterattack against Earth, the Secret Service in consultation with the Joint Chiefs decided to err on the side of caution. They determined to transfer the President and his staff to a nuclear shelter. Just to be safe, they decided to evacuate the cabinet and all of Congress too.

THE MILITARY DOES NOT refer to nuclear shelters as "nuclear shelters." It refers to them as government relocation centers. Most of these were built in the 1960s at the height of fears that the Cold War would become hot. The crown jewel of the system was "Greek Island," a mammoth shelter in the beautiful mountains of West Virginia, built at the suggestion of President Dwight D. Eisenhower during the period before he became a dinner plate.

Greek Island took two and a half years to build and cost approximately $86 million. It was located sixty-four feet underground, with five-foot-thick concrete walls and twenty-five-ton doors. It had a power plant, water purification system, and television studio. Department of Defense plans called for the President, the cabinet, and certain key civilians—one thousand people in all—to be evacuated to the facility in the event of nuclear attack. Once there, they would remove their clothing, take a high-pressure shower, and then be issued uniforms, underwear, canvas shoes, and a toiletry kit.

The Defense Department plan contained several substantial flaws. The shelter had a fresh air supply that would last only seventy-two hours, after which time airborne radiation would seep into the bunker. The food supply was more substantial, but still good for merely sixty days. By contrast, the half-life of uranium 235, the nuclear fuel used for *Little Boy*, is approximately 704 million years.

The television studio was also wrongheaded. A study by a sociologist at Yale concluded that in the event of nuclear war very few people would watch television. The notable exceptions were a core of middle-aged women in unaffected areas, mostly in the Midwest, who would keep up with their soaps.

THE TOILETRY KIT INCLUDED a tiny toothbrush, a small tube of baking-soda toothpaste, one ounce of mouthwash, a comb, four aspirin, a fingernail clipper, two Maalox-brand antacid tablets, six Q-tips, two alcohol-based sterilizing cleaning pads, an after-dinner mint, eye shades, and a pair of foam earplugs.

Retail cost at CVS: $17.98.

DoD contracted price: $2,111.37.

WHILE THE ABSENCE OF adequate food and air were shortcomings of the program, the location of the shelter was inspired. The defense department built Greek Island under the lavish Greenbrier resort. This meant that after the war ended, and the radiation cleared five or six hundred years later, Congress could emerge for a quick round of golf.

When the residents of White Sulphur Springs became suspicious as to the nature of the construction, the DoD devised a sly cover: Greenbrier was constructing a hospital, one of those underground clinics with thick concrete walls that so many of the top country clubs maintain.

GREENBRIER WAS NOT JUST any golf course; it was the home of professional golfer extraordinaire "Slammin' Sam" Snead, winner of seven professional majors, including three Masters. Snead was famously flexible, and through his late eighties could lift his legs above his head. Legend has it that while playing in the 1972 club championship, on the par-five twelfth hole Snead hit an errant tee ball, which descended into one of the ventilation shafts of the relocation center. When, after considerable searching, Snead and his opponent finally found the ball, it immediately became clear Snead faced a difficult shot. His golf ball had fallen sixty-four feet below ground onto the floor of the putative medical clinic, which appeared to be in fact a fallout shelter. Snead would need to hit the ball virtually straight up into the air, with enough spin so it would not fall back into the ventilation shaft, all with a restricted swing. Snead's opponent graciously offered to give Snead a free drop, on the basis that the fallout shelter constituted ground under repair. Snead refused.

"Play it as it lies," Snead said. "That's golf." On the first two attempts he failed but on the third try hit a spectacular shot that cleared the duct and, thanks to a favorable ricochet off an African gray parrot, landed on the green and rolled into the hole for a miraculous birdie.

THE PASSING PARROT HAD no earthly business either in West Virginia or at the Greenbrier Club Championship.

Happily, the parrot was not injured. He was merely stunned and soon returned to his business.

✳   ✳   ✳

In 1992, the *Washington Post Magazine* ran a story about Greek Island and the shortcomings of its design. Notable among these, the shelter was too small to accommodate families. Congressmen would need to leave their spouses and children behind. It was thus unlikely any government official would ever actually go to the shelter. To make matters worse, it cost a fortune to build and was expensive to maintain. These ongoing expenses included the salaries of several government agents who worked undercover at the resort as caddies.

After public pressure mounted, the Pentagon deactivated the bunker and turned it into a tourist attraction. It did not do particularly well in this capacity. More people played golf at Greenbrier in a day than visited the shelter in a decade.

Greek Island may have been discredited, but the government still needed shelters. When time came to build a new one, the Department of Defense came up with a creative idea: build the new shelter directly under Greek Island. It was the perfect cover. Greek Island I, as the original shelter came to be known, had been such a financial and conceptual disaster, no one would ever expect another shelter to be built in the exact same spot. As the Secretary of Defense explained, people do not expect the government to repeat mistakes of such magnitude.

Greek Island II shared many of the same features as Greek Island I. It also had five-foot-thick concrete walls and twenty-five-ton doors. The main differences were Greek Island II was 128 feet underground instead of 64, had better ventilation and more food, and was large enough to accommodate the members of Congress and their families. The new kitchen also had a cappuccino maker. Other than these subtle distinctions, one could not tell the two shelters apart.

As one of the DoD contractors put it, "One Greek island looks pretty much like another." He was referring to his travels with his wife in the Mediterranean, but the comment just as readily applied to the nuclear shelters.

Protocols at Greek Island II were much the same as at Greek Island I. Upon threat of nuclear war, all of Congress, the executive branch, key civilians and their respective families would be evacuated to the facility. Upon their arrival at the shelter, prospective inhabitants would remove their clothing, take a high-pressure shower, and then be issued uniforms, underwear, canvas shoes, and a $2,000 toiletry kit.

MUCH ATTENTION WAS DEVOTED to the toothpaste to be included in the new, revised toiletry kit. This was strange in a way since one toothpaste is pretty much like another. In fact when *Consumer Reports* reviewed toothpastes in 1998, it rated 30 of the 38 toothpastes tested as "excellent."

For business reasons, the executives of Gleaming toothpaste pushed hard to get their brand adopted at the new nuclear shelter, the location of which was a closely guarded state secret. The toothpaste executives argued that the granulated baking soda–based toothpaste used at Greek Island I had been grossly inadequate. They made this argument despite the fact no one had ever used the toothpaste at Greek Island I, and the fact that one toothpaste is pretty much like another.

It was nevertheless decided, finally, by the relevant government procurement officer after a long dinner at Morton's, pleasant conversation with several representatives of the Young Executive Program in the Champagne Room of the Capital City Playhouse Club, and the coincidental loss and recovery of a BMW convertible, that Gleaming would be the toothpaste of choice, thus positioning it desirably, in the view of the company executives, as the dentifrice of choice in postapocalypse America.

By the by, Gleaming was one of the eight toothpastes not rated "excellent" by *Consumer Reports*. In fact it was the only one rated "bad." The testers said it had a faint odor of foot rot.

BACK TO OUR HEROES. Some people might have been daunted by a flight to an underground bunker in the face of a nuclear holocaust, but the President did not appear to be fazed. In fact he appeared to regard the whole matter as a great adventure. He sat aboard Air Force One and dabbled at a Sudoku puzzle. At one point, he turned to Ralph and said, "I understand in the event of nuclear attack they give you a toiletry kit and clean underwear at this shelter. Could you make sure they have the right kind?"

Ralph said, "Yes, Mr. President."

"I wouldn't want to have to deal with a bunching problem while we're down there."

"No, Mr. President."

"What about a treadmill? Do you think they'll have a treadmill?"

"I don't know, Mr. President."

"This could be a great opportunity for me to really get in shape."

"Yes, Mr. President."

"Make sure they have a treadmill, Ralph."

"I shall, Mr. President."

THE PRESIDENT WAS THINKING about Sudoku and treadmills, but Ralph had only Jessica on his mind. In the weeks since they had met at Blimpway, Ralph and Jessica's relationship had blossomed into deep, abiding love. Their physical attraction had grown even more intense. More important, though, Ralph had the complete conviction that Jessica was the best person he had ever met. After she left school, she never looked back. Not once did she express even a whit of regret. Rather she tried to encourage Ralph to devote his energy to his own passion, whatever that might be. More and more, he found this to be Jessica herself, without whom he could not imagine living.

Jessica, for her part, loved Ralph intensely, but she continued to feel powerfully drawn to Tibet and continued to make the elaborate plans required to move there. In the meantime, while she waited for her visa, she went to work for a nonprofit organization based in Arlington, Virginia, that placed pets in the homes of teenage children. Where the child's home could not accommodate a living pet, he or she would be given a high-quality stuffed animal. In every case, the student was trained to care for the animal, which would be periodically examined, and was asked to make reports on its development and exploits.

What the organization found was that the students who participated in this program did better in school, were far less likely to get into trouble, and that, remarkably, these benefits accrued whether the student had been given a living animal or stuffed. The process helped the students learn empathy and responsibility. For her part, Jessica realized she loved working with children and all kinds of animals and didn't miss law school one bit. She also discovered she loved Ralph more than she had ever imagined she could love someone.

RALPH MANAGED, WITH CONSIDERABLE difficulty, to secure Jessica a space in Greek Island II. Since the slots at the shelter were reserved for the members of Congress and the cabinet and their immediate families, this required Ralph to claim, untruthfully, that he and Jessica were engaged to be married. It also required him to convince Jessica she should set aside her substantial objections to the President and live with him in an underground shelter for an unspecified, and likely substantial, period of time. Jessica insisted she would rather live in a nuclear wasteland than a bunker with the President and Congress, which she described colorfully as a "gaggle of fat, old, bald men, who pay lip service to serving God but care only about eating pot pies and padding their pockets with cash."

"Why pot pies?" Ralph had asked.

"I don't know," she said, snarling, "I just think old fat men like pot pies."

"The President isn't fat," Ralph said.

"Well, he should be," Jessica said. "And I bet he likes pot pies."

This was in fact true.

"Think about our children if we don't go," Ralph said. "They'll have three eyes."

"I don't care," Jessica said. "I'm sure they will be beautiful three-eyed children."

"Please," Ralph said. "I love you and I want you to be safe."

Jessica had no witty response to this. She agreed to leave work immediately if Ralph called to say an evacuation order had been issued and drive to Greenbrier, West Virginia. So when he did in fact call, she did not protest and said she would leave straightaway.

"Be safe," Ralph said, "but get there quick."

"I shall fly on the wings of love," said Jessica.

Ralph blew her a kiss through the phone. "Thank you," he said.

As Air Force One took off from Andrews Air Force Base, on its way to the Greenbrier airstrip, each of its passengers worried about something. The passengers were in this respect no different from every other sentient creature in the universe. Sentient creatures worry. This is arguably the defining characteristic of sentience.

The President was worried about his Sudoku puzzle. He was beginning to suspect he had misplaced a 9 in the upper left-hand box and that this faulty premise, upon which his entire solution was based, would require him to redo the entire puzzle.

An aging chef at a fine London restaurant could not recall whether he had already seasoned his stew with paprika. He worried about the stew and his diminishing memory. Losing one's memory can be a very disconcerting experience.

Both Sting and I were working on and worrying about the same Sudoku puzzle as the President. By coincidence, I had misplaced the same 9 as the President. Sting was solving the puzzle correctly, though he was bothered by his dinner, which seemed to have been seasoned too heavily with paprika.

On Rigel-Rigel, Professor Fendle-Frinkle was unwinding with a three-dimensional base–47 Sudoku puzzle. These could be ambitious undertakings, and he worried he might not finish before the end of the universe.

Also on Rigel-Rigel, the Ambassador worried about Earth and regretted how badly things had gone. Ned worried about the same thing. He also worried about his beloved Maude, who had taken the car out for the first time since the accident. Ned knew how crazy drivers could be.

Finally, back on Earth, aboard Air Force One, Ralph Bailey worried that his beloved Jessica would not get to Greenbrier in time.

21

ONLY THE RUSH HOUR
HELL TO FACE

COASTING DOWN THE HIGHWAY, Nelson Munt-Zoldarian was breathless with excitement. He had staged dozens of accidents in his career, but this one felt different. He recalled the anticipation he felt as a young man when he left the mob and struck out to blaze his own path of fraud. In those early days he would stay awake at night worrying about the details of his plan, whether it would go well and, though he knew he should not, daring to think what he would do with his earnings. That jubilant engagement in his work, like many aspects of his youth, had vanished long ago, beaten out of him by the routine of professional life.

Here on Earth, though, it all came rushing back. He lay awake in his motel room for hours, going over all of his plans, wondering whether he would be able to prove himself anew. Staging car accidents is a young man's game, after all. But it wasn't about money anymore, and this reality was in itself liberating. The excitement of the project rekindled his youth. Nelson saw these positive feelings as validation of his decision to forgo retirement and continue his career, regardless of how things turned out.

On the morning of the big day, Nelson woke up well before the alarm he set in his room at the Colonial Inn in Haymarket, Virginia. He got dressed, walked to the diner on the corner, and ordered coffee and a donut. In his four weeks on Earth he had become quite fond of donuts. He particularly enjoyed the ones filled with jam. When he finished his breakfast, he walked out to the interstate and nervously paced the highway in the manner of an expectant father.

Nelson was nervous, but he was also a professional. He had thought through every detail of the plan. He secured a driver's license for himself. He purchased a used Toyota Camry in red, which is the hardest color to see at sunset. He then replaced the brake lights with lower wattage bulbs, making them all the more difficult to see. Then he selected a segment of highway just over the crest of a hill where drivers would have the least visibility. This section of road, upon which Nelson now drove, was on the westerly portion of I–66, which emanated from Arlington and carried D.C. employees to their suburban homes after long days at work, when they were tired and least alert.

When he satisfied himself that every detail had been taken care of, he walked back into town to kill the rest of the day. He read the *USA Today* and ate at Sizzler where they had a pretty good lunch deal. You could get a steak, fries, and garlic bread for $6.99. Nelson liked the garlic bread a lot. Lunch made him sleepy so he went back to the Colonial Inn and took a nap for an hour. He got up and drowsily watched *Dr. Phil* for a few minutes, but couldn't concentrate. So he got out of bed, took another shower, and then counted down the minutes until he got into his car and back to work.

SIZZLER IS A RESTAURANT chain that got its start in Culver City, California. It serves steak and seafood and puts out a nice salad bar. In the late fifties it had several hundred locations throughout the United States, but closed most of them in the East in the mid 1990s. This is strange since the food was surprisingly good. It is also strange that one of the few surviving locations is so close to Manassas Junction, the site of the First and Second Battles of Bull Run, two of the key skirmishes of the Civil War. This makes for a peculiar juxtaposition. It is easy to imagine a soldier in the Union army thinking about what the world will look like in the future. If we could communicate with him, we would tell him, "In a hundred and fifty years' time, there will be no more slavery. Furthermore, on this site, there will be a monument to your efforts: a restaurant serving steak and shrimp and garlic bread that is quite good."

AROUND 5:15, ABOUT AN hour after she got the momentous call from Ralph, Jessica was driving in the right-hand lane of I–66, keeping up with the flow of traffic but going no faster. Her trunk and backseat were packed with hundreds of stuffed animals, which she kept in her car for work. Before leaving D.C., Jessica thought about unpacking the car, but she didn't want to take the time and thought, in any case, the people at Greck Island could use a few stuffed animals in the days ahead. It was a good thing Ralph told her she would be issued fresh clothes and toiletries when she arrived at the shelter. She had no space in the car to accommodate her things.

Jessica was a cautious driver, and never exceeded the speed limit by more than five miles per hour, even under the threat of nuclear war. She was such a cautious driver that in high school driver's education, on her first attempt at a left turn, she waited at the intersection for almost fifteen minutes before finding a comfortable opportunity. After the session, Jessica's teacher went to the school principal and retired. It was thus particularly odd that a Toyota Camry a few hundred yards ahead was going even more slowly than Jessica's own car.

AT APPROXIMATELY 5:17, JUST past Exit 40, the exit for Haymarket and the Manassas National Battlefield Park, Jessica struck the red Toyota Camry in the rear. She did not see the car until a moment before the accident. Like Maude Anat-Denarian, Jessica immediately blamed herself. Maude blamed herself because she had been distracted by the fiasco at Trader Planet and by the engaging program on broccoli. Jessica believed herself to have been distracted too, in her case by the prospect of a nuclear apocalypse.

ALSO LIKE MAUDE, JESSICA had been listening to the radio at the time of the accident. Maude had been listening to National Intergalactic Radio; Jessica was listening to Mix 107, a D.C. station that follows the "Jack" format. The Jack format replaces disc jockeys with a rotation of 60s, 70s, 80s, and 90s hits. Some people refer to it as the "MacKingization" of radio. This is a veiled shot at MacKing, which a lot of people really like. MacKing has really good fries and Dr Pepper in the soda fountain. At the time of the accident, the station was playing the REM song "It's the End of the World as We Know It." This song is a staple of the Jack format.

Nelson Munt-Zoldarian took great pride in his work. No one had ever been injured by one of his projects, other than some faceless insurance executives, and he did his best to ensure traffic was interrupted as minimally as possible. He considered himself a low-impact defrauder. But his first Earth project would have a greater effect on others than he anticipated.

When Jessica struck the back of Nelson's Camry, it caused the trunk of her own car to spring open. This in turn loosed the hundreds of stuffed animals that had been packed into the trunk and scattered them all over the road. Because the animals were of quite high quality and looked so real, the driver of the car behind Jessica's swerved to avoid hitting what appeared to be a nice bunny rabbit. This in turn caused the driver of the car immediately behind that one to brake hard so as to avoid another collision. One driver after another hit the brakes of his car, several thousand in all. Miraculously no one got hurt, but the resulting backup eventually stretched for more than eight miles.

This is an example of a chain reaction, an enormously powerful concept. For example, in the mid 1990s a few kids in the East Village of Manhattan began wearing these horrible shoes made of brushed suede and a crepe sole called Hush Puppies. Pretty soon everyone had to have some, and the company, which had almost gone out of business, sold millions of pairs. It shows how little things can make a huge difference. The point is similarly illustrated when a neutron strikes an unstable atom causing the release of additional neutrons. It sounds innocent enough, but the resulting energy can level a city.

Jessica stepped out of her car and went to check on the driver of the Camry. The man she hit introduced himself as Nelson. He was nice, almost professional about the whole thing. When she apologized about the collision, he told her in a sweet southern drawl that accidents happen and the insurance company would take care of everything.

Nelson said, "Isn't insurance a wonderful thing?"

"I suppose it is," said Jessica.

"It certainly is," said Nelson with conviction.

They turned and looked at the traffic behind them. From the crest of the hill they could see it stretched back all the way to the horizon, as far as the eye could see. In a curious way, it seemed rather beautiful, this river of cars.

"That's something, isn't it," Jessica said.

"Sure is," said Nelson. "I've been driving for more than fifty years, but I have never seen anything like this."

"Don't say."

Nelson smiled. "But that's the beauty of life, ain't it, sugar?" he said. "You think you've seen everything and then, one day, you realize you ain't seen nothing at all."

It may strike the reader as curious that Nelson Munt-Zoldarian speaks with a Southern accent given that he comes from the nation Shelbee on the planet Flossenberger, which is some 62,500 light-years from Earth. Similar to the conceit that mankind is the only sentient creature in the universe, this sentiment is another example of human hubris. The United States is hardly the only country with a South.

Viewed up close, the river of cars wasn't quite as beautiful as it appeared from a distance. After traffic on I–66 ground to a halt, people cursed and yelled. One driver honked because he was going to be late for his appointment with the chiropodist, who only had evening hours once a week. Another honked because he was late to meet his wife for dinner at Applebee's. Several others honked because they had nothing to be late for. After a while, though, when it became obvious no one was going anywhere, people resigned themselves to a long wait. They rolled down their windows and shut off their cars.

Then, a curious thing happened. The people got out and began to collect the stuffed animals that had scattered across the asphalt. They talked to one another as they did. Exchanges were made.

Stuffed bunny rabbits were swapped for teddy bears, and vice versa, to better suit the preferences of the drivers' children. A sweet and gentle scene evolved.

A half-mile back, a man pulled out his hibachi, which he had packed for a weekend camping trip, and grilled up some hot dogs and hamburgers. A second man brought out a case of beer from his trunk. The two organizers of this impromptu barbecue discovered they had been commuting on the same exact schedule for twenty-three years. They had driven past each other hundreds of times—perhaps on a bad day one had honked at the other in a fit of road rage—and never exchanged so much as a single word. Now they laughed and shared war stories of horrific traffic jams and missed Little League games and felt as if they had been friends for years.

When the mess finally cleared, hours later, the drivers departed feeling deeply attached to one another. In addition to all of their other identities and allegiances—American, Cornell graduate, Redskins fan, Democrat, Opraholic, shopaholic, hobbyist, allergy sufferer, human being—they were now members of the community of I–66, brought together unwittingly by an alien charlatan, stuffed animals, and a young woman with a heart of gold.

I MYSELF WAS STUCK in the jam on I–66, about a mile and a half behind Nelson's Camry. I was on my way to my friend's house in Nebo, North Carolina. Nebo is in the western part of the state about an hour east of Asheville. It's small enough that it's not on most maps. It has rolling hills and sprawling pastures filled with cows and sheep and the occasional alpaca. There's a diner that has good pie. It is quite peaceful. As yet there aren't many houses, but the developers are finding their way. Nebo is one of many places I have been that I worry will be ruined in the name of progress, such as it is. I feel this way too about Hawaii, Costa Rica, Alaska, Washington State, Maine, Vermont, New Zealand, and Balta.

LIKE EVERYONE ELSE I was at first annoyed by the delay, but soon enough I got into the spirit of things. A few stuffed animals made their way back to me. I handed a rhinoceros to a boy in the backseat of a Suburban and kept a little lamb to give to my girlfriend. The man in the next car ahead offered me a Chocodile, which I hesitated to accept as I had nothing to offer him in return other than a chipped cinnamon Mentos.

"Please," he said. "Many people have never heard of these, but they are quite delicious."

"Thank you," I said. Until that moment, I had heard of but never eaten a Chocodile. I gave it the once-over.

"Go ahead," the man said. "It's like a chocolate Twinkie. They're very hard to get. A lot of people think they stopped making them, but you can actually order them by mail. I just got a shipment delivered to me at my office today."

I smiled.

He said, "There are a few foods like that. Did you know that Mallomars are only made in the winter?"

"I didn't know that," I said.

"One needs to pay attention to the important things in life."

"Isn't that the truth," I said. I unwrapped the Chocodile and took a bite.

"What do you think?"

"It is really quite delicious," I said. And it was.

JESSICA TRIED TO CALL Ralph several times but failed on each occasion. Finally, she stopped trying. Jessica concluded that the problem was the unusual volume of calls coming from the same immediate area. It was true many of the people on I–66 were attempting to call home to say they would be late for dinner at Applebee's or whatever, but this was not the real cause of the problem. The true cause was a raccoon, which had made its home in the base of the nearest cell phone tower and chewed through the wiring, which it mistook for vermicelli.

AT GREEK ISLAND II, Ralph grew increasingly agitated. Jessica was more than three hours late. He tried her cell phone several times but she did not pick up. He paced around the facility. He tried to calm himself by drinking a glass of lemonade, which had been prepared from a powdered mix, but it did nothing. The operations people assured him cell phones should work from the bunker—"unless you got Verizon," one of them said with a laugh—but Ralph had his doubts. He paced for another hour and drank another cup of lemonade, which only seemed to be making things worse, and then finally demanded to be let out.

"Afraid we can't do that," said Major William Buckner, the commander of Greek Island II. Major Buckner's first decision had been to prepare a large tub of powdered lemonade to make the new guests feel at home. The major had a gentle, nurturing spirit, a defense mechanism against the revulsion people normally felt for him if they were from Boston, as he unfortunately was. This tender manner was particularly conspicuous in a military man. He knew how to make a fine lemonade, though, so his first decision was a big hit. His second decision, telling Ralph Bailey he could not go outside, was less popular.

"Look," Ralph said, "my fiancée is still out there and her cell phone isn't working. I think she was in an accident. I need to go find her."

"Don't think you understand, sir. The last of the congressmen arrived about a half hour ago. We're under lockdown now. The doors cannot be opened until the threat has passed."

"Is there any immediate threat?"

"None of which we are aware, sir, but those are the rules."

"This is crazy. I am just asking you to open the doors for a moment."

"I'm sorry, sir. The rules are the rules."

Ralph could see he wasn't going to get anywhere with Buckner. He sized up the situation and saw his only option was to go for one of the officer's guns and demand to be let out. He was seriously considering this course of action when the President walked into the command center to a chorus of "Good evening, Mr. President."

"I have been looking for you, Ralph."

Ralph muttered a reply of "Yes, sir." He wanted to make his case to the President, but he knew the chance of getting a word in before the President said whatever he came to say was precisely nil.

"Seems I have myself a case of the munchies," the President said. "I was thinking you might run out and get me a sandwich, Ralph. We looked it up and there's a Blimpway on Main Street that's open until nine. It's just a short walk."

Major Buckner intervened. "We can have the cook whip you up something if you like, Mr. President."

"Thank you, Major, but no. You guys have nothing but army rations. A man cannot live on that alone. Ralph knows what I like. It won't be any trouble at all for him."

"Sir, we are under lockdown as of nineteen hundred hours. Our protocols do not allow for those doors to be lifted until the threat has passed."

"Well, is there anything on the radar? Have the satellites detected anything?"

The major looked in the direction of a sergeant seated in front of a series of screens. The sergeant shook his head in silent reply.

"Not at the moment, Mr. President," Major Buckner said.

"Well then, it can't cause very much harm, now can it?"

"I'm just not sure it's a very good idea."

The President smiled and put his hand on the major's shoulder.

"Relax, Major. The world isn't going to end. And it certainly isn't going to end in the next twenty minutes. So why don't you listen to the commander in chief and let my assistant out to get me a sandwich."

The major followed orders, as he had been trained to do. He told the sergeant to open the twenty-five-ton doors so Ralph could walk into town and get the President a Blimpway sandwich. Ralph, who could scarcely believe his luck, could not get on his way quickly enough. As he hastened to leave, the President called to him.

"Make sure they put extra meat on the sandwich," the President said.

As fate would have it, these would be the last words the President would ever speak to Ralph Bailey.

22

A SUMMER SMOKER
UNDERGROUND

As soon as Ralph emerged from Greek Island II, he called Jessica on his cell phone. This time she picked up, and Ralph exhaled an enormous sigh of relief.

"Thank goodness," he said. "I have been trying to reach you for hours."

"I have been trying to reach you too," she said. "I was stuck in a horrible traffic jam on I–66. I couldn't get through to you on my cell phone. I guess everybody was trying to call at once."

"I was so worried."

"I'm sorry. There was nothing I could do." Sheepishly, Jessica said, "The worst part is I caused the whole thing."

Alarmed, Ralph asked, "Were you in an accident?"

"A guy slowed up at the top of a hill and I struck him in the rear. His car spun out, stopped across the lanes, couldn't move. It set off a catastrophic chain reaction. Traffic backed up for miles. It took hours for the police and tow truck to get through."

"Are you okay?"

"I'm fine," Jessica said.

"The car?"

"It's good enough. I'm moving now."

"Where are you?"

"I'm near Lexington, Virginia. I should be to you in about four hours."

"I'm just happy you're okay," Ralph said. "I was so worried."

At that moment Jessica, who was driving in a westerly direction, noticed what appeared to be a missile streaking through the sky at breakneck speed. She slowed down and pulled over to the side of the road.

"Do you see that?" she asked.

"I do," Ralph said. It was almost directly over his head, hurtling toward Earth. His heart sunk. He immediately understood the implications of this. Hundreds of similar missiles would be heading toward Earth to punish the planet for its transgressions. And the great irony was that the man responsible for all of it was safe and sound 128 feet underground behind twenty-five-ton steel doors. Ralph and Jessica, on the other hand, would be killed in the atomic blast or die from radiation soon thereafter because of a freak car accident and the President's taste for Blimpway sandwiches.

Ralph thought to himself, "Life is funny."

He said to Jessica. "I'm sorry. I wanted us to be together more than you can imagine."

Jessica's glow radiated from the phone.

"Don't fret," she said. "It's not the end. In fact it's only the beginning."

"I don't understand how you can know something like that."

"Just trust me," she said.

"I do," Ralph said, and he did.

"And love me," she said.

"I do," Ralph said.

And he did.

IN GREEK ISLAND II, Major Buckner sounded the alarm. The President arrived quickly, munching on some peanuts. Major Buckner informed the President that a missile had been detected heading toward Earth.

"Don't you mean missiles, Major?"

"No, Mr. President, just one missile. Furthermore, it appears the alien ship that launched the missile is returning to the wormhole."

The President considered the implications of this for a moment. "So this is the extent of the attack?" he asked.

"It appears that way, sir."

"What city is its target?"

Major Buckner checked the instruments. He said, "No major city, Mr. President. It appears to be heading toward West Virginia."

"Where exactly?"

The major checked the instruments again.

"Here, sir," the Major said. "It appears to be heading here."

The President stopped eating his peanuts. "How long do we have?" he asked.

"About twenty seconds."

"Oh," said the President.

TWENTY SECONDS IS NOT very much time to reflect on a life. The President had only four final thoughts.

His fourth-to-last thought was that he had forgotten to give Ralph money for the sandwich.

His third-to-last thought was that he had forgotten to pay Ralph for all of the other sandwiches.

His penultimate thought was to wonder whether, in the end, his father would have approved of him and the choices he had made in his life.

His final thought, just as the missile approached, was that he had ruined his last good pair of underwear.

THE MISSILE STRUCK WITH exquisite precision. Though it had been launched from a spaceship 400,000 miles away, the missile hit its target precisely, streaking down the very shaft up which Sam Snead had hit his miraculous shot many years earlier. It was a small missile, but it packed a wallop.

The missile killed all of the people in the bunker. However, it left their personal effects undisturbed. In addition to loathing violence, the Rigelians were quite neat and had a long-standing policy of doing as little property damage as possible. The Rigelian missile perfected the aspiration of the neutron bomb, the chic weapon of the 1960s, fashionable because its reliance on radiation rather than heat killed people while leaving buildings intact. The many items not destroyed inside Greek Island II included the President's peanuts, the stash of pornography the Speaker of the House always carried in his briefcase, and the remainder of Major Buckner's delicious lemonade.

Remarkably, the missile caused no disturbance to the golfers on the Greenbrier golf course. A player on the thirteenth green, who had struck a putt just as the missile touched ground, watched in eager anticipation as the ball stayed true to its course and fell into the cup for an improbable eagle. In fact, the missile might have gone completely unnoticed but for the small matter of its destroying the American government.

As THINGS TURNED OUT, the President's dying word was, "Oh." This bon mot would be lost for all time, as all of the people within earshot met their demise during the destruction of Greek Island II. So far as the annals of history were concerned, the President's dying words were, "Make sure they put extra meat on the sandwich." At the time he said this, he was unaware he would die in less than twenty minutes. If he had been so aware, one likes to believe he would have come up with something pithier.

DYING WORDS SAY A lot about people, just as the three things they would bring with them to a desert island do, and so too the manner in which they treat waiters and children.

Some people say things showing they really don't get it. On his deathbed, the obscenely wealthy entrepreneur and showman P. T. Barnum (d. 1891) grimly asked, "How were the receipts today at Madison Square Garden?"

On the other hand, some people say profound things suggesting they really do get it. For example, Humphrey Bogart (d. 1957) said, "I never should have switched from scotch to martinis."

Sometimes people display extraordinary grace. After being shot sixteen times, Malcolm X (d. 1966) said to his assassins, "Let's cool it, brothers."

Some are touching. On his deathbed, President James K. Polk (d. 1849) said to his wife, "I love you, Sarah. For all eternity, I love you."

Some are brilliant. Oscar Wilde's (d. 1900) dying words were: "Either that wallpaper goes, or I do."

Some forsake the process altogether. Urged by his housekeeper to speak his last words so she could record them for posterity Karl Marx (d. 1883) said, "Go on, get out—last words are for fools who haven't said enough."

Some experience revelations, such as film producer Louis Mayer (d. 1957) who said, "Nothing matters. Nothing matters."

Some die quietly, like Teddy Roosevelt (d. 1919) who said, "Put out the light."

And then there is Timothy Leary (d. 1996) who said, finally, "Why not? Yeah."

So far as I can determine, the English language has no word for a person's dying declaration. An "epitaph" is a summary statement of a person's life, the kind of thing that goes on a tombstone. A "thanatopsis" is a meditation upon death. It was also a poem by William Cullen Bryant. It comes close, but does not describe the pithy epigrams the Oscar Wildes of the world speak on their deathbeds.

I hereby propose we adopt "epitomb" to describe this familiar phenomenon. I am hopeful that along with the "Sneedle," it will be part of my lasting legacy to the people of Earth.

I have had a premonition of what my own epitomb will be.

I think it will be: "Oh shit."

I would rather it be: "This milk has turned bad."

Whatever it is, I would prefer the words be spoken in Latin. Anything is more elegant when spoken in Latin, particularly epitombs, such as John Wilkes Booth's "*Sic semper tyrannis.*"

Unless one lives in ancient Rome, of course, in which case it just seems ordinary.

While I did not mind knocking off the President and Len Carlson, I disliked killing Joe Quimble, who loved the Constitution, and William Buckner, who made such fine lemonade, and the press secretary Martha Jones, whom we hardly knew. I particularly disliked killing David Prince, who seemed like a nice person and who shared my geeky taste for science fiction movies.

In general, I don't like harming things. I am one of those people who picks up ants in the house and moves them outside. The crickets in my basement are made to feel at home. I do a lot of my writing outside on a laptop. Sometimes these little red gnats crawl across the screen. They can be a nuisance. I try to brush them off the screen gently, but in so doing I once killed one and felt bad about it for the rest of the day. You get the picture.

I made sure Sam Snead did not harm the parrot he hit with his golf ball and that Nelson Munt-Zoldarian did not seriously injure anyone with his reckless driving. But, in my opinion, the President and the cabinet had to suffer for the sake of the story.

War is hell.

So as not to grow too attached to these people, I kept the descriptions of them sketchy. I did not discuss their families, for example, though they each had one. I purposely chose not to give them hobbies or toupees or any of the many things that make people human. I left them as caricatures.

The argument could be made that my depriving them of depth was itself tantamount to murder since I deprived them of the opportunity to develop into fully realized human beings. But I did not want to knock off people to whom I—and you—might feel attached.

It is true I could have invented a fantastic scenario to get some of these people out of the bunker, which in fairness is precisely what I did to save Ralph. But this would have taken some doing. I suppose all of the nice ones could have developed a case of the munchies at the same time. They could have all gone to Blimpway together and been having a fun time eating subs just as the missile arrived. As it is, it was a stretch to get Ralph out of the bunker. So I just made the best of an imperfect situation, which I suppose is all anyone can ever do.

I do feel guilty, though, and am quite sorry these concepts of living creatures were harmed in the writing of this story. It may be small consolation, but I have tried to leave things as neat as possible.

23

PEANUTS,
PEANUTS, PEANUTS

To prevent the catastrophic contingency of the entire government being destroyed in a nuclear attack, it has been American practice since the dark days of the Cold War to send, on ceremonial occasions where its leadership is gathered in a single place, one government official to a separate, secure location. This person is referred to as the "designated survivor." It is a gloomy, ominous term, but being the designated survivor is not such a bad deal. The person is generally spared a tedious function, such as standing up and sitting down a hundred times during the State of the Union address, or shivering through the presidential inauguration. Furthermore, arrangements are made to provide the lucky official with an assortment of snacks and beverages.

During the 1980s and 1990s, the threat of catastrophe was taken less seriously. This is evidenced by the number of times the secretary of agriculture was designated as the survivor during the State of the Union address (five; excluding President Bartlett's designation of his secretary of agriculture, Roger Tribbey, during his delivery of the State of the Union in the first season of *The West Wing*).

In 2001 by contrast, at the height of the terrorist threat, it was the then–vice president who was designated as the survivor. He watched the speech from a comfortable, secure location. Speculation abounds as to his choice of snack, though he has a well-known fondness for Diet Sprite, now called Sprite Zero, which is not of the caliber of Diet Dr Pepper, but by all accounts a fine beverage.

IT IS ONE THING to be the designated survivor during the State of the Union address, and quite another to be the designated survivor when the entire government is gathering in an underground shelter because of impending Armageddon.

All things considered, the designated survivor, Henry Moleman, undersecretary of commerce, took the news quite well.

Before leaving the White House, the President called and said, "Moleman, you are the designated survivor."

"What's the occasion, sir?" Moleman asked. "It isn't time for the State of the Union."

"The occasion is that an alien race is about to launch a nuclear attack against Earth," the President explained. "The government is heading to Greek Island II. I have designated you as the survivor."

Undersecretary Moleman thought about this for a moment and then asked, "Do you think the term is appropriate in this case, sir?"

"That's a semantic question, Moleman. I don't have time to debate that right now."

"I see, Mr. President."

"Thank you for your service."

"Yes, Mr. President."

HENRY MOLEMAN TOOK THE news as part and parcel of the sense of resignation he felt about his political career. Like everyone who enters politics, Moleman had lofty aspirations at the start. But, as with anyone who does anything, life dragged him down. He was also the victim of substantial bad luck.

First of all, Henry Moleman is not the best name for politics. And Moleman came from Wisconsin, which has a great tradition of candidates placing placards on people's front lawns. During has first political campaign, when he was still a political science professor at U of W, Henry Moleman placed dozens of such signs across his district. Each said:

MOLEMAN
FOR CONGRESS

It was not eye-catching. Moleman's political consultant urged that he change his name back to the German original, Mahlman, but Moleman would not hear of it. He won in spite of his name, because of his well-deserved reputation for integrity and intelligence, earned over the years as a college professor and community activist. His constituents respected him and reelected him to Congress nine times.

But twenty years later, when Moleman aspired to the governorship of Wisconsin, his name became more of an obstacle. It was his bad luck to launch his gubernatorial campaign in the same week as the release of *The Mothman Prophecies*, an account based on real events of supernatural sightings preceding the collapse of a bridge in Point Pleasant, West Virginia. The opposition used "Moleman sightings" as a catchphrase to link prophecies of doom with tax-and-spend liberalism.

Now I know what you're thinking: few people saw *The Mothman Prophecies* and certainly no one in Wisconsin. Not true and not true. Do not underestimate Richard Gere, do not underestimate Laura Linney, and never ever underestimate the power of that combination in Wisconsin. The people of Wisconsin saw the movie in droves, and they paid heed. Unfortunately, this filtered into ill will for the gubernatorial candidate based on the similarity of his name to that of a fictitious character. Needless to say, this was irrational. But Moleman lost and that's really all that matters. Voters, like history, are under no obligation to make sense.

So Moleman ended up returning to the House of Representatives, where he had a reputation as something of a curmudgeon, and likely would have remained there for the remainder of his career but for the Internet Pornography Reduction and Apricot Price Protection Act. The President wanted it and needed Moleman's vote. The President didn't like Moleman, but offering him the position as number two in the commerce department seemed a small price to pay to ensure passage of such important legislation.

For his part, Moleman had grown tired of Congress. Taking the job in commerce felt in some ways like selling out, but he deplored Internet pornography, and though he disfavored price protections, the United States did not grow many apricots. It seemed a small compromise, and Henry Moleman very much liked the idea of being in the presidential order of succession, albeit at number 733. It would be a long shot for the undersecretary of commerce ever to be called upon to serve as president, but one never knew.

UPON THE DESTRUCTION OF Greek Island II, it was determined by the sergeant-at-arms, chief protocol officer of Congress, that the first 732 people in the presidential order of succession had been exterminated in the attack. The presidency thus fell to number 733, Henry Moleman. The sergeant-at-arms called Moleman at his home in Madison, Wisconsin, where Moleman had chosen to wait things out. The sergeant told him Congress and the cabinet had been destroyed together with Greek Island II, and that he, Undersecretary Moleman, needed to return to the White House immediately to assume the Presidency of the United States.

"Oh," said President-designee Moleman.

This could have been a fortuitous twist of history. Henry Moleman would have been an outstanding president. He might not have been a great orator like Kennedy or an ideologue like Reagan, but he had sound values and, after two decades in Congress, an impressive breadth of knowledge about how government worked. In the moments after the sergeant-at-arms telephoned, Moleman thought about how he would make peace with the aliens and use the outreach to repair America's standing in the international community. He also had a neat little plan for ending poverty, which had been dismissed by his peers, but was just crazy enough to work. Unfortunately, Henry Moleman never made it back to Washington because of that bane of the universe, the PTA.

STAY WITH ME HERE. Around the time *Earth's Hope* set out for Rigel-Rigel, Mrs. Moleman, Clarabella, launched her own political campaign to become the president of the East Madison High School PTA. A key plank of her platform: provide brownies at the meetings. Mrs. Moleman was a legendary baker and understood, as any good politician does, the key to winning elections is to offer good snacks.

In preparation for the vote, Clarabella Moleman prepared a giant tray of brownies and a giant tray of lasagna, each of which she stored in the family kitchen.

The complicating factor in this story is that Henry Moleman had a severe allergy to peanuts. Mrs. Moleman knew this, of course. So she wrote a large note on a sheet of loose-leaf paper and taped it to the tray of brownies. The note said:

PEANUTS!

Unfortunately, during the evening the Moleman family raccoon got into the brownies. The raccoon was not a pet in the conventional sense of the word. In fact the Molemans had attempted to evict the raccoon on several occasions. But raccoons have a way of finding their way back home, even if they are trapped and driven off several miles and deposited in the woods, as the Molemans had done several times with their pesky friend. Each time he found his way back and remade his home in the attic. Finally, after several failed eviction attempts, the Molemans accepted the raccoon's presence. In time, they began to think of him as part of the family.

Usually, the raccoon did not venture into the kitchen, but raccoons love sweet treats and this particular raccoon found Clarabella Moleman's brownies irresistible. During the night, he helped himself to half a tray of brownies. In the process, the raccoon dislodged the note, which attached itself to the lasagna.

Later, in celebration of his ascendancy to the presidency, Henry Moleman decided to indulge in one of his wife's delicious brownies. He checked for warnings, saw one on the tray of lasagna, but none on the brownies. Satisfied as to their safety, Moleman took a healthy bite of chocolaty goodness, then keeled over and expired.

HENRY MOLEMAN WAS AN intelligent man who spent his life thinking about weighty matters such as poverty, world peace, and how to get the Chinese to stop exporting so many *tchotchkes* to the United States, but he had the most ordinary of dying thoughts.

Henry Moleman often spoke to himself, a habit developed during his lonely years in academia, and he did so on this occasion. His last thought thus qualified on its face as an epitomb, but may not have truly met the criteria for dying words since they were choked out and, hence, inaudible.

In any event, Henry Moleman's last thought/epitomb was eminently ordinary. It was: "Why would lasagna have peanuts?"

FOLLOWING HENRY MOLEMAN'S UNTIMELY demise, the sergeant-at-arms determined that numbers 734 through 948 in the presidential order of succession had also perished in the attack on Greek Island II. The presidency thus fell to number 949, the last person on the list, Ralph Bailey, assistant deputy to the chief of staff, best known in the White House as the president's attaché.

I ADMIT, READILY, THAT this is all implausible. But it's about time we had a young, idealistic man in the White House, and Ralph Bailey fits the bill. I could imagine only two ways to get him there. One was to invent a fantastic scenario in which a twenty-four-year-old ascended to the presidency and the Constitution's age requirement had been suspended. The other was to give Ralph a really good fake ID.

THE NEWS THAT HE had been designated as the president was communicated to Ralph by cell phone by the sergeant-at-arms. He said, "Sir, you need to return to Washington. The first nine hundred forty-eight people in the order of succession have died. You are now the president of the United States."

Ralph was, obviously, stunned. "What happened to the designated survivor?" he asked.

"He had a fatal allergy attack."

Ralph said, "Oh."

RALPH ACCEPTED THE NEWS without cheer. Since the missile struck, Ralph had been fretfully standing outside Blimpway, waiting for Jessica and wondering about his friends. Ralph counted the President among them. He did not see everything as the President did. He particularly did not agree with the President's decision to attack the Rigelians, who Ralph believed had the very best of intentions. But the President had taken a great chance giving Ralph this once-in-a-lifetime opportunity, and he had always treated Ralph with respect. Ralph was sad to learn of the President's death and, of course, the death of his friends Maude, Joe, and David.

And Ralph was sad, for the most selfish of reasons, to learn of the bunker's destruction. He, for one, looked forward to that underground existence. Jessica may have dreaded the idea of being locked underground with the American government, but Ralph romanticized it. He would be with Jessica every day, and this was all he needed to be happy. Now, life would resume, and soon enough Jessica would leave for Tibet, as she had planned all along.

For old times sake, Ralph drifted into the store and purchased a ham and cheese sandwich. Then he sat down on a bench on the sidewalk, ate the sandwich by himself, and wondered what the odds were against this day having ended this way.

IF THIS WERE AN episode of *Star Trek*, Mr. Spock would chime in at this point and say, "The odds, Captain, are precisely 386,323,497 to 1." But this is intellectual pretension. To structure an answer to a question of this complexity, certain premises need to be established.

For example, suppose the question is the chance that a Rigelian dollowarrie and an African gray parrot would be indistinguishable. Spock could offer an off-the-cuff estimate here, but it would be meaningless. The answer depends on several background facts. If we know, for example, that Rigel-Rigel and Earth have similar atmospheres and each has canopies of tall trees with nuts and berries then, given the principles of convergent evolution, the similarity of the birds is less unlikely. If we know the dollowarrie is the creation of my imagination, then the similarity of the two creatures is less unlikely still. Similarly, if we suppose God created all life in the universe, and that he had a thing for long-billed birds, then the resemblance would be eminently unremarkable. On the other hand, if the question is approached with the premise that the universe was created in a flash of energy, and the existence of life was consequently uncertain, let alone the life of someone with the time to write books and think of renaming parrots as dollowarries, then the whole thing seems mind-blowingly unlikely.

Assessing the improbability of Ralph's fate similarly depends on several key premises. For example, if we know the President, the cabinet, and all of Congress gathered in the same place under threat of nuclear war, and that the food in that place was not to the President's liking, then Ralph's ascendancy seems less implausible than it otherwise might. Furthermore, if we know in advance the undersecretary of commerce has a severe allergy to peanuts and a raccoon lives in his house—instead of these facts being tacked on in such a slapdash manner—then it seems less implausible still. If we know I made the whole thing up, the coincidence seems mundane. This would also be true if we again began from the premise of an omnipotent, predetermining God.

On the other hand, shifting even just a few of these core presumptions can make the scenario seem improbable. For example, if we presume the universe is shrinking at a rapid pace, far more rapidly than anyone has ever imagined, and thus if a twenty-four-year-old were ever going to become president of the United States it would have to happen in the next two years if it were ever going to happen at all, because after that time everyone in the universe will be fused together into a tiny singularity, then the whole thing seems like a fantastic long shot.

24

THEY SAY IT'S YOUR
BIRTHDAY

LIFE RETURNED TO NORMAL after the destruction of Greek Island II more quickly than one might imagine. After a few weeks, the citizens elected a new Congress. Many people did not notice the absence of the old one. Few people had heard of White Sulphur Springs, West Virginia, or the Greenbrier resort. This gave the events a kitschy, surreal quality. Still, the incident created a moment. People understood that the President and the United States had acted arrogantly, squandering an invaluable, historic opportunity. This created political possibility.

Ralph nominated Clarabella Moleman to be vice president. It was time to have a strong advocate for children in the White House, he argued. The new Senate confirmed her unanimously. With mixed feelings, Clarabella resigned the presidency of the East Madison PTA and accepted the position. For the reception following her inauguration, Vice President Moleman baked and served her hand-made brownies. Their superior quality and moistness made her an immediate hit with the new Congress and the press.

At Ralph's urging, Congress passed a comprehensive energy program. The revenue from a new gasoline tax paid for wind farms, home solar panels, and underground repositories for carbon dioxide emissions. A luxury tax on low-fuel-efficiency cars bonded the pur-chase of large chunks of the Amazon rain forest.

Congress funded a new orbital space station, which served a dual mission. It scanned for alien life while broadcasting a message of peace to the universe. It also housed a new astrolab, which stud-ied advanced questions in physics, including quantification of the rate of expansion of the universe.

In memory of Henry Moleman, the shortest-tenured president in history, Congress guaranteed to every American child health care, a college education, and, at President Bailey's strong urging, a stuffed animal. This was, so to speak, his pet project.

THIS RESEMBLES MY OWN legislative agenda, a coincidence for which I offer no apologies. That Ralph feels a persistent sense of duty is integral to the themes of the book, though the people and causes he feels a sense of obligation toward is of no particular significance. Nevertheless, one cannot underestimate the significance of milieu to a story. Though it would have no bearing on the plot, I expect you would feel quite differently about this book if instead of favoring a cleaner environment, universal health care, and the proliferation of stuffed animals, Ralph favored logging in national forests, tax breaks for the wealthy, and the stockpiling of nuclear weapons.

ABROAD, RALPH REPAIRED AMERICA'S damaged relations with its allies. He restored America's prestige in the international community, and earned a personal reputation as a principled voice of moderation. He made a special effort with France, and won over the French prime minister and people with his modesty and earnestness. On his way home, he stopped on the island of Balta, just in time to judge the first-annual Sinclair Lewis Memorial Model Plane and Tile-Grouting Competition. His global efforts produced a period of peace and trust that had no precedent in recent world history. It was the *Pax Bailey*.

But Ralph was not happy. Generally speaking, being president of the United States isn't all it's cracked up to be. Nothing can prepare someone for the complete isolation of the job. If anyone should have been prepared, it was Ralph Bailey, who had experienced the insularity of life in the White House. He worked long days during his tenure of service to the former president, arriving at six A.M. and often not leaving until nine or ten o'clock in the evening. But at least then he went home at the end of the day. He could walk to his apartment in Dupont Circle and feel the evening breeze on his cheek and watch the sunrise the next morning. The presidency, by contrast, confined him to the White House twenty-four hours a day. A team of schedulers arranged his every minute.

Although Ralph had a staff of dozens to attend to his needs, and even to his whims, he was constantly late. On one typical morning he was late for a photo opportunity with the International Sudoku Champion, late to visit with the prime minister of Nauru, late for a fireside chat with Sting about the Amazon rain forest initiative, late for a haircut, late to open the National Chocodile Eating Contest, late to cut the ribbon on the refurbished Mary Todd Lincoln Bedroom, and late to receive the leadership council of the Association of Parent Teacher Associations.

Ralph blamed his lateness on overscheduling, but this was a ruse. Overscheduling could not explain why in the evenings he ate quiet dinners by himself and watched sports on television. This behavior could only be explained by the overwhelming loneliness in Ralph's heart. He never let this on to Jessica in their e-mail exchanges and brief phone calls, lest it make her feel ambivalent about her own experience. Nevertheless, the fact remained that every moment of every day, Ralph missed Jessica more than he could bear.

HALFWAY AROUND THE WORLD, Jessica, in contrast to Ralph, had come to adore her life. She was conspicuously happy at the Tibetan orphanage in the foothills of the Himalayas. She rose early, and in the morning performed physical labor. She chopped wood for the furnace and helped prepare the breakfast of warm bread and lentils. She taught the students English in the mornings and basic mathematics in the afternoons. Later in the day, she and the children played games. After dinner, she helped them wash and change for bed. The work was hard, but the days had a pleasant rhythm to them. The students were respectful, appreciative, and loving. This sustained her.

She had a sense of purpose as never before. Jessica believed that one of the orphans would grow up, free Tibet, and bring peace to the world. She was not sure which one of the orphans it would be, and she loved them all, but she was sure one would, as sure as she had been of anything in her life.

She had no regrets about changing her professional direction. One day, a dispute between the orphanage and a neighboring farm over the ownership of a wandering cow reminded her of law school. She thought about the hours spent studying contracts and the aspirations of being an attorney, and thought to herself: How did I ever?

The only thing she missed about her old life was Ralph, whom she missed dearly. She wished he was with her and knew he would adore sharing the life she had created for herself, but she understood that he was finding his own way as best he could. She was furthermore quietly and completely confident—though she had no basis to believe this—that things would work out for the best between them and that one day, soon enough, they would be together.

This was all a matter of perspective, of course. One could just as easily view tending to Tibetan orphans as tedium and being president of the United States at the impossibly young age of twenty-four as a dream come true. It could just as easily have been Jessica feeling trapped in the Himalayas, pining away in wretched isolation, while Ralph soaked up the unique experience of governing the United States, with its abundant opportunities for travel and easy access to ice cream and fine pasta, and missing Jess, but accepting that she was finding herself and possessing the quiet confidence that someday they would be together. This could be true, but it was not. She was happy and he was sad.

HALFWAY ACROSS THE UNIVERSE, Ned could see all this. As part of his new assignment, Ned kept an eye on several planets with whom the Rigelians had made first contact. Ned kept a special eye on Earth, both because of how badly things had ended, and because of the special place Ralph had earned in his heart. Few people had touched Ned as Ralph had.

Ned was happy in his own new life. He had more time to spend at home and did not miss the travel one bit. He spent time with

Todd. As his relationship with his son blossomed, he thought back to all those months on the road and wondered to himself: How did I ever? But the developments on Earth troubled Ned deeply. Ralph's public comments and photographs might have seemed normal to an ordinary person. Ralph's impressive accomplishments would have created in the average citizen's mind an image of quiet confidence and competence. But Ned's discerning eye saw something else: a young man in despair. He began to lose sleep, sometimes tossing and turning in bed for hours. He could not bear to see Ralph like this.

Maude, in turn, could not bear to see her husband so distraught. One day over peanut butter sandwiches and Dr Pepper she said, "Instead of sulking around all the time, why don't you do something about the situation?" And so Ned did. The matter was not within his official purview. His office monitored the statistical metrics that correlated with the health of a planet and its people. These metrics were improving for Earth thanks to Ralph's efforts. Nevertheless, in his official report to the Ambassador, Ned included a surveillance photograph of the president of the United States, dressed incognito, with a baseball cap pulled down over his face, trailed by undercover Secret Service agents, wandering the streets of Chinatown in the evening, with what were, unmistakably, tears in his eyes.

THE AMBASSADOR HAD HIS own problems. He was absorbed in his next project, a vexing first contact with a species resembling bunny rabbits. They were highly intelligent creatures, with a rich literary tradition. Unfortunately, when they were not reading and writing they were generally either eating or having sex. Overgrazing and overpopulation threatened their survival with Malthusian viciousness. This was the impetus for first contact.

The problem was that the rabbit creatures were unwilling to respond to the problem because of a peculiar spiritual conviction: they believed the universe was filled with disembodied rabbit souls waiting patiently for a corporeal home, and that each had equal moral standing to a living, breathing physical vessel. Of course they did not think of these as "rabbit souls" since they did not think of themselves as rabbits. It was a sticky situation, and occupied much of the Ambassador's waking thoughts.

Still, he thought often of Earth. Ordinarily, only one or two things from a mission made a lasting impression on the Ambassador.

In the case of Earth, he had expected this would be his complete set of DVDs of *Chappelle's Show*. But the Ambassador could not get Ralph, the young president of the United States, off his mind. He had the nagging feeling he and Ned had done wrong by Ralph. He wondered whether their desire to better the fate of the planet, to do right by the many, had led them to ignore the needs of the individual. Ned's report confirmed his intuition, and he called Ned immediately. It was also a good excuse to speak with his friend, whom he missed dearly.

"Hello, Ned," he said.

"Hello, Mr. Ambassador. I am glad you called."

"How are you, Ned? How is Todd doing in school?"

"Much better, thank you. We made a deal. Todd is going to finish his traditional education, but he is also taking art classes in the afternoon. If he is still interested in art when he graduates, Maude and I have agreed to send him to the Rigelian Institute for the Study of Design."

"I thought you called art school a den of sex and drugs."

"We all evolve. You know that better than anyone else."

"Perhaps. And Maude?"

"She is just fine, thanks—gardening up a storm. And you, Mr. Ambassador? How are you?"

"I have my hands full."

Ned said, "I have been following your current situation. It is quite tricky. Is there something I can do to help?"

"There is no one I would rather have by my side, Ned, but that's not what I am calling about."

"What is it then?"

"I'm calling about Earth. I think we may have gotten something seriously wrong."

"The use of violence was regrettable."

"I don't mean that. The incident was indeed regrettable, but also unavoidable. Furthermore, I don't believe it will be a barrier to good relations with Earth in the future. It's Ralph who concerns me. I saw the photograph. I am worried about him."

"I was hoping you would say that, sir. Obviously I have had the same thought."

"I read your report, Ned. The planet's progress is substantial. And much of it is due directly to him."

"This is true, sir. Several of his initiatives have reduced the risk profile of Earth substantially."

"But he is miserable," said the Ambassador.

"This is also undeniably true, sir."

"This is tricky, Ned. We have no guarantee someone else would be able to step in and continue the progress Ralph has made. The peace is fragile, the commitment to the environment equally so. The metrics could easily turn negative again without Ralph's leadership. All of our policies say to leave the situation as is. We need to turn a blind eye to his personal suffering because of his substantial talents."

"Nevertheless, sir, this doesn't feel like the right course of action."

"Against my best professional judgment, I agree," the Ambassador said quietly. "Do you think we can fix it?" he asked.

"I do, sir. I think I have the perfect idea. Tomorrow is Ralph's birthday as it turns out."

"I see where you're going, Ned. The timing couldn't be better."

"Yes, sir."

The Ambassador paused for a moment. "Do you think we're getting soft in our old age, Ned?" he asked reflectively.

"No, sir," said Ned. "The truth is you have been soft all along, and I mean that as the highest possible compliment."

"Thank you, Ned. It'll be good to be in action together again."

"Thank you, Mr. Ambassador. The honor is entirely mine."

ON THE EVE OF his birthday, Ralph slept on the floor of the Oval Office. Prior to becoming president, Ralph had no trouble sleeping. Now he suffered from regular bouts of insomnia. On bad nights, Ralph carried a pillow and blanket down to the Oval Office and slept in the spot where he and Jessica had first picnicked together. He cradled his birthday gift from Jessica, a stuffed animal from Tibet: the Dalia Llama. Into the Llama's hump had been stitched the words, "I love you."

In the morning, Ralph woke early. The sunrise reminded him of the last bittersweet moments he and Jessica had spent together. On the eve of her departure, they celebrated in their favorite manner: by eating Chinese food off paper plates on the floor of the Oval Office. The following morning, over a breakfast of egg rolls, Jessica made one final effort at convincing Ralph to join her in Tibet.

"You have already done so much good as president," she said. "If you leave, no one could undo what you have accomplished. And think of all the good we could do together in Tibet. The Tibetans are in such need. To have the former president of the United States take up residence would make the most dramatic statement on their behalf. Most important, we would be together. We could take hikes, learn to make prayer flags, and drink yak butter tea. Think of how romantic it would be to be young, in love, and literally on the top of the world."

Jessica didn't need to say anything to tempt Ralph. Their several months living together in the White House, while Jessica waited for her visa to come through, had solidified Ralph's conviction in her. He found her more beautiful than ever, though he thought her the most beautiful woman in the world to begin with. He looked forward to their conversations. And he knew her to be the best human being he had ever met.

"Can't you wait?" Ralph asked.

"My flight is in three hours. And you know I hate traffic."

"I don't just mean a few hours. I mean can't you wait a long while, until after I'm finished being president. Then I can go with you without any sense of obligation."

"There are always obligations," she said. "I want to see the world and I want to see it now."

"What's the rush?" Ralph pleaded. "We're young. Tibet will still be there in a few years. There will still be children who will need our help. There's plenty of time."

"I don't think so," Jessica said softly, caressing Ralph's hair in the morning sun streaming in through the east-facing windows. "I love you. You have a heart the size of a Himalayan mountain. I shall think about you every day and write as often as I can. But I think it's later than you think."

Then, warmly and gently, she kissed him good-bye.

Now, on the dawn of his twenty-fifth birthday, Ralph wondered again why he had declined Jessica's invitation, and why he could not accept it now. Why did he feel such a sense of obligation to the nation and to the work he had started? It was not as if the honeymoon would go on forever. Many congressmen already were showing signs of succumbing to irresistible temptations: sumptuous dinners, luxury automobiles, high-level meetings in the Champagne Room of the

Capital City Playhouse Club. Soon politics would return to business as usual. And then this sacrifice would have been for nothing.

On the floor of the Oval Office, Ralph quietly cried. Why, he wondered, could he not bring himself to do what he wanted to do?

ALL IN ALL, PRESIDENTS get a raw deal when it comes to birthdays. Everyone thinks otherwise because of JFK. During Kennedy's forty-fifth birthday celebration, at Madison Square Garden, Marilyn Monroe sang him "Happy Birthday" wearing a flesh-colored dress with 2,500 rhinestones, so tight-fitting she literally had to be sewn into the dress. Afterward, JFK said, "I can now retire from politics."

Most of the other presidents didn't get it so good.

Truman's sixty-first birthday came on V-E Day, which was nice enough, but in all the commotion no one remembered to tend to the cake, and Truman ended up celebrating with peanut butter and crackers.

Eisenhower had his sixty-third birthday party at the Hershey Sports Arena, home of the Hershey Bears of the American Hockey League. He listened to some local marching bands, ate a fried-chicken box lunch, and tried one of the eight hundred cakes baked by local women for the occasion. The cake was pretty good, so good Mamie later invited the chef to Washington for tea. But there were no gifts, sadly. The sole and saving grace was that after the celebration Eisenhower got to ride the Zamboni.

Nixon's birthdays were even more low-key. He spent his last birthday in the White House, in 1973, alone with Pat, eating pot roast and listening to Engelbert Humperdinck records on the turntable. For the occasion, Kissinger gave Nixon a paperweight. This is the sort of gift that really makes a statement.

RALPH DRAGGED THROUGH THE rest of the morning. At noon, Ralph ritualistically took the mail from Mrs. Dundersinger. The routine used to be going for a sandwich, now it was leafing through the daily post. It was the only thing that anchored him to a normal existence.

In peacetime, mail is delivered to the White House, like any other office or residence, by a postman, the contents secured in a bundle by a thick rubber band. On summer days, the mailman stops to chat, and sometimes is invited in for a cool glass of lemonade. His deliveries consist mostly of catalogs, which have been a guilty pleasure of every inhabitant of the Oval Office since Coolidge. After the stress of tending to the weightiest matters of state all day, nothing is better to help one unwind than the latest brochure from Hammacher Schlemmer. Ford once ordered, and really liked, those bead things that go over the back of a car seat.

This day it was the usual: Ralph's cell phone bill, his student loan statement, an offer to consolidate his student loans for which he was in fact not eligible, a copy of *Men's Health* magazine, an offer from a real-estate broker for a free appraisal of his property. He almost did not see it between the time-share invitation and the new Pottery Barn catalog: a birthday card that warmed his heart. The card depicted a sweet scene from *Peanuts*. Snoopy was asleep on his doghouse and Woodstock was asleep on Snoopy's belly. Snoopy was dreaming of playing with Woodstock and Woodstock was dreaming of playing with Snoopy.

"Mr. President," it said. "It's time to catch up. The Ambassador and I miss you."

Signed: "Your friend, Ned."

25

WE ARE ALL MADE
OF STARS

THE FOLLOWING SUNDAY MORNING, a chilly winter day, Ralph donned a sweatshirt and jeans and enjoyed the long walk to Prospect Street in Georgetown. Without the suit and tie, and with his baseball cap turned backward, most people did not recognize the president of the United States. He looked more or less like every other college student in Washington.

On this walk, he went without Secret Service protection. Ralph understood, without Ned's saying so, the meeting needed to be kept low-key. This took some doing. Ralph explained to the Secret Service that he would not require their protection at brunch. They could inspect the restaurant the evening before, but they were not to accompany him to the meal. The agents protested vigorously, but Ralph said the matter was not open for debate. Besides, he assured the agents, his safety could never be less in doubt.

At the Peacock Cafe, Ralph found that his friends had already arrived. Ned was casually dressed much as he had been on their first meeting, in an Arcade Fire T-shirt, an unbuttoned blue oxford shirt, and khaki pants. The Ambassador wore baggy jeans, a FUBU sweatshirt, a doo-rag, and a series of chains and necklaces, which could only be characterized as bling.

Ralph said, "Hello, Ned. Hello, Mr. Ambassador."

"Hello, Ralph," Ned said.

"Yo, yo, yo, Rigel-Rigel in da hizzy," said the Ambassador. He placed his right fist upon his heart and tilted his right shoulder forward in an apparent effort to thump the chest of the president of the United States.

Ralph thumped then looked quizzically to Ned.

"The Ambassador has just discovered the wonders of Dave Chappelle," Ned said. "He is also quite a fan of *The Ali G Show*."

"*Da Ali G Show*," the Ambassador corrected. "Da brother is a genius, word."

"So that's where we are," Ned said.

THE AMBASSADOR LIKES MANY of the same things I like, a coincidence for which I offer no apologies. That the Ambassador finds humor in unlikely situations is integral to the themes of the book, though the people and things he finds funny are of no particular significance. Nevertheless, one cannot underestimate the significance of milieu to a story. Though it would have no bearing on the plot, I expect you would feel quite differently about this book if instead of favoring Woody Allen, Dave Chappelle, and Sasha Baron Cohen, the Ambassador admired Rita Rudner, Carrot Top, and Gallagher.

A WAITRESS ARRIVED AT the table. Ned ordered the multigrain waffle with fruit compote, the Ambassador ordered a bagel with cream cheese, and Ralph ordered the French toast, which he had heard was very good. All three ordered coffee. The waitress appeared nonplussed by the Ambassador's outfit.

Ned said, "We came back because we wanted to see how you are and because we wanted to apologize."

The Ambassador nodded. "My bad on the missile thang," he said. "A'ight?"

"You don't need to apologize for anything," Ralph said. "My

country attacked your planet without any provocation. You reached out to us in friendship and we responded with violence. If anyone owes an apology it is we who owe one to you. On behalf of all of Earth, I am truly sorry. I hope you can accept this."

"F'shizzle, my nizzle."

"Can't he speak normally?" Ralph asked Ned.

Ned shrugged.

"You see, that's prejudice," said the Ambassador. "There was nothing abnormal about the manner in which I was speaking. No *correct* way of speaking exists. People think because they do things in a particular manner this invests their approach with some cosmic significance. I hate to break the news to you, but it's all arbitrary."

"You're right," Ralph said. "I'm sorry."

"It's all cool, G," said the Ambassador.

The waitress delivered the waffle, bagel, French toast, and three cups of coffee.

"You are kind to be forgiving, but we really are sorry," said the Ambassador. "We don't like to kill anything for any reason, and your attack was no threat to our planet at all. Unfortunately, the missile your ship launched activated an ancient and automatic defense system. Anytime someone uses violence on or against Rigel-Rigel, the system generates a proportional response. It enforces precisely the appropriate punishment."

"You explained this," said Ralph.

The Ambassador waved his hand. "It was just a bluff," he said. "Our planet hasn't been attacked in ages. The threat of retaliation has always been enough. We haven't even had a crime on Rigel-Rigel in seven hundred years. I didn't know the system was still operational. Unfortunately it was active, your ship triggered it, and the system calculated a proportionate response. After that, everything was automatic. There was nothing we could do to stop it."

Ralph considered the Ambassador's words. "What do you mean the system calculated a proportional response?" he asked.

"The computer determines the exact amount of punishment an offender deserves," the Ambassador replied. "It then administers that precise penalty, no more and no less."

"How could any computer do that?" Ralph asked. "Suppose three men each steal a loaf of bread. One steals the loaf to feed his family but the family is a bit on the chunky side and could stand to lose a few pounds, the second steals it because he was orphaned as a child and no one taught him proper values, and the third steals it to send to starving people in Africa, but he's a kleptomaniac and also gets a thrill from lifting the bread. How could a computer determine what each one of these people deserves?"

"This one could," said the Ambassador. "The software is very advanced."

NED CHANGED THE SUBJECT. "It appears you have been doing quite well as president," he said to Ralph. "We have been keeping an eye on you."

"I'm doing the best job I can."

"Well, it is a superb job. Many of the things you have accomplished have lowered your planet's risk profile substantially. The environmental initiatives are very significant."

Ralph waved his hand. "Who knows whether they will last?" he said. "It could all be undone tomorrow."

"You don't seem very optimistic," Ned said. "You should be happy. You're the president of the United States, after all."

"You da man," said the Ambassador.

Ralph smiled but said nothing.

"We're worried about you," said Ned. "That's the real reason we're here. It's obvious to us that something is wrong. What is it? Is it Jessica?"

Ralph sighed and took a bite of the French toast. It was conspicuously good French toast. He quickly took another bite and then a third. It occurred to Ralph that it might have been days since he last ate.

"It is Jessica," Ralph said. "She has gone off to Tibet, and I am here in Washington. I miss her more than I can bear."

"So why don't you go and be with her?" asked the Ambassador.

Ralph considered the question as he devoured more of his breakfast. "The truth is I don't know," he said, looking up. "Sometimes I feel as if I am not in control. It's as if I am a character in a play. Some writer has scripted out the course of my life and I am just being put through the motions."

"And you find that depressing?" the Ambassador asked.

"Yes," Ralph said. "Wouldn't you?"

"One could find it depressing. Or one could enjoy the performance and find the humor and beauty in it. It's really a matter of personal preference."

"But how could you enjoy it if it had all been scripted, if even the fact of your enjoyment had been determined in advance?"

"I suppose it's a question of how seriously one takes one's own importance," the Ambassador said. "Besides, why are you so convinced it has all been predetermined?"

"What's the chance of all this happening?" Ralph asked. "What's the chance everyone in the chain of succession would be killed except for two people, and one of these two would die of a peanut allergy and the other, a twenty-four-year-old, would become president of the United States? And what's the chance that young man would be me? Seriously, what are the odds?"

"I suppose it depends how you look at it," the Ambassador said. "Things often seem quite improbable when examined after the fact. But one must remember that *something* has to happen."

Ralph nodded.

"Don't make too much of the fact this something happened to you. Whatever the chance of a twenty-four-year-old becoming president of the United States may be, it is no greater or less because it turned out to be Ralph Bailey. You humans make this mistake all the time. You're so invested in your individual and collective uniqueness. Imagine believing that in a universe of infinite proportions, life exists on Earth and nowhere else. No one should take themselves so seriously. I certainly don't."

WHILE THE AMBASSADOR DISCOURSED, Ralph continued ravenously devouring his breakfast. He neither knew nor could have known that the Peacock Cafe chef got his start many years earlier cooking breakfast on Amtrak trains. Furthermore, while Ralph could have recognized it as the best French toast he had ever eaten, he neither knew nor could have known it was the best he would ever eat. He just knew it was excellent French toast.

TAKING A BREATHER, RALPH looked up from his breakfast toward the Ambassador.

"May I ask you a question?"

"Anything," the Ambassador said. "Shoot."

"Do you have some more of that Bundt cake?"

"Why do you ask?"

"I'm not sure how to put this," Ralph said, massaging his chin. "After eating that cake, I experienced what I can only call a moment of clarity. All of these things that used to be so important suddenly seemed trivial. Career. Money. In that moment, I had no regard for what other people thought about me. I didn't even see 'me' as having any special significance. I just felt like part of the universe—totally at peace. It was wonderful.

"And then we drank the punch and everything went back to normal. Politics mattered again, as did acting responsibly toward others. Now I feel completely removed from that clear-minded state. The woman I love is in Tibet working in an orphanage, and all I want to do is be there with her. But I feel compelled to stay here in Washington and fulfill the duties of my office. So do you have any more of that cake?"

The Ambassador appeared rather sheepish at this point. He fidgeted in his seat and swiped the cream cheese back and forth across his bagel. He turned to Ned to offer an answer to Ralph's question.

"It's funny you should ask," Ned said. "As it turns out, we had a bit of a mix-up with the cake and the punch. By mistake, I took the wrong punch mix. The altered substance ended up being served at my wife's PTA meeting."

"So we drank what?"

"Regular fruit punch. And we're pretty sure you got the wrong cake too. My wife baked two, one for the presidential dinner and one for her Mah-Jongg game. The night before I left for Earth she set them both out on the kitchen counter. The one for the President had a big sign on it that said in capital letters:

GENETICALLY MODIFIED BUNDT

"But we've been having trouble with lockernobbles in the house. One of them got into the kitchen at night and knocked the sign off. It's fifty-fifty whether I took the right one."

"What's a lockernobble?" Ralph asked.

"It's a cute but pesky creature," Ned said. "More or less like a raccoon."

"They're almost impossible to get rid of," the Ambassador added.

"Once you get one in your house, it's there for life. One time my neighbor got one in his attic. He didn't want to kill it, so he trapped it and flew it by spaceship to a planet more than fifty light-years away. Darn thing was back in his attic three days later."

"I DON'T UNDERSTAND," RALPH said. "More than thirty people were at that dinner. Everyone I spoke with reported a similar experience to mine. They ate the cake and experienced a moment of lucidity. Then they drank the punch and everything went back to normal."

"That's remarkable," said the Ambassador.

"Surely it means we ate the altered cake and drank the right punch."

"Perhaps, though not necessarily."

"You mean to tell me thirty people ate the same thing and had the same exact exprience and it was nothing more than a coincidence?"

"Maybe," the Ambassador said. "Coincidences happen all the time. I told you before, Ralph, lots of things happen in the universe. Coincidences are inevitable."

"But this—"

"Would be extraordinary, which is why we're discussing it, but that doesn't prove it is anything more than a coincidence. Let me give you an example. You're wearing blue jeans, aren't you?"

"Yes."

"So am I," the Ambassador said. "That's a coincidence and it has now been duly noted. What has not been noted is the many differences in our appearances. You, for example, Mr. President, are not wearing a doo-rag or any bling, so we are not similar in these regards. But these facts have not been commented upon."

"I suppose," Ralph said.

"Besides," the Ambassador said, "the cake didn't seem to have much of an impact on the President."

"That's true," Ralph said. "But suppose you're wrong and this wasn't all a series of coincidences. Suppose it wasn't just random luck that thirty people experienced the same exact transformation at the same exact moment. And suppose it isn't chance that not just any twenty-four-year-old became president, but me in particular. You make this whole big deal about disbelieving in God. Wouldn't this force you to reexamine your own beliefs? Wouldn't it compel you to believe?"

The Ambassador smiled. "I never said we disbelieved the existence of God."

"But at the state dinner you told the president you didn't believe."

"Not believing and disbelieving are two different things," the Ambassador said. "What I tried to convey to the President is that an excess of conviction can be detrimental to the long-term welfare of a species. We don't happen to be religious, but we are respectful of all beliefs. More important, we are open to the infinite array of possibilities. Depending upon how one defines god, there may be many gods with many different powers. The universe is a big place. For all we know someone really is scripting the entire story. We just don't worry about it."

"You don't worry about it?" Ralph asked incredulously.

"It would be pretty funny," the Ambassador said. "Imagine these people, we'll call them missionaries, were reaching out to a new alien species whose planet was in jeopardy. To impress upon them the error—or danger—of their ways, they bring a substance—in the form of a cake—that can alter the aliens' state of mind. Only at the last minute one of the missionaries takes the wrong cake and the right one ends up going to his wife's Mah-Jongg game." The Ambassador howled. "That is rich," he said. "One can't make that stuff up."

"Vonnegut could—or Woody Allen."

"Yes," the Ambassador said, pointing to Ralph in a gesture of affirmation. "Perhaps Mr. Allen is God. If he is, I hope it's the younger, funny Woody Allen and not, you know, the *Interiors* guy."

The Ambassador continued laughing for a while before he wound down, finally saying, "That's a good one."

"How can you laugh?" Ralph asked. "Doesn't any of this worry you?"

The Ambassador composed himself. "No," he said. "It's best to just try and find the humor in it."

"So if it's all coincidence, that's fine," Ralph said. "And if it is all preordained, and we're just objects, then that's fine too."

"Yes," the Ambassador said soothingly. "Like I said, you cannot take yourself too seriously. You need to be able, every so often, to step outside of the situation and appreciate it from an objective standpoint without fixating on your place in the whole thing. Otherwise, life is misery."

"Besides," the Ambassador said, "we're probably not objects or characters in a story. The coincidences aren't that remarkable. You must remember each of us ultimately comes from the same place. In the end, we are all just made of stars."

RALPH SAT FOR A good while considering the Ambassador's words, watching as the Ambassador schmeared his bagel, now with verve. Finally, he turned to Ned and asked, "What happened at the Mah-Jongg game where they served the other Bundt cake?"

"Nothing too unusual," Ned replied. "Although my wife did report greater than normal enthusiasm for the new cards."

"How is she? Has she recovered from the car accident?"

"She is fine," Ned said. "And you are kind to ask. It turns out the man she struck was a charlatan. He would set up situations in which people would rear-end him. Then he would collect on their insurance policies."

"That's terrible. Jessica was just in a car accident too. She rear-ended someone," Ralph said, looking toward the Ambassador in challenge. "Isn't that a strange coincidence?"

"I don't know," Ned said. "There are lots of car accidents."

"Still, it is always a very upsetting experience."

"To say the least," Ned said. "But in this instance some good came out of it. My wife had extra time and worked through some things with our son. I have restructured my professional life so I can spend more time at home. I am no longer with the First Contact division. I do follow-up work now. This is the first time I have been on the road in the past several months."

"That is good to hear," Ralph said.

"Enough about me. We're worried about you. Are you going to be okay?"

"I don't know," Ralph said. "My brain tells me everything that happens in Washington matters. My heart tells me that Jessica is the only thing that matters. I guess we'll have to see which one wins out."

"I sympathize," Ned said. "Looking back on it, I'm not sure what enabled me to muster up the courage to change my own situation."

"But you did," Ralph said, "and that's all that matters."

Ned smiled. "You'll do whatever is right for you."

"I'm not so sure," Ralph said.

"Well, we are," said Ned. "You're a good person. The Ambassador and I meet all kinds. You are one of our favorites."

The Ambassador nodded in agreement

"F'shizzle," he said.

RALPH PICKED UP THE check and the party rose to say farewell.

"Mr. President," the Ambassador said, "you have our lasting pledge of assistance whenever you require it. We are sorry things got off on the wrong foot and hopeful that someday our planets can start a relationship anew. We believe we will be great friends, when the time is right."

Ralph said, "I believe that will be very, very soon."

"It would be our pleasure," said the Ambassador.

"Tell me something before you go, Mr. Ambassador. What should I take from this conversation? Do you have any advice for me?"

The Ambassador rubbed his chin.

"I have one tidbit to offer," he said. "It won't sound like much, maybe even trite, but it really is profound if you think about it."

"Please," Ralph said.

"It's this," the Ambassador said. "You should eat more slowly."

AS THEY WALKED DOWN K Street, Ralph believed this advice would be the Ambassador's peculiar epitomb, but the Ambassador was a man of surprises. He extended a small package toward Ralph. "We got you something for your birthday," he said.

Ralph accepted it. "Thanks," he said.

"Tell me, Ralph, what do you have in your pocket?" the Ambassador asked.

Ralph produced a key chain from the Chinese restaurant Eat Here Now, where he had gone with Jessica on their second date.

"Funny," said the Ambassador as he produced from his pocket an identical key chain. "Quite good food," he said. "Excellent egg roll."

Then the Ambassador turned and waved and uttered his true epitomb, at least with respect to his relationship with Ralph: "Peace out."

BACK AT THE WHITE House, the package was put through security despite Ralph's protestations that such measures were unnecessary. The package was tested for explosive materials, viruses and other biological threats, illegal plant and animal content, narcotics, forbidden Chinese exports, and finally determined to be safe. Then it was placed on the Resolute with the daily collection of catalogs and credit card offers.

Ralph thereafter opened the box and found it contained a small slice of Bundt cake, preserved in plastic wrap. The package also contained a greeting card, on the cover of which was a pencil sketch of a parrot. Inside the card was a note, in what Ralph knew to be Ned's handwriting. It contained a simple message. It said,

Mr. President,
Be Happy.

Ralph began eating immediately, slowly, savoring every bite.

26

COME TOGETHER,
RIGHT NOW

JUMPING AHEAD A BIT, in the moments before the universe collapses, a buffet dinner is held where people from all over the universe come together and find they are connected in random ways. For example, Sting and Gordon Lightfoot discover they have each spent a fair amount of time thinking about their names and the influence they have had upon their respective careers.

Over shrimp cocktails, I and the insouciant two-year-old who eviscerated my work meet and discover we both enjoy a card game called Oh Hell! We put aside our differences and sit down for a match. The game is tense. The boy trumps me at an inopportune moment and I consider banishing him to another recursion. He is spared only by the timely arrival of Kurt Vonnegut, carrying a miniature spanakopita. Vonnegut enjoys Oh Hell!, we learn, and asks if he can join us. We are only too happy.

"Here is a man who knows how to write," the boy says.

I wholeheartedly agree.

Vonnegut crushes us.

The President reconnects with his father. Each has been existing for some time as spiritual energy in a domain of the universe referred to as Boca. The rabbit creatures had it right, as it turns out. Souls exist before birth and after death and are, with the exception of telemarketers, all worthy of being treated with respect. Boca is one of several repositories of disembodied souls. It is a big place, though, with no public transportation to speak of, and until this moment the President and his father have not met in the afterlife. Over hot hors d'oeuvres, they discover they share many interests, including fly-fishing and tennis and a taste for egg rolls. The father says he is sorry for not having been more loving and attentive. The son accepts his apology.

Together they meet their god, who has elbowed his way toward the spicy mustard, into which he dips his cocktail wiener. He is "retired" too and also living in Boca, though in the swankier Jewish section, which explains why none of them have crossed paths before. They chat for a while. The former god, who goes by the name of Howie, finds it ironic that they have been worshiping him. He does not consider himself special, as he has something of a self-esteem problem, which comes from being an only child with an absent mother and an authoritarian father.

Many people from many different parts of the universe meet their gods and have similar experiences, experiences that might, under different circumstances, be characterized as disillusioning.

Nelson Munt-Zoldarian, placed for adoption as a young child, discovers he has a brother who is an executive for an insurance company, in charge of the fraud abatement division. The siblings share a taste for the onion tart, of which I too am fond.

Professor Fendle-Frinkle meets Albert Einstein over a tray of miniature quiches. Neither is interested in talking about physics. Instead they spend most of the time talking about baseball. They agree this could finally be the Cubs' year.

Helen Argo-Lipschutzian and Clarabella Moleman meet at the crudités and compare notes about PTAs. Each agrees that, as institutions go, they could stand improvement.

David Prince meets Millard Fillmore at the sushi station. He is everything David had imagined, and more.

Hanukapi Puli offers Joe Quimble a Chocodile. Taking a bite, Quimble wonders to himself, "How did I miss these?"

Everyone enjoys the macaroni and cheese, pleasing Stanley Smithers of the Kraft Corporation to no end. Lucian Trundle is gratified most of all to see the food is being eaten off the Eisenhower base plates. Eisenhower, clad in running shorts and a singlet, pauses from his jog to look at an empty plate in Trundle's hands.

"Excellent likeness," he says, and then is off, faster than light.

At the bar, Armando Tanzarian meets Claude Eatherly, who is getting himself a Dr Pepper, and they compare notes about launching atomic weapons.

"Were you ever able to make sense of it all?" Tanzarian asks.

"No," says Eatherly, looking out the window at the abundant sunshine. "But it looks like it is going to be a very fine day tomorrow."

"Very fine indeed," Tanzarian agrees.

In the background, the Heavy Shtetl Klezmer Band performs. For the final set, Chaim Muscovitz calls the President to sit in. The President protests, saying he does not know how to play the accordion, but Muscovitz is reassuring. "It's inside you," he says. When the band gets going, the President finds, to his amazement, that he is more than able to keep up. Chaim Muscovitz nods enthusiastically. "See," he says. "You can really swing." Later Sting joins in on the clarinet. Then Andy Summers takes up the *groyse fidl*, Stewart Copeland the *poyk*, and Lennon the hammer dulcimer. Paul McCartney sings in the strong and sweet voice of his youth. It is a jam session for the ages, and everyone, sharing the love of the music, dances in jubilation, reveling in their connectedness. There are many, many connections—more connections than the mind can conceive—more connections than there are stars in the sky or all of the money in the universe taken in pennies.

Many of these connections make no sense at all.

Some are ironic.

Some are sad.

Some are funny.

Some manifest evidence of universal justice.

Most do not.

BACK IN THE PRESENT, or the then-present, the buffet to end all buffets is still in the future. At the moment, President Bailey is onboard Air

Force One en route to Tibet. With him are Vice President Clarabella Moleman and His Eminence the Dalai Lama. The staff is on edge. President Bailey has not told them why they are going to Tibet. Only Vice President Moleman knows. He has not told his chief of staff or the Dalai Lama or even Jessica. She has heard on Voice of America that the president of the United States is flying to Tibet. She is excited, of course, but also nervous something is wrong, and rushes to the airport.

Everyone around the president is fretful, but Ralph is at peace. He is staring out the window of the plane at the Himalayas, piercing the clouds. At this height the air is richly blue and crystal clear. Virginal snow covers the soaring peaks. It is the most magnificent sight Ralph has ever seen. He calls the cockpit and asks the pilot to circle the mountains again. In the adjacent seat, the Dalai Lama smiles.

"It is enough to make one believe in God," the Lama says. "He does so many horrible things, but then he also does this."

Ralph nods.

After its second orbit, the plane descends into Lhasa Airport and lands. Though this is not an official state visit, the vice premier of China and the governor of Tibet are on hand, together with an honor guard of hundreds. They have gifts for President Bailey, which have been arrayed in an elaborate and colorful display. Ralph ignores them. He descends the stairs, walks directly to Jessica, and gives her a long and passionate kiss.

He gestures for the Dalai Lama to step out of the plane. The Chinese gasp. The Dalai Lama has not set foot on the soil of his home in forty years. He slowly walks down from Air Force One, setting foot on the tarmac, which is not soil, but rather a composite of tar, concrete, and resin. All the same, the Dalai Lama begins to weep quietly. The Chinese are visibly uncomfortable.

President Bailey speaks without a microphone, but everyone hears. "I am resigning the presidency of the United States as of this moment. My intention is to live here in Tibet for the foreseeable future. I am very grateful that you have made me and my good friend the Dalai Lama so welcome. I am sure he looks very much forward, as do I, to living here in peace and with freedom."

Ralph turns then and offers a handshake and a hug to the new president. In the excitement of the moment no one notices the his-

tory being made in that transfer of power from the first president to
break one barrier to the first president to break another.

"Good luck, Madame President," he says.

"Good luck, Mr. President," she says.

"Please make sure to implement my last executive order."

"Of course I shall." She says the words warmly and Ralph knows
it will be done.

RALPH PUTS HIS ARM around Jessica. "So which way to that orphanage of yours?"

They walk slowly out of the airport and through the dusty streets
of Lhasa. It is a long walk to the orphanage, but they have nothing
but time.

"Will you miss it?" Jessica asks.

"Not at all," Ralph said.

"Nothing?"

"I got to meet Sting," he says. "That was pretty cool. And I
played golf with Arnold Palmer. I think that was the highlight."

"But you don't play golf."

"We played mini golf and went for hot dogs. He's a great guy."

Jessica smiled.

"So what was that last executive order you mentioned?"

"We're giving a stuffed animal to every child in the world—that
and two hot meals a day for every hungry man, woman, and child."

"Can you do that?"

"What are they going to do—kick me out of office?"

Jessica felt pride and love in such abundance that she thought
she might burst. She had only one question.

"Why?" she asked.

"Because I wanted to be with you," Ralph said.

"I mean why now?"

"I just thought the time was right."

"What time is that?"

"Now."

IN MANHATTAN, KANSAS, MARGARET Stoopler puts down her book.
She is obsessing about the passage describing the historic transfer
of power. "I understand that Mrs. Moleman was the first woman
president. But what was historic about Ralph's presidency? I figured

it was just that he was the first president under thirty-five. But maybe he was black or Latino? Why did I even presume he was white in the first place? His physical appearance was never described. And, besides, the president's attaché on *The West Wing* was black. It's very upsetting. You'd think the author would have had the decency to say something earlier."

She does not realize she has been speaking aloud.

Not looking up from his Sudoku puzzle, Allan Stoopler asks, "What are you reading?" He appears to have no recollection of ever having discussed the book before.

Margaret explains, "A book that is making a surprising commentary on race."

"Is it *Tom Sawyer*?"

Margaret is momentarily confused. "I think perhaps you mean *Huckleberry Finn*."

"Right. I have always wanted to read *Huckleberry Finn*. Do you like it? Is it good?"

Margaret thinks about this question long and hard.

"Yes," she says. "It is quite good."

ON RIGEL-RIGEL, TODD ANAT-DENARIAN is in physics class. As is often the case during physics, he is staring out the window and daydreaming. His inattentiveness is exacerbated by the presence of a dollowarrie on the sill and the beauty of the day. It is not merely a beautiful day, but a magnificent, splendiferous, refulgent, top-ten-in-the-history-of-the-universe type day. If people knew what it was like, they would flock from all over the galaxy to bask in the abundant sunshine of this Rigelian springtime miracle.

It is rare to see a dollowarrie at this time of year and Todd thinks that he would like to sketch it. He could do this from his seat, of course, but he has gotten in trouble for this before, and in any event would like to draw it while sitting outside so he could enjoy the gorgeous weather. Achieving this, however, seems grossly impractical. Professor Fendle-Frinkle is lecturing about his new approach to solving multidimensional matrices, a revolutionary technique with applications to solving certain sticky problems in interdimensional matter transport and complex Sudoku puzzles. The Professor seems to be quite absorbed in the subject matter, as he often is. One doesn't just blurt out that a teacher should end class, but Todd is gripped by an irresistible sense of urgency: he must sketch this bird and enjoy this day.

He raises his hand. The Professor is surprised since Todd rarely participates in classroom discussions.

"Yes?"

Todd starts timidly. "I was wondering," he says, "since it is such a beautiful day outside, really an extraordinary day, whether we might conduct the remainder of class outside or perhaps, though I hesitate to suggest this given the importance of the subject matter of this lecture, end class a few minutes early so we might enjoy a few hours of this precious, dare I say, once-in-a-lifetime type afternoon."

As soon as he speaks, Todd regrets it. He wonders what has possessed him to say something so foolish and futile. It would be better just to pick up his books and walk out of the class—and the school—and to admit once and for all that he finds physics boring, math insufferable, history interminable, and that he cannot hold up his end of his bargain with his parents, not even for another day, and that all he wants to do with his life is to design greeting cards, draw cartoons, and sketch the occasional bird. This would surely be better than the humiliation that is certain to follow.

But Professor Fendle-Frinkle does not humiliate Todd. What he does is look outside and see for himself that it is indeed a beautiful day. Rather than become angry, the Professor wonders why students have not made similar requests of him before. At a regular school they would. At a regular school they would hound him incessantly to cancel class or attempt to distract him by asking him stories about himself so they might shave a few minutes off the start or end of the period. But the high achievers never do anything like this. They are too worried about scoring well on their standardized tests and advanced placement exams. Sometimes it seems as if they do not notice the weather at all.

With respect to the students in his own class, this strikes the Professor as particularly ironic given what he has taught them about the impending demise of the universe. Whether he is right or not—and, of course, he is quite sure he is right—just thinking about the concept of the universe ending should force these young men and women to think about the difficult question of how a life should be spent. It seems only natural to expect that, when forced to confront this reality, one would view time, and life itself, as more precious.

But the students fail to see things this way. By all appearances they continue to be fixated on grades and getting into the best university. Rather than supporting their classmate's proposal for an early end to the day, they appear somewhat peeved by it. To the Professor, this is a gross confusion of priorities.

The Professor is aware some observers might say he himself is guilty of confusing priorities. His attitude regarding the end of the universe could be characterized as indifferent, perhaps even callous. But it is a mistake to think that because he has calculated the end of time with exquisite precision he is indifferent to the facts. He has simply accepted, long ago, the futility of railing against unchangeable fates. This is in large part how he has managed to remain married for twenty-seven years to the most difficult woman on Rigel-Rigel, where divorce is uncomplicated and common but one loses certain parking privileges. By his own measure, the Professor has lived life to the fullest, which until that moment has meant thinking day and night about the most challenging problems in theoretical physics, but at this moment takes on a new meaning entirely.

The Professor looks outside again and appreciates the full splendor of the day. He sees it is not just nice out but sublime, and thinks he too might enjoy spending some time outside. He has not spent a day outside in a long time. He could go down to the lake and lie in the sun or take a swim. As a boy he enjoyed swimming and fishing, but it has been decades since he allowed himself time for these trivialities. Now the idea of swimming takes on a sense of urgency, as it never has before, and the formerly fanciful notion of spending the rest of the day outside becomes an irresistible imperative.

So to Todd's surprise, the Professor does not reprimand Todd or chastise him. To the contrary, he gives the young man the warmest of smiles and says, "You're right, Mr. Anat-Denarian, it is a beautiful day." Then, with a liberating sweep of his arm, he says, "Class dismissed."

HERE, WHERE I AM, it is also a beautiful day, perhaps not as nice as on Rigel-Rigel, but beautiful all the same. It is August and the sun is shining. It will be hot later, but now it is pleasant and not at all humid for this time of year. The sky is clear and a robust breeze keeps the air fresh and cool. I am sitting in my backyard. The lawn mowers were active earlier, but they have quieted now, and there is only the sound of the occasional airplane, and nature. The crickets are chirping. A host of sparrows are sunning themselves on one of the holly trees that line my deck. A tiny one is exploring the bird feeder I maintain. After much deliberation he finds a seed to his liking, plucks it, then flies off happily to rejoin his friends and pass the time. I have been working for a long time, quite happily too, but seeing the sparrow reminds me of priorities, and this is the kind of day that demands to be enjoyed. So I am going to stop writing now and take a walk.

You should too. It's later than you think.

ACKNOWLEDGMENTS

ANYONE WHO DOES ANYTHING creative knows that producing a work of art is in large part a matter of perseverance. The fate of the work, however, is in similar measure a matter of luck. It is mostly happenstance whether one's screenplay sits on a shelf or becomes a major film, pure chance whether a bust of Pallas sits in the attic or is displayed at the Louvre. I have been luckier than anyone I know.

My agent, Janet Reid, miraculously appeared in my life five years ago saying that she loved my book and would sell it for money. I scarcely believed it then, but since that day she has been my steadfast supporter and a caring friend. She sold that first novel and then the next. No writer could ask for a better champion. Somehow Janet got this book to Christopher Lehmann-Haupt. Somehow Christopher read it. Somehow he passed it along to Carl Lennertz. Somehow you are reading it today.

Anyone who is even cursorily involved in the publishing business will appreciate in reading these names how astonishingly lucky I have been. Christopher was the senior daily book reviewer at the *New York Times* for three decades and is a novelist in his own right. He is also a gentleman, a respected critic, and, not unimportantly, a fine poker player. Having his imprimatur on my book is almost certainly the reason you have read it.

Carl Lennertz is a legend in the publishing universe and is the author of a sweet and charming memoir of his childhood. He is also the best editor I have encountered in my writing career. He shared the sensibility of the book, and it is substantially improved for the attention of his careful eye. Carl's fundamental decency and devotion to his family are obvious to everyone with whom he works. It is an honor to have my books associated with him.

Meeting Janet, Christopher, and Carl were substantial strokes of luck, but the truth is my good fortune began long ago. At East Meadow High School in Long Island, I met three teachers who made impressions on me that last to this day. James Connolly, my English teacher and the advisor to our school newspaper, had an infectious joy for books, writing, and life that I carry with me still. Ralph Henderson, our revered social studies teacher, taught me to love history and find the humor in it. Finally, Roslyn Goldstein, my guidance counselor, shared with me her love of books and music and theater. She remains to this day my best example of comportment, intellectual engagement, and my very dear friend. My life has been infinitely enriched by knowing her and her wonderful husband, Sy.

Before Mr. Connolly, Mr. Henderson, and Mrs. Goldstein, I had my parents, both schoolteachers in their own right, who gave me the greatest gift any parent or teacher can give to a child: they made me believe I could be anything I wanted to be. My father has been my patron, friend, and role model, my mother my staunchest advocate. She is my first and best reader and my most enthusiastic fan. A wonderful lifelong actress, she understands the arbitrariness of success. On my best and worst days, she has said to me the most important thing that anyone could ever tell a writer: "Keep writing."

My aunt and uncle Lynne and Michael Cohn have been consistent and gracious supporters of my career. Lynne and my father are my remaining connection to my grandmother Be and grandfather Matty. Matt's jubilant, youthful spirit is the soul of this novel.

I am blessed with the very best of best friends, Ira J. Kaufman, whose own brilliant sense of humor suffuses this book (and who can indeed be found at the McDonald's on seventy-first and Broadway most Sunday mornings, buying a bacon, egg, and cheese biscuit).

Finally, my greatest luck of all has been to meet and marry the love of my life, Valli Rajah. I never dreamed that I would have such a fulfilling relationship. As if that were not enough, Valli has been generous enough to share with me Eamon Vanrajah, the kindest, sweetest, and funniest boy I have ever met, my favorite driving range partner and bunny searcher; Suria Vanrajah, whose indomitable spirit awes me each and every day; and most recently, the miraculous

Mattea Erin Rajah-Mandery, who rendered invaluable assistance editing the final version of this manuscript and who is the very best reason to get up in the morning (and the evening). My greatest hope is that Eamon, Suria, and Mattea will each read this book someday and think to themselves that their dad was out of his mind.